MW00776615

want
you
still

CE RICCI
usa todaybestselling author
MARLEY VALENTINE

Editing: Ink Machine Editing
Proofreading: Amanda Mili of Amandanomaly
Cover Design: Kate Farlow of Y'all. That Graphic
Cannon Beach Photos: CE Ricci

5/7/53

lieve Piety en broer Piet, vorige jonge

Dinsdag

waarop vermeld stond dan

Ik feliciteer jullie broer

maar heel

Hoe is het met je Pi

Ik hoop dat i

Oma

trots

een

daarom

For all the inexplicable connections
that withstand the tests of time and distance.

"I want you to promise me something:
If you love someone, you tell them.
Even if you're scared that it's not the right thing.
Even if you're scared that it will cause problems.
Even if you're scared it will burn your life to the ground.
You say it, and you say it loud.
And then you go from there."

— Dr. Mark Sloan, *Grey's Anatomy*

theme song

All I Have Left To Give — Thousand Below

ce ricci's playlist

Photographs And Gasoline — Framing Hanley
Just Pretend — Bad Omens
Without You — Palisades
THE DEATH OF PEACE OF MIND — Bad Omens
Drunk Enough — Angels Fall
Erase My Mind — Siamese
Doomed — I Prevail
Without Me — Dayseeker
Heavenly — Broadside
Glass Heart — Caskets
Memories — Beyond Unbroken
Ornament — nothing,nowhere.
Gravity — Holding Absence
Stay — Sun Never Sets
There's No Such Thing As Accidental Infidelity — You Me At Six
Who are you? — Bad Omens
Somebody else. — Bad Omens
Dial Tone — Catch Your Breath
alone (out of my head) — Thousand Below
Stop Myself (Only Human) — Calum Scott
Slow Burn — The Word Alive
Take Me Back To Eden — Sleep Token
Hopeless — Too Close To Touch, TELLE
Before I Cave In — Too Close To Touch
What I Wish I Could Forget — Too Close To Touch
Silent Season — Thousand Below
Modern Love Affair — Too Close To Touch
The Fountain — Bad Omens
Give — Sleep Token
harder to lie. — elijah
Where I Want To Be — The Dangerous Summer
Dancing On My Own — Calum Scott
Better Off — Sunsleep, Jonny Craig

Listen to CE Ricci's playlist on Spotify

marley's playlist

War Of Hearts — Ruelle

Come Back Home — Calum Scott

Locksmith — Sadie Jean

I Remember Everything — Zach Bryan, Kacey Musgraves

illicit affairs — Taylor Swift

All You Had To Do Was Stay (TV) — Taylor Swift

This Love (TV) — Taylor Swift

drunk text me — Lexi Jayde

august — Taylor Swift

Enchanted (TV) — Taylor Swift

To Love Someone — Benson Boone

A Little Bit Yours — JP Saxe

Listen to Marley's playlist on Spotify

author's note

As storytellers dedicated to depicting real-life situations in our works of fiction, we've done our best to portray all aspects of military life and Army regulations as accurately as possible. However, sometimes rules, when applied in a fictional setting, need to be bent to fit within the narrative, so some creative freedoms and liberties were taken for plot purposes within this book.

The views in this book have been fabricated as to not represent or reflect the principles, policies, values, or facilities of the United States Army, or any other branch of military, as it is a work of fiction.

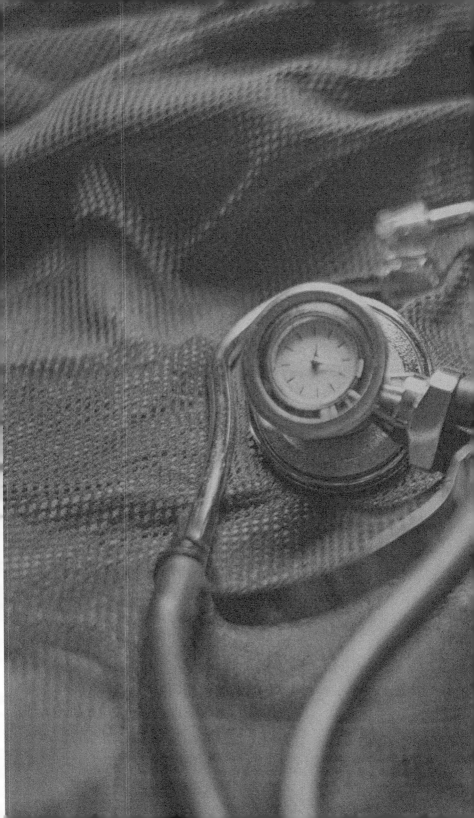

PROLOGUE

Will

Everything I am—every ounce of strength, every set of morals, every piece of me—was shaped by the greatest man I've ever known.

My father.

Even when I was thirteen, and his work took him to far-off ends of the world, I held on to the values he taught me. To be the man of the house when he wasn't around. To put my family above all else—the way he did in order to provide for us.

To take care of those I love.

When he passed away a few short years later, I finally put those lessons into action at full force. Becoming the rock my mother and sister needed to get through the rough patches. Comforting them, supporting them, being whatever they needed me to be. Being the glue that held what was left of our family together.

And it never felt like an obligation. It was only done out of love.

Something similar happened with my brothers-in-arms when I joined the military at eighteen, following in my father's path even after he was gone. Through them, I learned what true selflessness was. How to help those in need, not just with my medical expertise, but even during the moments of homesickness or loneliness that would creep in through the nearly unbearable nights half-a-world away from home.

And through it all, I've worked to become a person—a son—my father could be proud of.

Every word, lesson, value, and moral he and the military instilled in me continued to infiltrate my decision-making until I'd become the embodiment of what it meant to not just be strong, but to be Army Strong.

It gave me the ability to endure and withstand any task, trial, or tribulation put before me.

But none of it would ever prepare me to stand at the crossroads I find myself at in this moment. Toeing the line between my own desires and the feelings of others. Lingering in the gray area between right and wrong, salvation and damnation.

Maybe that's because, never in my wildest dreams, did I think I'd have to withstand...*him*.

"I want you."

Three words, whispered against my lips in a hot, seductive dance, are almost enough to undo me. But still, because of my strength, I endure.

"You're drunk," I murmur back, clenching my jaw. "Which is why you should call a cab and go home."

Two firm hands anchor themselves on my hips, and he pulls me impossibly closer, grinding his erection against my rapidly thickening cock.

"But we're supposed to be..." he slurs slightly. "...getting to know each other."

I let out a sharp laugh, the irony not lost on me. "Not like that."

"Mmm, no. You're right." But his actions don't match his words when his tongue flicks out, swiping over my top lip in a wicked caress that would bring weaker men to their knees. "Except we already *do* know each other like that," he says, his voice somehow full of snark and sorrow. "Don't we, *Will?*"

My eyes sink closed, fists balled at my sides. I don't dare touch him. Not when I know I'll never be able to stop if I do.

I turn my head, trying to reduce the temptation. "Don't do that."

"Do what?"

There isn't time to answer before teeth sink into the flesh of my neck, making me gasp at the unexpected contact. It sends a bolt of desire straight to my aching cock, now harder than granite behind my jeans. A fact he doesn't fail to notice when a free hand slips between us, cupping me through the denim.

"Fuck," I say on a groan as his palm rubs against my length.

His touch heats my blood with fiery lust, mixing with the whiskey already burning through my veins. Tempting me in ways I've never felt before as he continues to torment me with his mouth on my neck and hand on my dick.

Goddamnit.

Forget the alcohol I've consumed tonight. I could get drunk off him alone. It didn't even take that much to succumb to my desire for him the first time I saw him.

But things are nothing like they were back then. A harsh truth that won't shake free, and it's enough to sober me.

"Pierce, stop," I manage past the baseball lodged in my throat. "You have to stop."

He gives my dick a rough squeeze through my jeans before flicking the button open. "Why?"

"Because…" There's another long lick down the column of my neck, and *Jesus take the fucking wheel.* "Because—"

"That's not a reason, Will."

Every single time he says my name, my brain completely short-circuits. It takes me back to before all this, to the moments he sighed it in my ear as he came. It's a sound I could never forget, no matter how hard I've tried. No matter how many times I've *begged* to.

His mouth moves up to my ear again, and his breath as he speaks causes goosebumps to break out across my skin. "Don't you want me too?"

My eyes sink closed.

Desperately.

"Pierce, you're drunk. You don't know what you're saying. Think about—"

"I don't want to think." He nips at the vein in my throat that's pulsing beneath his lips before bringing his forehead to rest against mine. "I want to *feel.*"

With the way he's touching and licking and biting at me, it's a wonder I haven't combusted entirely. Or worse, given in to the desire that's sure to send me to an early grave.

And God, how I almost want to do just that, because it would be a mercy to not have to live like this. In pure torment, plagued by want and desire for what I know I can never have.

My jaw tics, and I feel water welling at the corners of my eyes as the battle between my head and heart rages on, an ending nowhere in sight.

I've been to war, and as a flight medic, I've seen the devastation firsthand. Heard my brothers' screams of agony to be put out of their misery as I tended to their wounds. Going as far as bringing them back from the brink of death, even when they begged me not to.

But nothing I've seen overseas made me feel the way I do right now.

Decimated and obliterated. Completely gutted by shards of shrapnel no grenade or IED could ever be capable of. I'm being torn apart from the inside out, because my loyalty and honor are being tested by the desire I hold for the one man in this world who has always been so much more than just another warm body.

It makes me sick. Physically ill with the need to feel the lines and planes of his body beneath my palm or taste the salty sweat on his skin, while knowing *he isn't mine.*

It's a wonder I'm able to even think, let alone speak.

But I manage a single word.

A plea. For just a little more of that strength I hold within me.

"Pierce."

His hand leaves my cock, and at first, I think he's listening. Seeing reason. Allowing me to keep the tiny shred of sanity I have left by stopping this before it goes somewhere we'll never come back from.

But instead, his hand moves to wrap around the back of my neck, anchoring us together, close enough that the sliver of air between our lips is practically non-existent.

And then he whispers a single, gut-wrenching word.

"Please."

The word is a blade slicing through my heart, and it's then I realize, there's no hope for me. After all, even a diamond—one of the strongest materials known to man—will break, crack, shatter into a million tiny pieces under the right pressure.

I'm strong, but I'm no diamond.

A truth never more apparent than when all it takes is one more desperate whisper of my name from his lips…and my willpower comes crashing down around me like a house of fucking cards.

My mouth collides with his in a brutal crash, and this first little taste of him already has me craving more. Needing to remove every possible thing separating us until there's *nothing*.

I don't just want his lips and tongue battling with mine. I want *all* of him.

Every inch of smooth skin and toned muscle beneath me as I sink inside him. Every dirty word that spills from his lips between pants and gasps while we give each other just as much as we take.

I want to fuck him hard and relentlessly, if only to give him half the pain I feel every moment I see the two of them together. Sink my teeth into his flesh, as if leaving those brands is enough to stake a claim on him—mind, body, and soul—forever.

Drink in his moans like they're the very fucking thing I need to survive.

Because they are.

So I do just that. I take, and I take, and I take it all. Everything he has to give, knowing it will leave nothing but devastation for both of us once it's over.

But even as I take his body, he takes something far more valuable from me.

My strength, my honor, my loyalty. The very pieces of myself I pride most.

Now all I have is an empty bed, messy, cum-soaked sheets, and a burning sensation lingering on my skin from the cool metal of his wedding band.

And I hate myself for it. For being so weak.

But more than anything, I hate knowing this isn't the way it's supposed to be.

Because, even for the briefest of moments, he was mine.

He was mine *first*.

part one

the coast

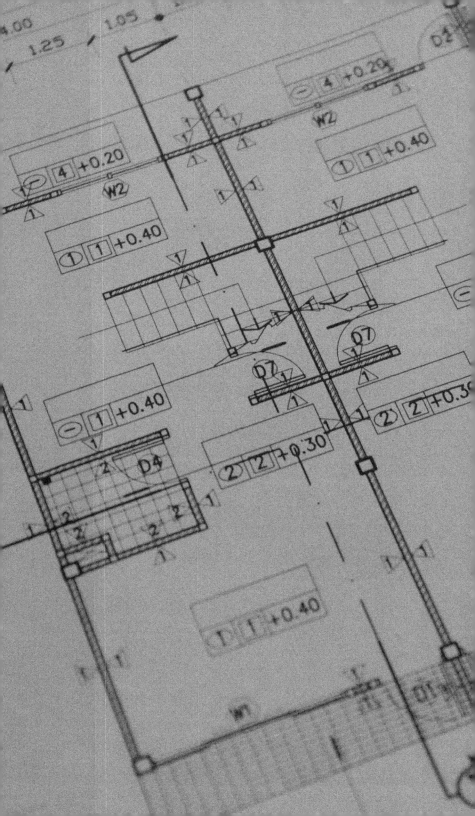

ONE

One Year Earlier — September

Pierce

"**C**an I get you another one?"

The bartender's gruff voice startles me, and I glance down at my drink, surprised by the almost empty glass, then back up at him.

How many of these have I already had?

Debating if I should order yet another round, I take my eyes over the man in front of me.

He's tall with wide shoulders, a firm chest, and biceps big enough that, if he wanted to pick me up and throw me around, he probably could. And if the hunger in his eyes and knowing smile are anything to go by, he definitely wants to.

Not waiting for a response, he adds three cubes of ice to a new glass and reaches for the bottle of single malt whiskey, pouring a little over two fingers.

"I'm Nick." He pushes the drink in my direction before resting his forearms on the wooden bar top and leaning in. With a lick of his lips, there's no mistaking the intention of his introduction.

Neither does the blatant invitation that comes next.

"I finish up here in an hour."

The words hang in the air and I meet his gaze, taken aback by his forwardness, but not enough to dismiss the offer entirely.

It's why I made the detour to Cannon Beach in the first place, wasn't it?

Well, not this exact reason, but a pit stop of sorts. An intermission before my big move to Seattle. A few days in a beautiful coastal town, where I could just relax and exist.

Reset.

Let loose.

And while Nick isn't necessarily my type, it doesn't mean he can't be. I hadn't set out to find someone to warm my bed tonight out of necessity, but the longer I sit here, drink in hand and contemplating life, I realize this might just be exactly what I need.

I'm on edge. Have been all night, and the hope that alcohol would ease my anxiety has long since gone. There's no doubt I'm overwhelmed by the magnitude of this move, but with a new job, the need to make new friends, and no family, it's to be expected.

Everything about this next chapter in my life is such a cliché, and yet the need to leave everything I know behind felt unavoidable. Only, the mask of confidence I've been wearing since accepting the job offer is slowly slipping, and I'm in desperate need of a reason to let it fall off completely.

Allow myself to just…fucking breathe.

Curling my hand around the glass, I raise it to my mouth and tip my head back, needing the smooth, cool liquid burning down my throat to make my decisions for me.

I place the empty tumbler on the wooden surface and glance back at Nick, pushing the glass toward him expectantly. My acceptance of his offer is on the tip of my tongue, but I'm interrupted by a flurry of movement in my periphery.

The stranger clumsily places an army-green duffel bag onto the bar top before pulling out the stool beside me and dropping his body on it in an exhausted heap.

"Long day?"

It takes me a few seconds to realize the voice is mine, and thanks to the alcohol running through my bloodstream, I let the errant question slip past my lips. Unable to swallow back the words now, I watch him patiently and wonder if he'll acknowledge or ignore me.

More importantly, wondering why the hell I even care.

He sighs. Loudly. Irritated almost, before he turns his head toward me. And just like that, any embarrassment or regret I feel over my wayward tongue evaporates into thin air as hazel green eyes—damn near the color of his bag—surrounded by thick, long lashes, study me quizzically.

I take stock of every single inch of his face, slowly dragging my gaze down the slope of his nose, then across to the sharp angle of his jawline. Dark, week-old scruff covers his cheeks, framing his perfect, peach-colored lips in a way I can't help but appreciate. Enough that I'm quickly imagining my fingers sliding through his brown hair and hauling his mouth to mine.

I feel my pulse quicken, the warm, liquor-infused blood rushing through my veins and arteries…straight to my dick.

Damn. I can't take my eyes off of him.

His tongue peeks out, licking his bottom lip, and my gaze darts up to meet his.

Busted.

The corner of his mouth rises in a cocky, all-too-knowing smirk, and I find myself wanting to kiss that sexy, smug look right off his face.

"What can I get you?" Nick's voice interrupts as he leans on his elbows between us, and I'm reminded of his offer that I'd yet to accept.

The stranger tips his chin up at me. "I'll have whatever he's having."

Begrudgingly, I drag my eyes away from him and back to Nick. "Make that two."

Nick knocks on the bar top, a clear look of irritation passing over his features, before pushing off the wood. "And there goes my plans for tonight," he mutters.

I open my mouth to appease him, only to close it just as quickly. What am I going to say? *I'm sorry?* I may have been interested, but I never agreed to anything. I don't owe him an apology. But I know neither of those facts will soften the sting of rejection, so I keep my mouth shut instead.

Glancing back at the stranger, I watch him take his turn at brazenly eyeing me. His gaze moves from my face down the length of my body and back up again, and I catch his hint of curiosity.

I raise a brow. "Like what you see?"

Another question asked.

He smiles.

And another question unanswered.

This time his smile is small. Reserved. Far less cocky as he asks, "Here after work?"

I narrow my eyes at the question, and the man gestures to my clothes. I'm wearing black tailored dress pants and a white button-up shirt, sleeves rolled to my elbows. Looking down, I see how he's made that assumption.

People don't usually wear business attire unless they have to.

Me, on the other hand, I thrive on putting my best foot forward. I dress in what I'm most comfortable in, and what I'm most comfortable in is the man these clothes turn me into.

Secure. Assured.

Confident.

Some days I need the clothes to convince me of who I am. A suit of armor, of sorts. Today's one of those days. But since I have no plans to explain any of this to him, I simply nod.

"You?"

Before he can answer, Nick returns, wordlessly handing over our drinks and a scowl reserved just for me.

The stranger's smirk returns, eyeing the exchange between Nick and me with clear amusement. "Friend of yours?"

"Did I miss the memo where you're the only one allowed to ask questions and I'm supposed to answer them?" I blurt out, irritated by his third dismissal.

His dark brow arches, that sinful grin growing. "I didn't say you had to answer them."

My knee starts bouncing, and I find myself biting my bottom lip, equally irritated and interested. I'm definitely out of my element with this guy, and I'm not sure I like it.

I'm usually the one with the upper hand. I hold the cards and call all the shots. Being this off-balance…it's new to me.

"What's your name?" he asks.

Trying not to focus on the fact that, once again, I'm answering his questions, I clench my jaw to give myself a few seconds before answering. As if I could pretend I'm not already becoming putty in his hands.

"Pierce."

"Pierce," he repeats as he slides off the stool into the space between us. A space that doesn't offer much room to his tall, muscular frame. If I turned and widened my legs, it would take less than a step for him to be standing directly between them. And the steady thrum beneath my skin lets me know I want him there.

He plants one forearm on the bartop and extends the other. "I'm Will."

Keeping my eyes locked with his, I take his hand, but rather than shaking it, I just hold it. Feeling the warmth of his skin has me wondering how the rest of him would feel pressed against me. And I have no idea what to do with those kinds of meddling thoughts.

I force my eyes to dart away, breaking the connection, and let them land on his duffel. "What's with the bag?"

He chuckles, releasing my hand. "The answer to that is going to require more than one drink."

Rising up off my own stool, I slip my hand into my back pocket and pull out a few folded bills. Counting them, I throw down three twenties.

"I think that'll get me at least the beginning."

Facing one another, I realize we're almost the same height. And also that closeness between us now is a little unusual for strangers, though not enough for either one of us to move.

Will's eyes shift to something behind me before lowering his mouth to my ear. My body shivers the second his warm breath touches my skin, and I can hear the amusement in his voice when he asks, "Why does the bartender look like he wants to kill me?"

A frustrated groan slips out of my mouth, and I mutter back, "I was thinking about letting him fuck me after he finished his shift."

Will rears his head back to look at me, a devious glimmer in his eyes.

"And now?"

I shrug nonchalantly. "You tell me."

He's silent for a moment, contemplating, before he picks up his untouched drink and hands it to me. "Here, you have it."

"What? Why?" I ask, staring down into the whiskey glass.

"What if he put something in it?"

That earns him a laugh. "Somehow I don't think the loss of some ass is enough to warrant poisoning."

"I don't know," he muses, raising a shoulder. "Something tells me it's a nice ass."

As I bite the inside of my cheek to stop myself from smiling, I bring the tumbler to my mouth and finish the drink in one long sip.

"Listen," I say, putting down the glass and grabbing the cash. "Let's go somewhere else. I'll settle my tab here and buy you a drink that doesn't have you fearing for your life."

"Are you sure you don't need me to deal with the bartender?" He's surprisingly serious when he asks. Like he actually cares about whether or not I can handle myself, and this time, I can't help but let the smile spread across my face.

"I'm sure I can manage." I tip my chin at the exit. "Wait for me outside?"

He picks up his bag, hauling it over his shoulder before walking away, and my eyes follow his every step.

The pull of interest and curiosity he's got on me is unnerving.

If he said let's drop the pretense and just go straight to your rental, I wouldn't think twice. I doubt I'd even need to think once.

"Here's your bill," Nick says, interrupting my thoughts. Gone is the warm, seductive tone from earlier, and I push away the unnecessary guilt. I'm allowed to change my mind.

"Thanks, man." I put down all three bills I originally pulled out for Will—hoping the excessive tip alleviates the rejection—and offer a quick nod. "Have a good night."

I don't bother with any other niceties, too eager to be back with the sinful man waiting outside. Pushing away the nervousness and excitement sitting in the pit of my stomach, I leave the bar to find him leaning against the building.

Will's head is tipped back, gaze on the sky, with one leg bent at the knee to rest against the wall. I slow my steps and stare at him, hoping the crisp air cools down the uncontrollable heat that's running through my veins and straight to my dick.

He was gorgeous inside, but under the moonlit sky, he's perfection. The kind I want to spend all night exploring.

Subtly, I press a hand against my half-hard cock to adjust myself.

Of course, that's the same moment when Will's eyes land on me, and the wry grin on his face tells me he knows exactly what I just did.

He pushes himself away from the wall as I reach him. That's when I notice the cigarette behind his ear; something I hadn't seen earlier in the bar. Curiously, I pull it from its resting place, hoping to distract us both from my rogue dick.

"You smoke?" I ask. He pulls out a full pack just as I slip it between my lips.

"I quit," he says as he snatches it out of my mouth and slides the stick back into the packet.

Raising an eyebrow in question, I watch him shove them into the side of his duffel and ask, "Am I going to have to buy you another drink to find out why you quit but still carry them on you? You're not exactly forthcoming."

The soft glow from the moonlight reveals the way Will's eyes dance up and down the length of my body. "You'd be right. But it's a good thing you're not interested in *talking* all evening."

I can't help the chuckle that leaves my mouth. "Right. I'm after something entirely different."

A devious grin paints itself on his lips as he closes the distance between us. His hand reaches for me, curling around my hip, and the heat from his palm sends goosebumps breaking out over my skin again.

"So let's skip the drinks."

Despite wanting exactly that, I straighten my spine and take a step back for some much-needed space, forcing his hand to fall. He's had the upper hand since the moment I laid eyes on him, and I'm still figuring out how to process that.

I'm used to wanting total control of the situation, and I'm certainly not used to enjoying *not* having it at the same time. Which is why, though I find myself wanting to act out of character and hand this stranger the reins, it seems impossible without a little help from some alcohol.

Well, some *more* alcohol.

"One drink," I coax. "And then you can have me any way you want me."

He steps forward, close enough that we're almost touching.

"One drink," he repeats, leaning in to whisper in my ear. "One drink and then I'm going to spend the rest of the night making you wish we skipped it altogether."

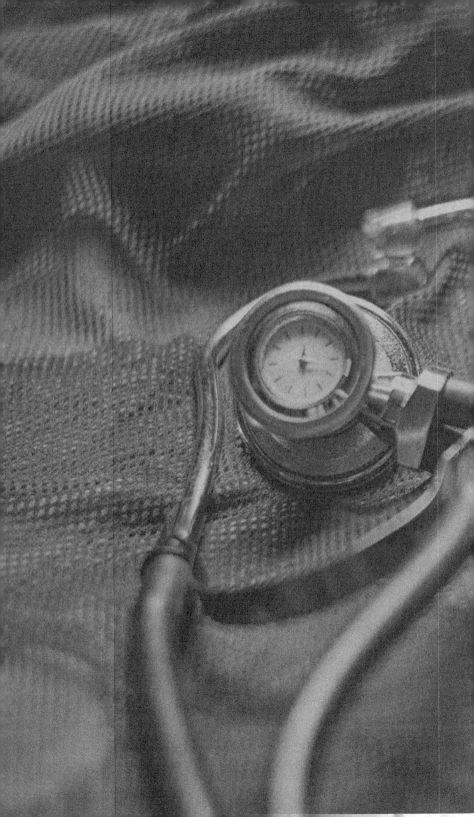

TWO

Will

"So. The bag."

We've barely been handed our drinks at the new bar when the words leave the mouth of my delicious companion; his not-so-subtle attempt to, once again, garner more information from me. But hell if I'll let him off that easily.

"Ah, yes," I murmur, swirling the amber liquid in the glass before lifting my gaze to collide with Pierce's. "How could I forget?"

Small divots form on either side of his mouth at the same time his brows draw down, another hint of irritation crossing his expression. For whatever reason, it makes him all the more attractive.

"You're not good at giving up details."

"And you're not used to being challenged," I surmise, taking a swig of the whiskey.

The frustration in his eyes is now laced with heat, and the acute interest has begun roaring to life like a wildfire. I'm not sure if the warning, hidden within the flames, is supposed to deter me or not, but I've always been a bit of a risk taker.

I'll take my chances on getting burned.

"I'm also not used to being the one who does all the talking," he points out, a small amount of bite in his tone as he runs his fingers through his short, onyx waves. "And generally speaking, I like to know *something* about the person I'm planning to sleep with. More than just their name, at least."

My lips quirk, knowing I'd take him to bed entirely nameless, before finally relenting. "I just arrived in town. That's why I have the bag."

A dark brow arches. "And you didn't think to leave it in the car?"

"Not a chance," I say, locking eyes with his sapphire blue ones. "I knew it'd be the perfect conversation piece if I needed to save a sinfully gorgeous man in a suit from going home with the bartender tonight."

His lips twitch almost imperceptibly, but he keeps his tone dry. "And the real answer?"

Because I didn't drive here would be the answer he's looking for. But the way he's trying to fight my charm causes me to smile before countering with a question of my own.

"Who's to say that wasn't the real one?"

A row of perfect white teeth sink into his bottom lip before he shakes his head and lets out something between a scoff and laugh that goes straight to my dick.

"Are you planning to play coy all night with me, Will? Because at this rate, we won't be going anywhere before last call."

My gaze latches to his lips as he says my name, and I can't help loving the way it sounds coming from his mouth. I'm sure it'll sound even better when he cries it out while I'm buried deep inside him later tonight.

The thought alone causes my own lips to hitch up farther, becoming more of a devilish smirk, as I lift my gaze to collide with his.

"Playing coy isn't my style. You know what I want from you, Pierce. I'm just waiting for you to give it to me."

His nostrils flare slightly, eyes heating a little more. "And as tempting as that might sound, it's not happening until you give me what *I* want."

Stubborn fucking bastard.

"Fair enough," I mutter, taking another swig of my drink. "What do you wanna know?"

He drums his long, lean fingers on the bar top before asking, "Is this your first time here?"

The question is so unexpected, I almost laugh. Or maybe it's the idea of this being my first time to Cannon Beach when it—and the entire Oregon coast—has been a staple in my family for as long as I can remember. Even with living hours away in Seattle.

It's probably the entire reason I chose to spend my last week stateside soaking in what the northwest has to offer. The crisp, clean air with that faint hint of salt from the ocean. The brisk breeze coming off the water. The fog rolling off the hills and mountains in the early morning.

All the things I'm sure to miss when all I'll see around me are the deserts of the Middle East in barely over a week.

"No. I've been here more times than I can count. We came here a lot when I was younger, especially as a teen. Once a month during the summers, maybe more."

"And just like that, I've learned something about you." There's a triumphant glimmer in his eye. "That wasn't so hard, was it?"

"Like pulling teeth, actually."

That earns me a laugh. "So you're from around here, I take it?"

"Seattle." His features twist into some sort of peculiar frown at mention of the city. "What? You have something against Seattle?"

"No, it's just a small world, 'cause I'm moving into my new place in Seattle next week. This was a pit stop on the way to my final destination." He pauses, a more pensive, thoughtful expression crossing his features. "Who knows, maybe we'll be neighbors up there."

I can't explain the flip in my stomach at the mere thought of that being true.

It might be the heat in his gaze or the tension zapping between us like electricity, but I know one thing: even without truly getting my hands on him yet, the idea of living anywhere near this man could be my undoing.

Too bad the chances of that being reality anytime soon are a whopping zero.

But there's always tonight, and I'm not about to ruin it or the mood by dropping a heaping dose of reality on us.

"Maybe," I murmur, turning on my stool to face him.

"Could be nice to have a friend before I even get there," he adds as I lay a palm on one of his thighs.

The second I touch him, even through the fabric of his dress pants, my pulse begins pounding out of control. Want and desire risk taking over, the desperate need to touch and feel more of him.

All of him.

"I'd have to agree." I slide my palm up a little higher on his thigh, the heat from his body nearly scorching me through his slacks. "But, Pierce, the things I'm planning to do to you tonight are far, *far* from friendly."

His eyes flick up to mine, and I find they're filled to the brim with lust.

It's nothing new—the desire in his gaze has been unmistakable since the moment it locked with mine earlier tonight. Right before I saved him from making a *terrible* choice in bedmates for the evening. Ice blue flames licked at every inch of my body as he checked me out, nearly incinerating me on the spot.

Now, only inches away, the heat has only amplified.

But so has the warning.

"You keep touching me like that, and I'm not gonna be able to walk out of here."

My tongue darts out over my bottom lip, wetting it before leaning in to whisper, "If you're worried about my hands, just wait till you see what I can do with my mouth."

The temperature between us ratchets up another twenty degrees, fueled by the tension and electricity crackling in the air. It's charged, ready to short-circuit with the flick of a switch that I'm sure as hell ready to flip.

"You're quite sure of yourself."

"Easy to be when I can back it up." I skate the finger on my free hand along his arm, stroking the bare skin from his wrist to his elbow.

The anticipation of this moment's been building in the air all evening, and Pierce is the first to waver from it, breaking our eye contact in favor of grabbing his drink. I watch as he slams the remaining whiskey in a single swallow before turning back to me.

His eyes flare with heat when he murmurs, "You ready to get out of here?"

Finally.

The grin spreading over my face can't be helped as he rushes to toss some bills on the bar.

"I thought you'd never ask."

In no time at all, I've gathered my bag, and we're weaving our way through the tables until we reach the door. Anticipation builds more with every step I take behind him, and I feel each thread of composure I have falling away, only for it to be gone entirely once we reach the sidewalk.

The need to touch him—really fucking touch him—is dire at this point.

And now we're finally alone, so I allow the craving to take hold of me.

The second we hit the corner of the bar, I grab his arm and drag him down the dimly lit alleyway. My sudden change of direction must take him by surprise if his slight gasp is anything to go by, followed by another when I slam his back against the bar's exterior.

Two wide eyes bore into mine, shock mixed with desire swirling in their depths.

"What're you—"

He doesn't get the question out before I drop my duffel and slam my mouth to his.

No more preamble; I'm done with the flirting and teasing.

Instead, I let need and desire take over at full capacity.

My body crowds his against the wall, caging him in like an animal. One hand digs into his silky, black hair that's just as soft as I figured it to be, while the other grips his jaw, tilting his head so I can dive deeper into the kiss.

It takes him a moment to find his footing, but once he does, he's meeting me with just as much enthusiasm.

The ridge of his erection digs into my hip, and I shift to grind my own throbbing length against it. Pierce lets out a soft gasp into my mouth at the friction, and I'm quick to greedily swallow the sound down.

I'm impatient to know what other noises I can drag from those sinful lips throughout the night.

It could be minutes or hours that we devour each other, groping and touching as much as we dare while still very much in public. Honestly, I don't even care who might walk by and see at this point. I'm damn near ready to turn him around and fuck him here and now, consequences be damned.

Pierce is the first to break away, gasping for air while his lips still lightly brush against mine in a taunt.

"I wasn't done yet," I pant, rolling my hips against his again before stealing another quick kiss.

"Fuck," he mutters, his hand snaking between us to cup my cock through my jeans. "I want this inside me."

A soft laugh escapes me. "You're the one who's been edging me all night with your game of twenty questions instead of letting me take you straight to bed," I murmur back. "If you'd have let us skip the drink like I suggested, we'd already be on round two."

He gives my throbbing dick a light squeeze. "Cocky."

"Confident," I correct, emphasizing the point with another sensual press of my hips into his palm. "And don't worry. I have the skills to back it up."

This time, he's the one to laugh. "Then I think it's about time to put your money where your mouth is, Will."

Goddamn.

My name on his lips will be my undoing.

But not before I unravel him first.

Accepting his challenge, I slide my hand between us, knocking his own out of the way before palming his length. I lean in, rubbing his shaft through the fabric of his slacks, letting my proximity work in my favor.

"Don't test me, baby. If I wanted to, I'd have you coming in your pants right here. All without sliding down your zipper."

Turning my head, I let my teeth skitter along his jawline, scraping against the dusting of stubble there as I work my way back to his lips. We collide into each other, the same way I hear the waves crashing over the coast off in the distance.

Relentlessly.

I tease his cock, finding that sensitive spot below the head and giving him just the right amount of torturous pressure there. Rubbing and rolling my thumb against the nerve in time with each swipe of my tongue against his.

He must be more turned on than I thought, because not even a minute later, I feel his dick twitch and pulse in my hold, signaling I've got him right where I want him—teetering right on the edge of release. And from the way he's arching into my touch, he's desperate to jump into freefall.

But instead of surrendering to the lust, he wraps his fingers around my wrist to halt me.

"You've made your point." He pulls back so his lips are a breath away, eyes glazed over with desire.

I lick my lips before giving his cock another squeeze. "What was that? I don't think I heard you right."

Something between a laugh and gasp escapes him as he surrenders. "You win. Happy now?"

"Mhmm," I hum as I release my hold on him. "For now."

"Thank God." Another soft laugh leaves him as his head slumps back against the building. "My place or yours?"

The question pulls me out of the lust I've been drowning in, if only for a moment.

After the day I've had, the last thing on my mind was booking a hotel for the night on the way down. Foolish, even if we're about to go into the off-season for the coast. But now, with this sinful man standing before me, it seems I won't need one. At least, not for the night.

My teeth roll over my bottom lip before I lift my bag up off the ground, ready to really get this show on the road.

"Yours." My eyes flick to his. "Definitely yours."

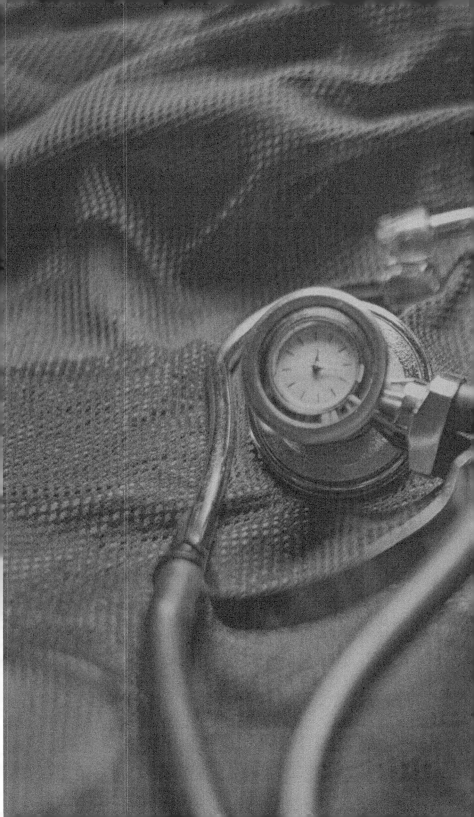

THREE

Will

I slam Pierce against the door of the beachfront rental house the second we're inside, my mouth locked on his, like I'm trying to breathe the oxygen straight from his lungs. When his back collides with the wood, a loud thud echoes through the otherwise empty house, and I'm thanking any god that exists for finally being alone—really, truly alone—with him.

Not waiting another moment, I drop my bag and immediately make better use of my hands. They slip down between us, tugging his shirt free from his pants before traveling up to the collar.

"Fuck," he mutters into my mouth before spearing his tongue back between my lips for another carnal kiss.

Fuck is right.

The whiskey on his lips and the scent of his cologne work together as the best kind of aphrodisiac, and I'm already hard enough to cut steel. Granite. Fucking diamonds.

He's driving me mad with want.

My fingers quickly work at his tie, loosening the knot before moving to the buttons of his shirt, but I'm so keyed up—ready to bury myself inside him—and my patience is too thin to undo them all blindly. So I grab both sides and yank the fabric apart instead.

The buttons fly free, and the sound of them pinging across any surface in their path before falling to the floor sends another bolt of lust straight to my already aching cock.

Pierce pulls back, brows drawn together as he looks at the mangled remains of his shirt.

"Did you just—"

"I'll buy you a new one," I mutter before grabbing his jaw and crashing my mouth back to his.

My tongue slides against the seam of his lips, and he opens immediately, allowing it to tangle and dance with his own in some combination of a ballet and a duel. The give and take is as frustrating as it is blissful, because we both know it's not enough.

Not what we crave.

Pierce's hands anchor in my hair to pull me closer, deepening the kiss in the sexiest, most commanding way I've ever experienced. It's rough and brutal, and before long, we're like two feral animals, desperate to rip each other to shreds. Clawing at each other's clothes to find smooth, bare skin, and not a single damn to give about the wreckage we leave in our wake in finding it.

I yank him away from the door, slipping the tattered shirt from his shoulders as I do. He follows with ease, stripping my belt from the loops while keeping his lips glued to my own. We only break apart to rip my shirt over my head before colliding together again.

We crash against every available surface as we move deeper into the house. A vase topples to the floor, shattering on impact. I knock a few photos off the wall, too, before Pierce finally pushes me against the back side of the couch.

At this rate, the entire place will be in shambles before I'm inside him.

"What do you like?" I ask in harsh pants against his skin as I strip the last remaining layers of clothes from our bodies. "How do you want this to go?"

He shakes his head, staring at my naked body like he's ready to devour me. "It doesn't matter. You can do whatever you want to me, Will. Just get inside me."

I've never been fond of desperation. Hell, *I've* never felt this kind of desperation myself, but with him, I can truly say it doesn't matter to me either. If he wanted to fuck me instead? I'd let him. Even though I rarely bottom, I'd do it right here and now.

God, this level of lust is doing something stupid to my brain.

My tongue wets my lower lip as I step into his space and wrap my fist around his shaft. I give it a firm squeeze, drawing out another one of those sinful gasps. A bead of pre-cum appears at the tip, and I swipe my thumb over it, gathering the liquid before bringing it to my mouth.

The salty tang of him makes my mouth water for more.

"I think I wanna taste you first."

He shakes his head as a tortured, miserable laugh leaves his lips. "That can be round two."

The need and desire laced in his tone matches my own, and I smirk. "I think I can deal with that," I murmur before nipping at his jaw.

My hands and lips trace over the endless miles of warm, soft skin, touching and tasting him. Learning every inch and crevice I can, wishing he'd let me bring him to the edge of impending ecstasy over and over with my mouth before sinking into his firm, tight—

"*Will*," he rasps as a hand tightens painfully in my hair and pulls my mouth away from his flushed skin.

A small bout of frustration ripples through me, and it takes more willpower than I thought I possessed to step back, grab my discarded jeans, and slip my wallet from the pocket. Pulling two foil packets free, I toss my pants haphazardly to the ground again and stride back to the sinful, naked man waiting for me.

"You came prepared," he says, eyeing the condom and lube in my hand before his gaze lifts to mine.

For a second, I don't know where the self-assured sexiness he's had all night went. The apprehension in his eyes doesn't fit with the picture he's painted for me since I sat next to him at that bar.

My brow hitches and I tear the condom packet with my teeth, letting the lilt of judgment in his tone roll off my back. "Call it the Boy Scout in me. Is that a problem?"

Pierce's nostrils flare as his eyes drop to my cock, watching as I roll the barrier over my length. That's all it takes for the carnal lust to reappear in his features, and any glimmer of hesitation is gone.

"Not at all, actually. I'm glad one of us was."

I cock my head to the side, unexpectedly surprised that this seemingly straight-laced guy would forget something as obvious as protection. "You mean to tell me that you were planning to let that bartender fuck you raw?"

Something of a sheepish grin appears on his lips, and that's all the answer I need.

Taking another step toward him, I plant a hand on either side of his hips, my palms resting on the back of the leather couch.

"Well, I'm glad to see I saved you from making more than one mistake tonight," I growl before taking his mouth in a brutal kiss. It's all teeth and tongue and pure, addictive carnage.

"Guess that makes two of us," he mutters, all airy and breathless.

I can't help the smirk from sliding on my lips. "Good. Now, turn around and bend over the couch. Ass up."

His cock twitches against my stomach at my command before he obeys, turning in front of me and placing his hands just inside of mine. My own dick aches at the sight of his perfect, round ass, but not nearly as much as it does when I spot two little divots just above each cheek.

Venus dimples.

I don't think those can be classified as a kink, but if I'm wrong, I'm pretty sure I've just unlocked a new one.

"Oh, this is going to be so much fun," I muse, two fingers caressing down his spine before diverting to those two little indents. "Your body is a work of art, and I plan to admire it all fucking night."

Pierce shudders slightly under my touch, and those little tremors create a sense of power I've never experienced before. A feeling of control and command that only serves to turn me on more than him bent over like this does.

I don't know what it is about this guy that's flipped some sort of switch inside me. All I know is…I'm really enjoying it.

"Spread 'em wide for me, baby," I murmur. Leaning forward, I scrape my teeth across the freckles dotting his shoulders. "I wanna watch as every inch of my cock sinks inside you."

Fuck, just the idea of it has me primed and ready to explode.

Pierce's back trembles some more against my lips as he follows my request, shifting his legs apart so I can stand between them. The head of my cock glides up and down his crease, and more than anything, I wish I could feel him clamping around me bare instead.

"Perfect," I muse while gliding two fingers up and down his spine again. "Now stay just like that for me."

Tearing my body away from his is nearly impossible, but I manage in order to rip open the packet of lube, quickly applying a generous amount to my shaft before rubbing the excess down his crease.

A low groan leaves his throat as the tip of my finger teases around his hole, spreading the lube over the puckered rim. It's a taunting caress that doesn't let up until he's pushing back into my hand, begging for more. With a wicked grin, I indulge his silent request, sliding into the tight heat of his body until the digit is fully sheathed.

"Fuck me," he groans, head dropping down as I pump my hand.

"Make no mistake, that's exactly where we're headed," I tell him, curling my finger until I press against that little spot of bliss inside him. A small string of expletives leaves his lips as I caress the nerves there, playing him like Mozart plays the damn pianoforte.

I add a second finger, and it doesn't take long for him to loosen for me after that. Even less time for him to start pushing back against my hand with every thrust, to the point where I have to grab hold of his hip to control the pace.

"Fuck, fuck, *fuck*," he hisses when the pad of my fingers press against his prostate.

My lips curl into a grin at the sound of him coming undone so quickly, and I press a kiss to the space between his shoulders. "If this is how well you take my fingers, I can't wait to see my cock in their place."

His ass squeezes around my fingers at my praise, and if anything, he starts thrusting back even more enthusiastically. I've never been with someone as eager or responsive as Pierce is right now, waiting and at my mercy.

Or impatient, because he turns his head to aim a glare at me that could melt ice.

"Then stop fucking around and give me your cock, Will."

Under normal circumstances, I wouldn't take well to him bossing me around...but I'd be a damned liar if I said I hadn't been waiting for this exact moment. Which is why I find myself pulling free from his body, only to replace my fingers with the tip of my dick.

"Last chance to back out," I whisper, pressing a little harder against his rim.

"And why the fuck would I do that?"

A smile lifts my lips and I murmur against the shell of his ear, "Because, baby...I'm about to ruin you for anyone who'll come after me."

And with that, I press my hips forward, impaling him with my length.

His body envelops me in a tight heat, and I rest my forehead between his shoulder blades as I wait for him to adjust to the intrusion, all the while praying to keep it together and not start pounding him into the sofa cushions.

Only, it seems that's exactly what he wants me to do when he pulls forward before pressing back into me. Too bad for him, the hand still anchored on his hip won't allow it, but it still doesn't stop him from trying again.

"More," he commands, glancing at me over his shoulder. "I want more."

"Demanding, aren't you?" I raise a brow when his glare turns molten. "Just who do you think is in charge here, Pierce?"

I don't wait for him to respond before pulling back, only to slide all the way home in a single, unrelenting thrust. Every squeeze and clench his ass makes while adjusting is nothing short of heaven.

Pure fucking nirvana.

"Oh, fuck." A low growl rumbles from deep within my chest as my head drops back. For a moment, I'm completely lost to the world. It doesn't exist.

Nothing does except me and Pierce and this moment right here.

My hips begin moving of their own accord, pulling back and slamming into him again at breakneck speeds. Our tempo increases, nothing but the sound of our harsh breathing and the slap of skin on skin filling the living room.

That is, until the filthiest, most sinful sounds start leaving Pierce's mouth.

Not just the normal moan or curse word. I'm talking groans and pants that would put a porn star to shame.

And it does everything for me, spurring me on to fuck him harder. More ruthlessly. Anything to draw more of those noises from his lips.

"Fuck your fist for me, baby," I murmur in his ear before nipping at the lobe. "Pretend it's my mouth and that you're punishing me for making you wait this long to be inside of you. Push it so deep down my throat, I've got no choice but to gag around it."

He doesn't need to be told twice, taking himself in hand and stroking his length like his life depends on it.

"Oh, Jesus Christ," he pants when I draw his body back against mine, changing the angle on him. It must hit him in just the right spot too, if the tortured groan that leaves his lips is anything to go by.

His back bumps into my chest with every thrust, and I run my lips and tongue over the pale, dewy skin of his neck and shoulder.

"You feel so fucking good," I rasp, the words coming out in staccato with every thrust.

My pace is downright brutal now, pounding and grinding and pistoning my hips. Pierce doesn't mind, though. From the way he's meeting me thrust for thrust, I'd dare say he's enjoying this just as much as I am. Maybe even more.

I lean back, hands trailing over the smooth, muscled lines of his back and ridges of his spine. He feels perfect in my hands—too fucking perfect—and I'm quick to lose myself in him. In the pleasure he's drawing from my body and pouring into his own.

"That's it. Make me pay for it." My hips move faster, pistoning harder, while I lean back in to murmur sinful words in his ear. "Picture me on my knees in front of you, completely at your mercy."

I'm not sure if it's the filth leaving my mouth, the way my cock keeps swiping over his prostate, or some combination of the two, but Pierce lets out a choked moan as more and more pre-cum leaks through his fingers.

Our new position allows me to trace my tongue over his pulse, exploring his throat while he frantically chases his release.

My own climax hits me hard and far sooner than I'd like, forcing me to still while pressed deep inside him. I grapple for purchase, hands dancing across his heated skin as cum fills the condom, and I bury my face into the arch of his neck and shoulder.

His ass clenches my softening dick, squeezing me to high heaven. Another wave of pleasure ripples through my extremities, causing me to shiver.

"Fuck, I…*Will*," he rasps, head dropped back in ecstasy.

As much as I'd like to watch him get lost in pleasure, memorizing the lines and planes of his face while he comes, there's something else I want just a little bit more. A desire—a taste—for a little more of him, which is why I pull out and drop to the floor, my knees colliding with the laminate.

His hand around his dick stutters at the sudden loss of my cock, but he doesn't have a chance to get the words out before I'm urging his hips to turn. He spins in place, and the fire in his eyes ignites in a blaze when he sees me kneeling before him.

Liquid seeps from the head of his cock as he continues jacking it haphazardly, and my tongue flicks out to lap it up. The salty tang bursts over my taste buds, flooding my mouth.

And like an addict, I'm instantly hooked, desperate for more.

I lick at the head some more while his fist pumps the shaft before his hips cant forward, brushing his tip over my lips. They part on instinct, and if I thought his eyes were two blue balls of fire before, it has nothing on the way they look when his dick disappears between my lips.

Cupping his ass in my palms, I urge his hips forward to pick up his pace from before. It's not long before his movements become jerky and more sporadic, signaling he's right there. Hanging on the edge.

His hand moves to the back of my head, only for his fingers to claw at my skull when I moan around his shaft and his climax slams into him like a runaway train.

And the second I get a real taste of his cum on my tongue, I know I'm in fucking trouble.

FOUR

Pierce

My body slowly stirs at the first hint of sunlight, eyes heavy and struggling to open, yet refusing to stay closed. A few blinks rid me of the morning haze, and the weight of a body half-atop of mine has the pieces of where I am snapping into place. And who I'm with.

Will.

My eyes automatically drift down to the naked man beside me. While I slept on my back, he managed to wrap himself around me like a vine. Tucked beneath my arm, his head rests against my chest, the heat of his gentle breaths coasting over my skin. His muscled arm is draped across my torso, and he's slipped one of his legs in between mine.

I've never done the morning after, but I'm sure the way he's comfortably curled into me isn't the usual.

My gaze continues to trace over him, and I find myself absentmindedly running my fingers through the short strands of his hair, enjoying the softer version of the man who ravaged and ruined me more times than I can count.

We somehow made it to the bed last night—or rather in the early hours this morning. And despite the heavy layer of exhaustion I can feel deep in my bones, my dick twitches and goosebumps break out over my skin as vivid flashbacks play in my mind.

Him touching me.

Tasting me.

Fucking me.

It was hands down the best sex I've ever had, and despite being well and thoroughly fucked, I find myself *still* wanting those things. Wanting him. Wanting us to stay inside these four walls, on this bed, naked, until there's nothing left of me but my spent cock and the smell of sweat and sex and him on my skin.

My nerve endings start prickling with awareness, and my pulse begins to pound erratically. The memories of us together taunt my body, threatening to give my wayward thoughts away if I don't lock them down soon.

Or stop touching him.

My fingers go still in his hair, and I attempt to pull my hand away from his head before he wakes and notices. God knows it might make things weird, and that's the last thing I—

"Don't," he says, his voice groggy and muffled.

Embarrassment rushes through me at being told to stop touching him. A little panic seeps in too, that maybe the night wasn't as good for him as I thought it had been. I quickly try to drag myself out from underneath him, but he holds on to me tighter, locking his arm over me like a vise.

"Where are you going? You didn't even let me finish the sentence." He tilts his head up, resting his chin on my chest, and tired eyes meet mine. "*Don't stop* is what I was going to say. Someone playing with your hair is a nice way to wake up."

The way he's looking at me and the words that leave his mouth have me swallowing hard; even without the sex, I'm very much fascinated by this man. In the juxtaposition between who he is right now and who he was last night. Seemingly content, he places his head back down on my chest. As if we've slept this way a hundred times.

"Sorry," I say, cautiously threading my fingers back through his hair. "I didn't mean to wake you."

"You didn't," he answers, nuzzling his scruffy cheek against my pec. "I'm just a light sleeper."

Knowing now he isn't one for personal questions, I bite my tongue, fighting the urge to ask him about himself. Instead, we lie here in a surprisingly comfortable silence, both of us seemingly lost in our own thoughts, a little slow and sluggish in the sunlight.

"Regretting it already?" he eventually asks.

My hand stills in his hair once more. "Not at all. Do you?" I say in a worried rush.

He holds me tighter, pressing himself into me, his dick half hard against my thigh. "What do you think?"

Relief at knowing I didn't imagine just how great we were together has my own dick thickening. Something that doesn't go unnoticed either, because I feel his stubbled cheek lift in a smile against my skin as his hand skates down my bare chest. It dances down my abs, passing my happy trail entirely, before his palm is brushing over my hard length.

My sharp inhale is the only sound in the room as he wraps his fingers around me.

"I thought you'd be tired." His voice is still raspy from sleep, but the seductive lilt in his tone is unmistakable while his hand lazily moves up and down my shaft. "I can stop if you are."

"Please, don't stop," I say, and again, it comes out a little too quickly. The desperation in my voice isn't even a surprise anymore; clearly, it's my default reaction when it comes to him. I should be embarrassed, but the need to have his hands on me trumps all of that. I'm already too turned on and keyed up.

He presses a few open-mouthed kisses to my skin before pushing himself up on one elbow. His gaze darts down to my cock and then back to my face. Heat and hunger fill his eyes, and a confident smirk stretches across his face.

He still wants me.

I sink my teeth into my bottom lip so he doesn't hear the audible sigh of relief that tries to leave my mouth. Submission to a stranger is so foreign to me, but submission to *this* stranger lights me up like a Christmas tree.

Especially when he looks at me like that.

Last night, I wanted all of him. His words, his attention, his touch. I wanted him as unhinged and unprepared as I'd felt. And so, I gave myself permission to indulge.

This morning, though?

I'm a glutton for him.

Starving and ready to devour.

I've never wanted someone the way I want him, and that alone should be cause for concern.

Like magnets, my eyes follow his every move as he climbs up over me, his body straddling high up on my thighs while his sac lightly grazes mine. His hand returns to my cock as my palms glide up his legs, settling on his hips, and my thumbs circle the skin there.

So much more of him is visible in the light, starting with the fact that his hair isn't nearly as dark as I thought it was last night, lingering somewhere between light brown and blond. Green eyes peppered with dashes of golden brown stare down at me, flicking over my face while I trace my thumbs down his sinfully defined V.

But the thing I notice most is the pale scarring on his left pec and shoulder. They streak and dot across his tanned skin like a constellation; some raised ridges and others indented pits.

All of me wants to ask about them. Maybe trace my fingers over them to learn how they feel under my touch, but I know now's not the time.

I'm certain about one thing, though, as I stare up at this nearly flawless god of a man.

Even with the imperfections, he's fucking edible.

"Damn, you look even better the morning after," he says, eyes mapping over my body beneath him. Apparently, I left myself open to his perusal while I've been dragging my gaze over him, and I'm stunned to find myself preening at his approval.

"Stole the words right off my tongue," I murmur, watching as he continues to lazily stroke my shaft. My muscles tighten in anticipation, already responding to his touch. Glancing down, he moves his hand to line us up, and I'm wrapped up in the perfect view—his hard length against mine.

Skin on skin.

Lust met with lust.

His hand moves over us, up and down in a slow rhythm. Squeezing our crowns together, he smears the mixture of our pre-cum down the length of our shafts. It feels fucking exquisite.

"How long are you here for?"

"W-what?" I stammer.

His hand circles us, his eyes never leaving mine.

"How long are you here for?" he repeats, completely unfazed.

"A week," I answer, struggling to concentrate on his question when he's touching me like this.

I watch him work his throat and then expertly drop a string of saliva onto our joined cocks, rubbing it into our skin. The added lubrication has my dick twitching in his palm.

"And you're going to Seattle straight from here?" he asks, as if he's not turning me inside out with every touch.

I reach for him and still his hands. "Are you serious right now?"

"What?" His eyes are full of mischief as he knocks my hand away. "I thought you loved playing twenty questions."

I gape at him for a moment, unsure if I'm imagining things when this playful version is such a contradiction to the man I brought home with me last night.

I'm having a hard time trying to work out which one I like more.

"I'd rather play twenty ways we can make one another come," I retort, arching a brow.

He raises one back. "Twenty ways? Sounds like something that could take a while."

"Are you in a rush?" I challenge.

"No. I'm more curious as to what number one on your list is." He says it nonchalantly, but I don't miss the flicker of lust in his eyes or the way his thighs have tightened around me.

With bravado I don't truly feel, I hold his gaze and wrap my hand around his cock, stroking him slowly. I'm determined to take control. To take what I want from him.

To try and satiate this growing need that I have no business feeling.

I rub my thumb over his crown, smearing his pre-cum before slipping it into my mouth, needing to taste him.

His tongue grazes his bottom lip, gaze boring into mine. He rises up on his knees, holding his cock and reading my mind. "You want this in your mouth?"

Propping myself on the pillows, I curl a hand around each of his thighs and wordlessly encourage him forward. He shuffles closer, grabbing the headboard with his free hand to hover over me.

I tip my head back to take in his closeness and meet his hooded gaze. He's all skin and muscles and happy trails. His cock is directly in line with my face, glistening right in front of my lips. He's a wet dream—*my* wet dream—and I can feel my own dick jerking and leaking against my lower stomach, desperate for some form of release.

"Tell me," he coaxes. "Tell me you want my cock in your mouth."

I want his cock. *Desperately.*

I want my mouth all over him. I want to feel every single ridge and pulsing vein underneath my tongue, but keeping him on edge is worth the wait.

"I want to hear you say it," he says, his tone calm and measured, a complete contrast to the sex-filled air surrounding us.

His gaze burns into me as he brushes the tip of his cock across my lips, and a groan reverberates in my chest. My hands slide further up his thighs before slipping around to squeeze the tight globes of his ass.

"I wanna taste you," I tell him, my voice soft and purposefully gentle. "I want your dick in my mouth, down my throat. I want you to fuck my—"

The word dies on my lips as one of Will's hands drops into my hair, tugging my head back, as the other shoves his dick in my waiting mouth.

His thrusts are hard and fast from the start. Rough and needy, a crazed ferocity seeping out of him. My blood thrums as I watch him, his calm and collected mask sliding right off his face.

"Fuck. Fuck. Fuck," he chants as he sinks himself into my mouth, his tip repeatedly hitting the back of my throat. Making me choke and gag around him. My eyes water from the brutality of it.

It's exactly what I asked for.

"Is this what you want? Want me to use you?" Will's pupils dilate at my gasping breaths, and if possible, his thrusts become faster. More frantic.

Unhinged, even.

"Fuck," he growls. "You make me feel so fucking crazy."

Words tumble out of his mouth.

All the words.

No control, no cohesion.

He's as caught up in his euphoria as my body is caught up in him.

Moisture pools at the corner of my eyes, and the sight of them must be what has Will slowing down. His thrusts become deep but unhurried. Almost an indirect power exchange as I begin bobbing my head up and down his length. My cheeks hollow out as I suck him enthusiastically, loving how thick and hard he is in my mouth.

I let him slip from my lips, only to circle his crown with my tongue and taste the salty beads of pre-cum in his slit. My head tilts, giving myself better access to his sac, sucking on each of his balls.

"Your mouth is magic," he says, his voice hoarse as he pushes himself back in between my lips. "Just like that, baby."

My own hand reaches for my shaft at his praise, needing release like it's my next breath. I stroke myself rapidly, wanting to push us both toward the finish line. To find the ecstasy we're both craving.

Drawing his length deeper into my mouth, my cheeks hollow as I eagerly lick and suck. I press two digits right behind his balls, my fingertips massaging his taint as I continue to work my throat and mouth over his length.

"Don't stop," he breathes out. "I'm gonna come."

With no intention of stopping, I rush to please him. Neglecting my own cock, I circle my hand around his hip, stilling him. My fingers slip to his taint and massage his prostate, my lips and tongue working him over until I feel his body stiffen and hands tighten painfully in my hair.

"Fuck," he cries out, as spurts of cum begin to fill my mouth. I greedily swallow the salty liquid, my own body coiling in anticipation as I grip my shaft, fucking my fist furiously as I suck him dry.

Taking note of my frantic movements, Will hastily moves down my body, slapping my hand away from my dick and wrapping his lips around it. It doesn't take more than just the feel of the heat of his mouth for me to spill onto his tongue with a throaty groan.

"Holy shit," I pant, my body slumping into an exhausted heap against the mattress while I try to calm my erratic breathing.

My fingers slide into Will's hair, playing with the soft strands while his tongue greedily licks my softening cock until it's completely clean. Once he's satiated and satisfied, he crawls up the length of my body so we're flush against each other. His mouth brushes across my collarbone and neck before nipping at the corner of my mouth.

He captures my lips, sliding his tongue against mine.

"See how good you taste," he mutters before kissing me again.

My hands cradle his face, everything about us quiet now that our thirst has been quenched. It's not a battle of wills or a fight for control anymore, just a slow, languid kiss. His arousal mixes with mine, the taste of both of us sinfully potent.

We're good together.

Too good.

Scarily good.

After a playful slap to his ass, I sit up, needing to put some distance between us. It has the desired effect, and he shifts off me, but not before giving me an eyeful of scars dotting the back of his left shoulder too.

Or his tight, firm ass.

Fucking hell.

I was going for casual. Lighthearted. Unfazed. Everything opposite to how hard and forceful the organ inside my chest is thumping as I head toward the bathroom.

Chancing a glance at him over my shoulder, I find him watching me as I walk away, his eyes fixated on my ass, and the pounding against my ribs only grows.

But rather than letting it show, I wink and give him a grin.

"I still think you taste better."

FIVE

Pierce

Walking out of the bathroom, with nothing but a towel wrapped around my waist, my eyes immediately land on Will. He's dressed again in last night's clothes, sitting on the edge of the bed with his cell in his hand. His fingers fly over the screen and the material on his body makes it seem like he's put up a wall between us; the loss of intimacy and attention creating an uncomfortable lump in the pit of my stomach that I choose to ignore.

The very last thing on my mind as Will and I raced to get one another naked last night was to bring the bag I packed inside. Dragging my eyes away from him, I search for my own clothes before noticing they've been tossed on the bed beside Will, who must've brought them into the bedroom while I was in the shower.

I grab my shirt and shrug into the sleeves before reaching for the first button, only to realize I'm missing most of them. That's right. Will ripped them off when he went at me like a starved animal going in for the kill.

"Probably should've thought that one through, huh?"

I tip my head up at the sound of his voice, my stomach doing somersaults with his eyes back on me again.

Get a grip, Pierce.

"It's okay, I have other clothes in the car," I tell him, switching out the shirt for my pants. My stomach rolls some more as I let my towel fall, playing with fire and desperate to poke the bear. Will's eyes drop to my dick immediately, and I pretend to be completely unaffected by his perusal of me as I push my legs into the pants. He's certainly affected, though, and I don't miss the way his Adam's apple bobs or the way he bites the corner of his bottom lip.

"You're staring," I murmur, meeting his gaze again.

"Is that a problem?"

I shake my head, unable to hide the little smirk forming.

While I've never been one for compliments—always feeling uncomfortable when they're given to me—when they're coming from his lips, I find myself wanting to earn another.

Maybe because it feels like a victory.

For what? I don't know.

But I don't care either.

In the less than twenty-four hours around him, I lost both my head and my senses, and it doesn't look like they're returning anytime soon. I'm feeling bold and reckless, and I like it. It's a feeling I want to hold on to. And if he's the reason behind it, well…

"I'm gonna grab the rest of my clothes from my car." I pull up the zipper of my pants, eyes meeting his. "You know you can shower, right?"

He looks surprised by my offer. "Oh. I was just waiting around to let you know I'm heading out."

It's then I notice his infamous green duffel beside him on the bed, packed up and ready to go. I try to push down the irrational wave of panic that threatens to expand inside my chest at the mere mention of him leaving. One that defies all logical sense, yet it's there regardless.

"Okay, well, at least let me buy you breakfast," I suggest, aiming for a casual invite. "We both worked up quite an appetite."

"I—"

Will's stomach growls loudly, and my lips stretch into a smile at the perfect timing. "I'll take that as a yes?"

Indecision is written all over his face, but something tells me it has nothing to do with me. Attempting to keep things light, I tilt my head toward the bathroom door. "Look, I've got a few things to take care of this morning as it is, including how much damage is behind that door after last night. Have that shower if you want to, and if you're up for it, then we can get out of here."

With my offer of space and privacy, I step toward the hall to go grab my bag from the car, all the while hoping he'll choose to stick around. Even if it's only for a little bit longer.

After emptying my car and setting my suitcase and laptop bag inside the house, I find a freshly showered Will much more certain of his decision to have breakfast with me. He even offers up a recommendation for a place to eat, making it clear he's quite familiar with the coastal town of Cannon Beach. And it's also becoming apparent that, while it might not be my nature, I'm having no issue with him calling the shots.

Or maybe I'm still riding the high from last night. Of relinquishing that control to him.

It's a quick walk to the quiet, quaint café—the establishment fitting right in with the rest of the sleepy town. We're close enough to the ocean that the sound of the waves hitting the shore soothes me instantly, and I understand why this place is one of the top tourist destinations in the state.

My gaze settles on Will seated across from me, and I can't help noticing how the connection between us is now vastly different with clothes on and the absence of alcohol.

Instead of exchanging filthy words and heated glances, we've been talking about this being the best time to visit the coast, then moving on to what breakfast foods we prefer after I placed an order for pancakes despite his protest that the waffles here were far superior. The information might be seemingly meaningless, but I greedily gulp it down.

It seems the need to touch him—and be touched by him—has been replaced by a desire to learn whatever I can about him.

"So, you obviously visit here a lot," I hedge, restating the small amount of information he gave me last night while cutting into my stack of pancakes.

He nods. "It's my home away from home."

Mention of his home has my brain rerouting to the conversation we had last night. About a little tiny fleck of information he gave up—willingly or not.

"And it's kind of a small world that we'll both be living in Seattle."

Something crosses his expression that I can't quite place, but it's gone a moment later. Replaced with a wry little smirk before he says, "You, me, and almost 750,000 other people."

Fair enough.

"Were you born and raised there, or…?"

I leave the question to hang in the air as his lips twitch and he stabs at his hashbrowns, keeping his eyes cast down. "So, it's not just twenty ways to make you come after all? We're really doing twenty questions too?"

My words were meant to be cautious. To be anything other than overly intrusive. What I want to know doesn't matter if it means scaring him away.

"You don't have to answer that," I say, maybe a little too quickly, before awkwardly adding, "Unless you want to."

A throaty chuckle leaves his mouth. "I never want to talk about myself. I think I'm pretty boring and my life is very…" His face turns pensive, lips pursed together, almost like he's deciding what he will or will not say. "Let's say it's very rigid."

"And this place somehow makes you less rigid?"

Despite me asking the question, instinct tells me I already know the answer. I'm familiar with rigid. I'm familiar with pressure and expectation, and the distant look in Will's eyes tells me he is too.

"It's like heaven on earth here, don't you think?" His gaze focuses back on my face as he asks the question. But even though it's rhetorical—and a way to completely avoid my question—I'm still able to discern just how much this place means to him.

And for now, that's enough.

"I only stopped here because it was on my way to Seattle," I tell him in between bites, offering to switch the subject to myself instead.

Forcing questions on him won't make him trust me. In fact, it might have the opposite effect. Showing him that I'm willing to hand over pieces of me, on the other hand, might garner another reaction.

"On the way from where?"

My lips twitch as I swirl another piece of pancake in syrup, a small amount of excitement racing through my bloodstream. Apparently, I'm not the only one wanting to know more about the person I spent the night with.

"Are you joining in this game too?"

His eyes flash to mine. "It's only fair, right?"

"True," I agree with another nod, knowing I'll happily tell him whatever he wants to know.

"Then let's make a deal. We get to ask each other twenty *meaningful* questions. Follow-ups don't count. No topic is off-limits. No backing out of it, no mincing words."

The offer takes me aback momentarily, seeing as Will hasn't been all that willing to give up any personal details about himself. It's been like pulling teeth, to be honest, so the fact that he's offering up *twenty* personal pieces of himself is…shocking.

Surprise must be written in my expression too, because he arches a brow while waiting for my response.

"I…yeah. That sounds good."

Smiling, he cuts through his syrup-covered waffle and brings a piece to his mouth. "You don't have to look so shocked."

Swallowing hard, I shake my head and lie. "Just wondering what pieces of information you'll be asking for first."

"We can start easy, then. Where did you move from?" he asks, reiterating his question from earlier.

"Denver," I tell him, indulging in our newly made-up game. "This was a little break along the way."

"The coast is a couple hours out of the way—"

"Figuratively speaking."

"And this?" He gestures between us. "Was this in the plan? Picking up a stranger and taking them to breakfast?"

"Sort of," I answer honestly. "I'm not a one-night-stand guy, and I wanted to give it a try."

"And did it live up to your expectations?"

The side of his mouth lifts, and I reach for my coffee, bringing the mug to my lips in an attempt to hide my own smile. "I don't know, the bartender might've been a better choice."

Subtly clenching his jaw, he raises a challenging brow. "Is that so? You think he could've fucked you better?"

"Maybe," I say confidently, enjoying the tinge of tension in his voice. "Might have to pay him a visit and see if his offer still stands."

It's stupid to tease him, especially when I haven't gotten him to agree to spend another night with me like I'm craving. But I've been enjoying the back and forth we've found ourselves in. How, despite his decision to hold on to all his words, his facial expressions and body language tell his every secret.

Like the hint of jealousy I see etched there now, and it's electrifying to the point where I push a little further.

"We can go back to the bar tonight and see if he's up for it. Hell, maybe you could watch."

Leaning forward, Will licks his bottom lip while holding my gaze. "You know you're going to pay for that, right?"

My dick stirs at the idea, and I hitch a thumb at the door behind me. "Yeah? Do you want to go back to the rental?"

He shakes his head and stabs at his food. "Oh no. That would be too easy." His eyes flick up to mine before he adds, "Plus, we've got things to do."

"We do?"

"You were in the middle of telling me all about your mid-life crisis, and I was going to tell you why I came here."

I gape at him. "Who the hell said anything about a mid-life crisis?"

"You did, Mr. I've Never Had a One Night Stand," he answers with a smile, clearly pleased with himself. "Which you've now crossed off your bucket list."

"You're making me sound uninteresting and old as fuck."

"You're neither of those things," he says seriously. "Well, I guess you *could* be old, seeing as you've never mentioned your age. But definitely not uninteresting."

"I'm twenty-nine." I finish off my coffee and set the mug back down on the table. "Rolling into my thirties and just having my first one night stand. Like I said, old and uninteresting. But hardly a mid-life crisis."

"I'm twenty-six," he offers before his eyes fixate on his plate. "But I feel older than you are, and the number of one-night stands I've had is probably the most uninteresting thing about me."

That's an opening if I've ever heard one, and there's no way in hell I can stop myself from taking it.

"Well…" I murmur, arching a brow. "Then are you going to tell me what the *most* interesting thing about you is?"

The silence stretches between us, but this time I don't rush to fill it. Instead, I wait until his attention returns to me, only to hold his gaze while his thought process unfolds across his face. Analyzing the hue of his hazel eyes until his shoulders sag, letting me know he's decided to relinquish another piece of himself.

"I'm in the military."

My brows furrow, curious why something as simple as his occupation would be the most interesting thing about him.

"What?"

"I'm in the military," he repeats while shuffling pieces of his waffle around his plate absently. "Combat flight medic."

He doesn't give more, and I can already read him well enough to know not to push on this particular topic. It's clear as day in his body language.

So instead, I bring our conversation full circle.

"I'm assuming that's why you come here, right? For some much needed R and R?"

He swallows a bite of waffle, mulling over my words briefly. It's only when he's finished eating that his attention shifts to me, and he utters a sentence that damn near stops my heart.

"If you want to know why I come here, I think it's better if I just show you."

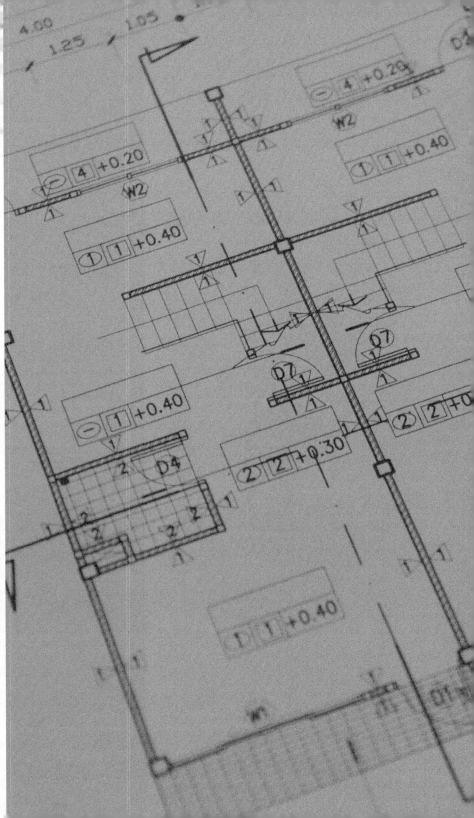

SIX

Pierce

"So…where exactly are we going?"

Will glances to where I'm about five feet behind him on the heavily-wooded path—the same one we've been trekking down for the past forty-five minutes. "You're the one who wanted to know more about me and why I come here."

I manage to catch my breath before answering, "That was before I found out you'd be leading me through the forest to an unknown destination."

He stops and turns toward me, lips lifting in the ghost of a smile. It forces me to stop too, or risk running straight into him. "Do you not trust me to get you there in one piece or something?"

I roll my eyes and adjust the pack slung over my shoulders. "Trust has nothing to do with it."

"Oh, really?" he murmurs with a laugh. There's a seductive lilt to his tone as he steps closer to me, and a hand reaches up to fiddle with one of the straps. "You're sure you haven't started thinking I'm actually a serial killer or something? Luring you to your death?"

"I wasn't…" I search his face, my gaze catching on his tongue wetting his lower lip. "But now that you mention it, this whole scenario feels like it's right out of a horror movie. Very *Wrong Turn*."

"*Wrong Turn*," he repeats slowly. From his tone, it's clear he's never seen or heard of the movies. Which is blasphemous, in my opinion, though we can deal with that little detail later.

Instead, I do my best to keep my face straight as I nod. "You could be leading me into a nest of inbred cannibals who want to string me up for dinner. Or you could *be* one of them, standing right in front of me while you picture how delectable I'll taste after being marinated like a steak."

He stares at me like I've lost my marbles, and I can't help but crack a smile…only for it to turn into full-blown laughter when relief replaces his bewildered expression.

"Please tell me that isn't a real movie."

"Don't worry, we can watch it tonight," is all I say, hoping he picks up what I'm putting down.

He looks like he wants to say something—maybe talk me out of forcing the best horror movie of my childhood on him this evening—when he just laughs and grips my strap a little tighter.

"You're just full of surprises, aren't you?"

I offer him an arched brow. "One night together and you think you've got me all figured out, Will?"

A wry smirk curls his mouth at the corner, and he shakes his head. Then he leans forward, his lips dancing over the pulse point in my throat before brushing against my ear. "Well, you're right about one thing. You do taste fucking delicious. But unless we're talking about death by orgasm, I think you're safe with me."

It takes every ounce of willpower in my body to not visibly shudder from the sin and sex laced in his words like an aphrodisiac.

Fuck.

He's potent, and he knows it too.

Just a few enticing words and provocative looks, and I'm ready to haul him against the nearest tree and maul him. A desire only fueled by the heat and filthy promises swirling in his irises as he takes a step back, then another.

I'm grateful for the much-needed distance, though it isn't enough to cool the fire now raging in my veins.

"C'mon," he murmurs, nodding his head toward the trail. "We've only got the downhill left till we're there."

True to his word, it's not more than ten minutes until we reach a set of steps leading down the cliff's steep edge to the deserted shoreline of Crescent Beach.

Something about him changes the second his feet hit the sand and he starts out toward the shoreline. It's like his whole demeanor transforms before my eyes as he stares out at where the sand meets the sea, a sense of peace overtaking his entire body. The lines between his brows smooth out, and the muscles in his back and shoulders seem to visibly ease, serenity enveloping him.

I'm completely enraptured by the hardened man beside me as he slowly softens. And I have the strangest feeling that this is a part of himself he doesn't reveal often.

Maybe even ever.

"This," is all he says after a few minutes of silence, attention still fixed on the horizon. But I hear the rest of his unspoken words loud and clear.

This is why I'm here.

Finally removing my attention from him, I follow his gaze to take in the scenery before me. The second I do, understanding washes over me, like the waves rolling on the sand.

The aptly named beach is shaped like a sliver of the moon, backed by a wall of lush, green forest, and capped on either side by stunning rock formations jutting from both the sand and sea. Waves crash and thunder as they roll toward land, and the salty breeze catches the fine mist they create.

The place is deserted, the two of us the only signs of life besides the gulls flying overhead, and it feels like we've stepped out into a prime example of pure, undiscovered beauty.

I've never seen anything quite like it, and it damn near steals my breath.

"Wow," I find myself whispering while taking it all in.

"Exactly."

My gaze shifts back to him, surprised to find him already staring at me. Intently watching with the same knowing scrutiny and discernment he used last night, like he's waiting for something. Maybe for me to put more pieces of the puzzle that is him together.

Too bad the only thing I can do is get lost in the greens of his irises.

A feat as easy as it is dangerous.

"Thank you. For sharing this with me, I mean."

His lips tilt up at one corner, and it's that tiniest hint of a smile that does something wicked to the organ in my chest, causing it to stumble for the briefest second. But it's got nothing on the way it crawls into my throat the second he takes my hand and starts leading me toward the rock formations off to the left side of the beach.

"Oh, Pierce," he says, a smile evident in his voice. "You haven't seen anything yet."

If I thought I saw a new side of him before on the trails and when we first set foot on the beach, I was sorely mistaken. Because the child-like enthusiasm radiating from him as he leads me through a cavern in the rocks bursting with sea anemone and colorful starfish clinging to the walls is unmatched. To the point where I'm starting to wonder how many layers of this man there are to uncover.

We take our time in the caves, leaving no nook or cranny unexplored, before coming out the other side. The second we're back on the beach, I see a familiar shape off in the distance. One that looks distinctly like—

"Is that Haystack Rock?"

His eyes lift to follow my gaze, and he nods. "Sure is."

My attention drags the length of the beach, noticing there's only a couple spots where the water is high enough to maybe reach my knees at this tide. My brain slowly puts the pieces together, clicking into place as I turn to look at Will and frown.

"Are you telling me we could have just walked the beach to get here instead of hiking?"

A devious smirk rests on his lips as he guides me back toward the main area of the beach. "Depending on the time of year, you can at low tide, yeah. Today looks like a day where we probably could've. But where's the fun in that?"

I'm not at all amused as I glare his way. "You're lucky I actually like hiking."

"I certainly wouldn't have pegged you for someone who'd be down for a hike, that's for sure. Even if you are from Colorado."

I frown. "What's that supposed to mean?"

Rather than answering, he continues on to where he said more caves wait for us to explore at the north end of the beach. I follow—of course,

I follow—and we walk the beach's length in silence while my brain does that thing where it starts reading between lines that probably aren't there.

Which is why, when he grabs my hand to pull me between two narrow boulders, I halt our progress until he looks at me.

"Seriously, what did you mean by that?" I ask when he arches a questioning brow.

"Nothing bad. Just that when I picked you up at the bar last night, you looked like you just came from a courtroom or *Fortune* 500 business meeting. Nothing about you screamed *I'm into the outdoors*, and then after breakfast when you pulled out a pair of hiking boots that were actually *used*...." He pauses, shaking his head with a wry laugh. "You're just not what I expected."

His response has a smile curling my lips upward. "The thing about people, Will? They have layers. And some of the deeper ones might be surprising compared to what's on the surface."

The grin he returns has my damn heart stuttering all over again, especially when his eyes dart down to my mouth. "So I'm beginning to realize."

"Just don't think I'm oblivious to what you're playing at here," I murmur.

His brow arches, the picture of innocence. "And what would that be?"

"Steering the conversation in a direction where you'll get more information about me without actually using your questions." From the way his lips twitch in a clear effort to remain composed, I know that's exactly what he's doing. "Yeah, thought so. That should constitute as cheating."

"Oh, really? And how would you like to rectify that issue?"

"Maybe knock a couple questions off. Make the punishment fit the crime and all that."

Will takes a step toward me, the heat in his gaze scalding. He backs me into the rocky wall of the cave before wrapping a hand around each wrist and raising my arms over my head, like I wasn't just the one mentioning punishing *him*.

We're only inches apart, his breath hot on my lips and the air between us thick. There's never any reprieve, the attraction and the chemistry weaving its way through every word, every look, every touch.

He presses a kiss to my jaw before blazing a path to my mouth. It's nothing more than a teasing brush of his lips over mine once he's there, but it must have the desired effect, because my mouth greedily chases his, desperate to crush our lips together.

He maneuvers my wrists together, holding them in one hand as the other trails down my chest before settling on my hip.

"That just made me wanna fuck you in this cave," he utters.

Tension builds and coils in my stomach, desire knotting itself there as his lips carve a path across my collarbone, the heat of his mouth slicing through me.

"Anyone could come down here."

"Mmm. But that's half the allure, isn't it? The possibility of getting caught?"

God, yes.

While I've never been one for public sexual encounters, the idea holds more appeal than I dare to admit. He challenges everything I know about myself, especially when he's shackling me like this, rolling his hips into me while his mouth unleashes wicked torment across my skin.

"I wanna take my time with you, though," he rasps. "Really draw out your pleasure until you damn near lose your mind from the need to come."

His words conjure up back-to-back images in my mind. My cock hard. My hands itching to touch him. Every part of me trying to decide whether it wants hard and fast or would prefer his brand of torture.

"Stay with me again."

He doesn't even miss a beat when he rears his head back and says, "Oh, I was already planning on it."

"Really? Without an invitation?"

Another smirk—one I'm starting to realize is as devious as it is sexy—curls his mouth up. "Maybe."

I arch a brow. "And how exactly were you gonna do that?"

"Well, if you must know, I have every intention of luring you into the hot tub to avoid watching that horror movie you so graciously outlined for me earlier." Fingers sneak beneath my shirt, dancing up and over the skin of my side in a feather-light caress. It creates a trail of heat beneath his touch; one impossible to ignore. "And then after ordering some pizza, I plan to drag you to the bedroom for a few more rounds of sweaty, earth-shattering sex. By that point, you'll be so satisfied, you won't even realize I spent the night until you wake up with your dick in my mouth tomorrow morning."

I gape at him, astounded. *His brand of torture.* "You've really thought it all out."

"I had a plan B too, if you wanna hear that one," he jokes.

I wish I was irritated with how cavalier he is, with the cockiness and obscene amount of self-assuredness he possesses. But if anything, it only makes him more attractive. It doesn't matter that in all other circumstances of my life, I'm the confident one. The role reversal draws me in deeper, flooding my dopamine-high brain with things it really shouldn't be thinking.

Opening my mouth to speak things I might regret saying.

And yet…

"Well, if you're going to that much trouble," I hear myself uttering, "then maybe you should just stay the whole week."

I flex my wrists in his hold as I glance away, not daring to look him in the eye and risk the sting of rejection. But he's not having it, using a finger to tilt my chin up. Forcing me to meet his gaze as his thumb brushes over my lower lip.

"Like I said," he murmurs, eyes searching mine. "Full of surprises."

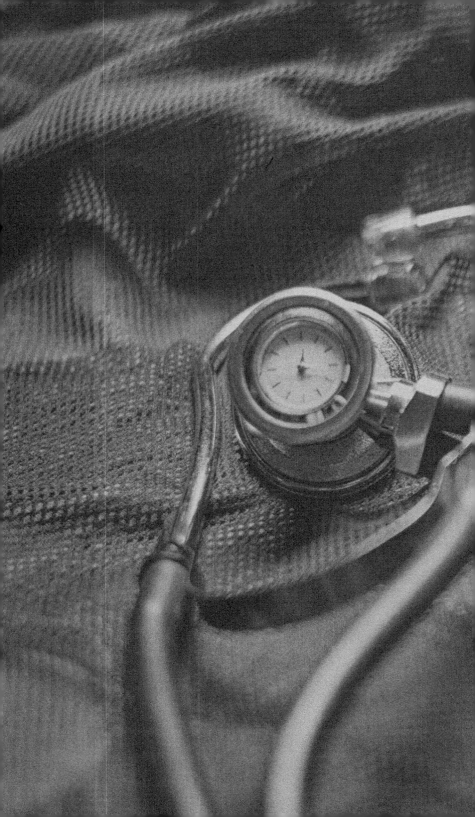

SEVEN

Will

Our hike back to the car is pretty uneventful, as is the drive back to Pierce's rental in town. There's been a small shift in Pierce's demeanor, though, and I'd have to be blind not to realize it.

It's like he's more relaxed.

And while I'm not so self-important to think learning more about me or my agreeing to stay the week with him is the cause, I also don't believe it's a coincidence.

Even as the front door falls closed behind me, I don't feel the nervous energy radiating from him the way I had been this morning after waking up together. Instead, it's easy. Comfortable, even.

Pierce starts toward the primary bedroom, but I'm quick to grab his wrist and stop him. I grin devilishly when his confused gaze shifts to mine.

"Where do you think you're going?"

He tosses a thumb over his shoulder, toward the bedroom. "To shower?"

Oh, that's cute.

Bewilderment slides over his features when I arch a brow and step in closer to him. "And tell me, Pierce. What's the point of getting cleaned up when I'm only gonna make you filthy all over again? Or have you forgotten our conversation from earlier about my plans to seduce you into submission?"

Heat flashes in his sapphire eyes and he wets his lower lip. "Believe me, Will. I've been thinking about it since the moment you said it."

"Then you better strip, because my seduction starts with you, me, and that hot tub on the deck."

Desire licks through my veins like a wildfire as I step back and pull my shirt over my head, not bothering to wait for a response. I toss it to the floor, feeling his lust-filled stare drag across my torso in a wicked caress. The rest of my clothes are quick to follow, as is his stare.

The way he looks at me is electrifying, especially when it's with the unchecked want currently smoldering in his eyes as I move toward the deck leading to the hot tub.

But when I glance back to see he hasn't made a single move to undress—attention too fixated on my ass to do much of anything else—I quirk a brow at him.

"You gonna come willingly, or are you planning to play hard to get?"

The question spurs Pierce into action, and by the time I've slipped into the steaming water, he's stripped down to nothing but the tight pair of black boxer briefs that cling and mold to his body like they were tailored to him.

But then he quickly sheds those too once he's out on the deck, and my dick immediately takes notice, stirring to life beneath the water's surface.

There's no mistake about it: I'm as affected by him as he is by me.

I just happen to be better at hiding it.

Not right now, though. At this very moment, nothing short of the world ending could pull my attention from his naked form as he slowly climbs the steps to join me, watching the way his muscles move and flex beneath his skin. He must feel the heat of my gaze, and his eyes lift to collide with mine.

It's at that moment I realize how quickly I've begun drowning in their blue depths.

He hisses when his skin touches the bubbling water before submerging himself from the neck down in the seat at the opposite corner of the hot tub. One too far away for my liking, but I don't mention it.

I don't act on the impulsive thoughts begging me to close the space between us or haul him into my lap so I can have my way with him either. And, God, how I want to touch him. Not just now, but all the time. Whenever or however I can get my hands on him, no matter who might be around or watching.

It's unsettling, like a strange sort of addiction. One I have no idea what to do with.

My attention sweeps over his face, studying the ridges of his cheekbones. The slope of his nose and taut lines of his shoulders Every inch of available skin, my gaze greedily devours as he leans his head back against the headrest and allows his eyes to fall shut.

"Fuck, I needed this," he mutters and rolls his shoulder again.

"Sore?"

A little grin pulls at his lips. "Honestly? Between hiking and the sex, I feel like I've been hit by a truck."

"In a good way, or…?"

He frowns and peeks an eye open. "In what world would being hit by a truck be a good thing?"

"Fair point," I say with a soft laugh. "But there's that delicious feeling you get when you're so tired and exhausted, you could just dissolve into a puddle of goo."

"Mmm," he agrees with a low hum.

Silence falls over us then, the only sounds coming from the jets of the hot tub and the nearby crashing of waves against the shoreline. And it's a peaceful sort of quiet; the kind where neither of us feels the need to fill it with small talk or our game of twenty questions.

We can simply exist together, enjoying each other's presence.

Yet even in comfortable silence, I'm hyperaware of every water and air molecule separating us, building until the need to touch him is unbearable. Unable to curb my addictive personality, I find myself sliding to the bench perpendicular to him and slowly close the distance between us.

Anticipation swirls in my stomach as I reach out below the water until my fingers make contact with his leg, all the while keeping my gaze locked on his face. He's smiling as he peeks at me with one eye again, only for it to fall closed again when I pull his calves across my thighs.

I work my fingers over the taut and overused muscles in his calf. Something between a moan and a sigh escapes him at my ministrations, and my cock jolts at the sound.

God, everything about this man turns me on. Turns me inside fucking out with little to no effort.

I train my eyes on his face, watching him visibly relax into my touch. Though it's only been twenty-four hours since we met, he's already become quite easy to get a read on.

Strangely enough, I find myself *wanting* to know everything I can about the man beside me. The big, the small, and all that falls in between.

"Question."

His grin grows, spreading across his face. "Answer."

"What's your favorite thing to do?"

"God…" Pierce releases a soft sigh as my fingers continue to massage his calf, loosening the strained muscles some more. "It's been so long since I've done anything besides pouring all my time into work. I don't think I even know what I enjoy doing outside it anymore. Or if I even know how to have fun anymore."

"Well, I think you're doing a pretty good job of it right now."

He doesn't respond, though his smile remains wide and unfiltered with his head tipped back. The sight is absolutely intoxicating.

Not unlike everything else about him.

It might've been his body that's drawn me in since the moment I saw him sitting on that bar stool, but I'd be a liar and a fool to think it's the only thing keeping me around anymore.

It's unexplainable, and if someone else relayed a story of how they met a man and became addicted to him in less than twenty-four hours, I'd laugh in their face. But Pierce is different. I don't know how or why, but he's found the cracks in my defenses—the walls nearly as high and impenetrable as Fort fucking Knox—and only continues infiltrating deeper as more time passes, pulling out pieces of information I haven't willingly given…fuck, anyone.

Ever.

And the more cracks he finds his way through, the easier it becomes to open up completely.

At this point, I don't think there's much I wouldn't tell him. All he has to do is ask. A fact that's nearly as terrifying as it is completely insane.

Maybe it's because I know this thing between us has an expiration date lingering over us like a guillotine ready to drop—effectively severing all connection from each other once we go our separate ways. Though that's a fact he's still entirely unaware of.

He lets out another low moan as I put more pressure on the long muscles of his calves, loosening them and kneading out the knots.

"That feels so good."

The sounds leaving his mouth are making it really hard to keep my hands to myself. Well, more to myself than I'm failing to do already. But no amount of self-restraint seems to be enough, and the need for more—for *him*—reaches the point of unbearable.

My fingers wrap around his ankle, just above the joint, and my other hand curls around his thigh. His eyes fly open, colliding with mine when I tug him toward me, his body cutting through the water with little resistance.

He's in my lap seconds later, settled between my thighs and resting his back against my chest like we've done this a hundred times before. My stomach does a strange little flip when his head leans on my shoulder, exposing his throat to me.

"Was there a problem with where I was sitting before?" he teases, and I glance down to find his eyes closed again.

"You were too far away."

His lips twitch, amusement evident in his tone when he asks, "Two feet was too far, huh?"

"Might as well have been two miles."

That draws a laugh from him. "Better be careful there, Will. I might have to kick you out if you start acting too clingy."

My mouth drops to the thin layer of skin at his throat, drawing it between my teeth. The bite elicits a soft gasp from him that has my dick thickening against the base of his spine.

"I'd like to see you try," I taunt, running my mouth up and down the length of his neck. "Better yet, why don't you try and climb out of the tub."

My hands find purchase on his hips, shifting his body enough that my rock hard cock is in line with his crease. A low hum leaves his throat when my fingers dig into his skin, holding on to him. Despite the taunting words that leave my mouth, I have a feeling I don't need to keep him here. Maybe because I *know* neither one of us is walking away from the other earlier than we have to.

He rocks himself against me, his ass sliding up and down my shaft, and even in the water, the friction promises us a night filled with ecstasy. Sliding my hand around his body, I wrap my fingers around his cock, loving how heavy and thick it feels in my hand.

Taking a deep, shaky breath, he drops his head against my shoulder as I begin to stroke him.

"I can't think when you touch me," he confesses.

His hands settle on my thighs as he continues to move his body back and forth, his crease sliding up and down my shaft, and his cock so desperate to fuck my fist. My mouth continues its trek along his neck, the pounding of his pulse underneath my lips in complete sync with my own.

"Feeling needy, baby?" I rasp before nipping below his ear.

A groan rumbles in his throat, the vibration of it against my mouth making my dick even harder. I want to slip myself inside of him, skin on skin, and feel his body snug around me. The thought of this being the closest to bare he and I will ever be has my hand moving faster and my mind wishing for more than we can have.

"Fuck, that feels good," he pants, more breathy noises leaving his lips.

Lowering my hand, my fingers graze his balls before giving them a quick squeeze, and he releases a desperate whimper.

"The sounds you're making are really testing my self-control, baby." My teeth nip at his throat again. "Making it really *hard* to be good."

His movements above me become a little frantic. "Who said you had to be good?"

God.

The temptation he holds is intoxicating. All-consuming, even.

And when things like that come out of his mouth, the way he wants me—full of taunting lust and desire—resisting him is next to impossible.

"Want me to fuck you?" I say into his ear.

"Yes," he pants. "But we aren't having sex in here."

"God, no," I agree, but that doesn't stop me from rolling my hips against him for the hell of it, letting him feel just how ready I am to sink inside him all over again.

"You don't seem too sure about that."

I realize he's right as my hand starts to move faster, a new desperation to sink inside him clawing at me. "And here I thought I'd mastered some sort of self-control."

"Will, if you don't stop—"

The threat dies on his lips as I release his cock, grabbing his hips to turn his body to face me. I curl a hand around his neck and slam his lips to mine in a quick but brutal kiss.

"Dry off and wait on the bed," I command against his mouth. "Spread yourself out for me."

His Adam's apple bobs, but there is no pushback or refusal, just undiluted lust emanating off of him. I grab my own dick, squeezing it, willing myself to calm down as I watch him step out of the hot tub, cock bobbing, rivulets of water accentuating his toned backside.

He's a fucking vision.

My restraint falters as I climb out after him, but I detour to the bathroom in search of condoms and lube instead of watching him dry himself. I rummage around in my bag, knowing I stashed them with my toiletries after repacking this morning.

Fuck, fuck, fuck. Where are they?

I tip the whole toiletries case out onto the counter, my eyes finally landing on the small travel-size bottle of lube and the string of condoms. Grabbing them both, I rush back to where Pierce is. With the comforter kicked to the bottom of the bed, he's sprawled out on his stomach, just like I asked.

But his eyes are closed, and he's…fast asleep.

My body deflates, the adrenaline quickly leaving my body. Under almost any other circumstance, I'd be annoyed to no end about being left hard-up and wanting. Especially if someone literally passed out on me before I was about to fuck him six ways to Sunday.

Yet for whatever reason, I huff a soft laugh, and my legs eagerly lead me to him. Placing the lube and condoms on the nightstand, I climb into the bed, the mattress dipping beneath my added weight.

"Pierce?"

Nothing but silence.

Naked and still smiling, I lie down beside him and pull the blankets over us. I map the soft lines in his face and the way his cheek is scrunched up against the bedsheet as his parted lips blow out soft puffs of air.

Even when he's asleep, I can't stop staring at him.

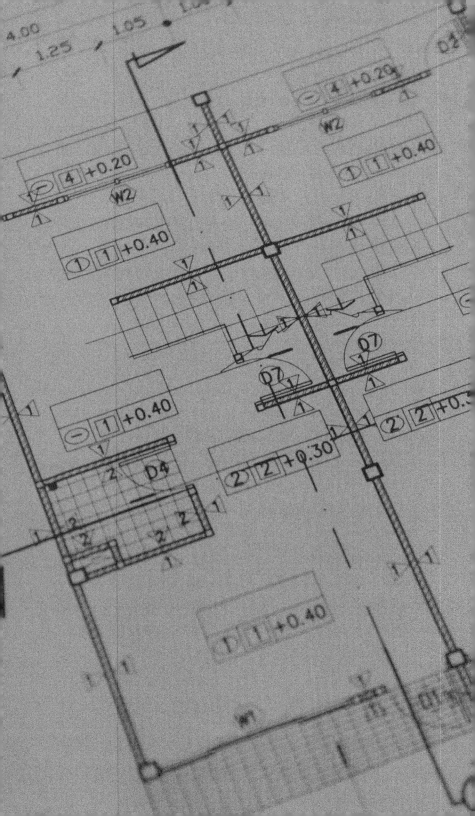

EIGHT

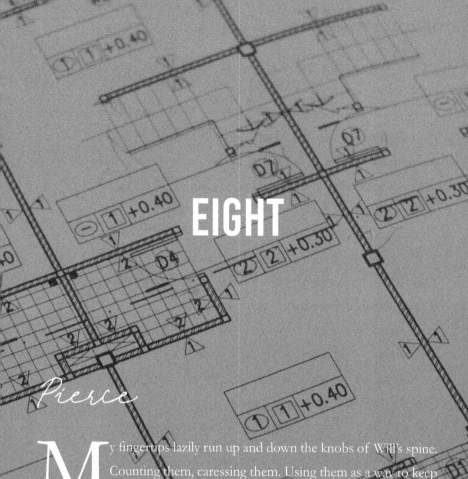

Pierce

My fingertips lazily run up and down the knobs of Will's spine. Counting them, caressing them. Using them as a way to keep touching him.

It's been four days, and waking up beside Will has become the perfect start to my mornings, with his body draped all over mine. There's no doubt I'm beginning to crave the way he curls himself around me, using me like a pillow. I'm becoming too comfortable with the way he presses his skin against mine and buries his face in the crook of my neck; literally and figuratively getting closer and closer with each sunrise that passes.

The attraction is no longer about how good the sex is, or how undeniably insatiable we are for one another. It's about all the other things Will has finally let slip through the cracks. The kaleidoscope of colors he's turning out to be; the variety of hues, dark and light, blending together to create someone unbelievably unforgettable.

There's no missing how the military has shaped him. His commanding presence and the way his confidence transfers to the bedroom has me turned inside out for the man. His mouth, his body, his cock; I am at his mercy—and will be until the very last goodbye. But it's his blinding core, shining through the dark exterior, that keeps drawing me back. That keeps me wanting things I have no business wanting.

It's the time between midnight and sunrise, when he's nothing more than soft skin and gentle snores. Nothing more than listless legs and arms seeking refuge and comfort, only to find it with me.

I keep reminding myself of the short time we've spent together, as if it'll make any difference at all. As if it changes the fact that this blissful little bubble we've found ourselves in is proving to be my favorite place.

It's a statement as large as it is insane, and it only multiplies whenever that moment of realization slips back into my consciousness.

That, just like we started this, we will be ending as strangers.

In a perfect world, this would be the start of something new and great. Something that could be *more*. But for now, I'm going to have to settle on being grateful I got to experience any of it at all.

"You're always thinking so hard in the mornings," Will says against my neck.

His correct observation has me smiling. "Know me so well already?"

Just like every other morning, he presses his half-hard cock against me as every part of him lazily wakes up.

"I know you some."

He knows me better than "some," and the worry that I'm so transparent to him in such a short time has come and gone. I'm an overthinker by nature, but with Will, his presence influences me to live in the moment, become someone different.

Because something about *this* is different.

I'm not the same man I was four days ago, and every bone in my body tells me Will isn't either. The connection between us is too hard to ignore; the days spent together feeling more like a lifetime. For so many reasons, our personal circumstances have never presented us with the opportunity to indulge in something so casual and consequence-free.

And if I can't have more than this week, I at least want that.

I want the days that are left and the memories that will keep me company in the days after.

He peppers kisses up my neck and across my jawline. "Did you sleep well?"

I rear my head back and meet his gaze. "The question is did *you* sleep well?"

"You mean after you finally made me watch *Wrong Turn* last night and ruined hiking for me?"

"I didn't actually expect it to scare you," I tease.

"Maybe I just needed a big, strong man to make sure no creepy cannibals were planning to snatch me in my sleep," he mutters before burrowing his forehead against my neck.

A smile creeps up on my lips. This is why mornings with him are my favorite. The physical affection he's so willing to give is a complete contradiction to how closed off he was when this started.

My arms wrap around him, shamelessly squeezing him to me. "Don't worry, I promise I won't let anyone snatch you away from me."

The words come out way heavier than intended, a promise of a different kind. One I shouldn't make. One I can never keep. I expect him to shift himself out of my arms, but he surprises me when he lifts his head up and those green eyes peer into mine.

They're two pools of honesty staring at me, an insurmountable amount of unsaid feelings sitting between us. Still holding my gaze, he brings his hand up to my face and brushes his fingertips over my lips.

"We have to get up," he says softly, a lot more reverently than I expect. "I made plans for us."

I raise a brow. "You did?"

He nods while moving himself off me and then off the bed, giving me the best view of his body and his hard cock.

"Eyes back up here, sir." He points to his face. "We have places to be."

"I'm sure those places will still be there after I get my mouth on you." I lean over to reach for him, but he slaps my hand away.

"I'm going to take a shower."

"I'll come—"

He shakes his head, cutting me off. "If you touch me…"

"If I touch you, what?"

He wraps a hand around his stiff length and strokes himself. "I'm going to rub one out in the shower while thinking of you, because if you touch me right now, I won't want you to stop."

I shake my head slightly. "I'm still struggling to see the problem here."

Frustrated, he bends down and presses his lips to mine, clearly trying to shut me up. "Just let me fucking surprise you."

In less than an hour we're down at the beach, Will introducing me to his friend, Easton, who will be our surfing instructor for the day.

Our surfing instructor.

I turn to face Will. "You booked surfing lessons?"

"Yeah." He stretches the word out while looking at me quizzically. "You said you wanted to learn."

I did say I wanted to learn how to surf, but it was an errant thought in a conversation that was about everything and nothing all at once. A simple fact, stuffed into the middle of other things about me that I had no expectation of him remembering, let alone acting upon.

Glancing back at Easton, I hold a hand up. "Can you give us a moment?"

"Sure." He nods. "I'll go ahead and grab the boards you'll be using."

Will and I watch him retreat before looking back at one another. His brows crash together, confusion crossing his face before he speaks.

"What's wrong?" His gaze flicks between my eyes. "We don't have to go surfing. I just thought—"

Grabbing the back of his neck, I haul him to me and slam my mouth to his, unable to contain my gratitude despite being in public. Despite having not a single claim over this man, and yet, wanting every single one.

With my eyes closed, I rest my forehead against his, trying to hide the depth of my feelings. "You really didn't have to."

"It's no big deal," he says, trying to downplay his gesture. "I knew Easton's surf shop offered lessons. It was just a quick phone call."

"Easton," I say, thinking of the surfing instructor's tattooed muscles. I rear my head back to get a better look at Will's face as an uncomfortable weight sits in the pit of my stomach. "You said you come here a lot. You and Easton haven't like…?"

Will's eyes dart between mine again before his head falls back, laughing loudly at my insinuation. "While your jealousy is amusing, I haven't slept with Easton. I'm pretty sure he's taken. And more importantly, he's not at all my type."

Glancing over Will's shoulder, I see the man in question walking toward us with two boards in tow. There's no denying he's a good-looking man, but an unwarranted rush of relief settles over me knowing he and

Will are truly just acquaintances.

"For the record," Will says, subtly pressing his hips into mine, his cock hard behind his shorts. "This is how I feel being around you. Only you. All. The. Fucking. Time."

"You two ready for your lesson?" Easton interrupts.

Will winks at me, adjusts himself, then takes a step back, leaving me speechless. "We are," he answers for us. "Just tell us where you want us."

NINE

Will

"**Y**ou two done for the day?" Glancing up from where I'm setting the rental surfboard in the sand, I find Easton eyeing me, an easy smile brightening his features. "I mean, you guys are welcome to just hang out, but it's too beautiful of a day to miss out on the waves."

He's right about one thing: today's the perfect example of why September on the Oregon coast is one of the best times to visit. The weather still clings to the last remnants of summer—bright and sunny with temps hovering around the seventy-five degree mark—and the tourism has died down, so we have a nearly empty beach except for the local surfers.

But I'm tired as hell after fighting waves for the past two hours.

"I think I'm done for the day," I tell him before shooting a look at

Pierce, who's working on the zipper of his wetsuit. The same one I've been dying to peel off his body since he put it on, seeing as it molds to his toned muscles like fucking cling wrap.

Still, I've managed to behave myself while we've been in public.

He catches me eyeing him, and he shoots me a small smirk before he looks over to Easton.

"Yeah, I'm pretty worn out too."

"All good. The first time is usually pretty taxing on your body. It can take a bit to get used to." His gray eyes dance between Pierce and me, and I get the sense he's trying to decipher what we are to each other.

As if either of us has the slightest clue ourselves.

"Yeah, I think I'm gonna be more sore from this than I was after my first day of basic," I say with a laugh.

That earns me a returning chuckle from Easton before he nods toward the boards in the sand beside us. "Well, don't worry about those. I'll take care of them when I'm done for the day."

"Thanks, man. And thanks for the lessons too."

"Believe me, any excuse to get out here is no hardship to me."

Easton leaves us alone and the comfortable silence we so often share settles over us. I shove the wetsuit down past my waist, eyes darting to Pierce as he does the same.

"Thank you," he says, gratitude dripping from those two words.

"You're more than welcome."

And I truly mean it. The idea formed the second I heard the bucket list item leave his lips. As flippant as it was when he said it, I didn't realize the weight of my gesture until this morning. The excitement I felt at surprising him, and the anticipation for his reaction to it.

I didn't expect for it to rattle the almost lifeless organ behind my rib cage. I didn't expect to be sad knowing this would be the only time I'd ever see that look of surprise and wonder aimed my way from him.

For it being his first time on waves, I feel like he did a decent job, though I'm far from a proper judge. But even if I'm way off base, I wanna know he had a great time, which was the main goal.

"Did you enjoy it?" I ask.

He runs a hand through his wet, midnight-black hair, his face splitting into a blinding smile that I can't help but match. "Today's been perfect."

Both of us smiling, we wordlessly drop down to the sand and soak up the hour or so that's left of the summer sun. Unacquainted with the overwhelming amount of emotions unfurling in my chest, I close my eyes, choosing to focus on the silence and enjoy just how fucking peaceful it is.

I wouldn't mind staying in this spot forever, but moments like this are transient at best. Unfortunately, just like Pierce and me.

"What're you thinking?"

I peek open my eyes to find him staring at me, gaze roaming over my face before tracing down my shoulders, chest, and abs. The heat of his perusal sears me, no matter how accustomed to it I've become this past week.

Sometimes, it's like he can see right through me.

Sometimes, strangely, I let him.

When I don't answer, Pierce moves himself closer to me, letting his fingers dance over my disfigured skin. Tracing the ridges and indentations left on my shoulder.

"That story counts as a question," I tell him eventually.

His fingers stumble over my pec, where he was tracing one of the more brutal scars—this one raised, jagged, and still a bit angry, even having been completely healed for a few years at this point.

"What makes you think I was planning to ask?"

"Your thoughts are pretty fucking loud, Pierce." I lift my hand to trace the ridge of his cheekbone with my thumb. "And your eyes like to speak the loudest."

"You ever think you might be reading into things?"

"You ever think you might be a shitty liar?"

His brows lift, surprise written all over his face. "I don't think you know me well enough to call me a liar, soldier."

"You're right," I say with a smirk, choosing not to comment on the new nickname. "But I have about fifteen questions left to rectify that."

He rolls his eyes and flashes me a hint of a smile. "You think you only need to ask twenty questions in order to know me that well, huh?"

"Don't even need them, baby. The way your body sings for me tells me all I need to know."

A hint of crimson tints his cheeks, and it's adorable considering all the far filthier things I've said to him in the past while we've been naked and devouring each other.

"Go ahead. Ask," I murmur.

My fingers skitter along the veins in his forearm, tracing them like a roadmap, as I watch the indecision warring within him. Surely debating whether or not the question is too personal to ask.

"Question," he says slowly, his fingers moving across my scars again. "How did you get these?"

"That wasn't so hard now, was it?"

Ocean eyes lift to mine, and when I offer him a sly smirk, he rolls them. "Obscenely, actually. So you better make it worth my while."

My smirk grows to a grin. The snarky, sarcastic demeanor he holds has become one of my favorite things about him over the past few days. Especially if I can pull it out of him unwillingly.

But then the reality of his question sinks in, and I'm instantly sobered. Remembering days like the one that permanently marred me—the ones where I almost lost my life—fuck, painful doesn't even begin to describe it.

"It was my last deployment to the Middle East. Shrapnel from an IED." I draw in a deep breath, recalling the moment like it was yesterday. The blinding pain of metal shards embedding themselves in my skin. Some of them, merely inches from my heart.

Some days, I find myself wishing they wouldn't have missed.

Regardless of the rules, I know he wants to ask follow-up questions, and yet I can hear his restraint not to in the silence, and I'm grateful for it. Sitting on the beach with him is such a world away from the horrors I've both endured and left behind, and that's where I want them all to stay.

Far away from this. Far away from *us*.

"Why are you moving to Seattle?" I ask, purposefully changing lanes.

His hand on me stills and something in his eyes change—the clear blue oceans darkening, like a storm has rolled in. For the first time since we met, it's obvious to me, I'm not the only one who's been keeping my cards close to my chest.

"I needed a change of pace," he reveals.

"Did you leave anyone behind?"

The question tumbles out, and instead of calling me out on it, in true Pierce fashion, he'll tell me anything to keep me talking. My heart pounds in anticipation of his answer, as if I have any right to his life before or even his life after.

"Just friends and family."

The nonchalant way he responds makes it sound like there's no love lost there, and it starts a vicious cycle in my mind of wanting to know more. Wanting to know everything.

He nudges my shoulder and I catch his knowing smirk. "You can ask more questions, you know? There's no actual punishment for being curious."

A small chuckle escapes me. If only he knew how just being curious made this imminent end feel like a punishment.

"You see, but I only have twenty. I have to make sure I use them wisely."

"I don't mind if you ask all the questions," he reveals, his fingers back on my shoulder, tracing patterns between my scars. "Since getting you to give me *any* personal information is like pulling teeth."

"I'm not that bad."

Wordlessly, he arches a brow, and I shake my head while laughing, every part of me feeling light and free. I want to remain in this moment and hold on to this feeling. Sink into it as much as humanly possible.

"You ready to get out of here? Go back to the house?"

"Sure." He presses his lips to my shoulder, right on my scars. "I'll go wherever you wanna go. Just lead the way."

TEN

Will

My eyes trail over the horizon, watching the storm as it rolls over the ocean toward the shore. It seems the luck we encountered with the weather earlier today has finally run out, and the moody, Pacific Northwest atmosphere is finally ready to move in for the winter months.

Or maybe the weather's shifted to match my mood, seeing as all I can think about is how, every time we're together, it's one moment closer to the last time.

The fact creates a strange mixture of emotions within me that I can't quite reconcile.

The sound of the shower's spray seeps beneath the door separating me from Pierce. No doubt he's warming up from our surfing lessons earlier, and every atom in my body is pushing me to join him.

Drawn to him in indescribable ways that edge on insanity.

And I go, like a moth to an open flame.

Pushing the door open reveals the expansive ensuite bathroom, complete with a massive custom tiled shower—more than large enough to fit four or five people beneath the rainfall showerheads. A clear pane of glass, now fogged with steam and condensation, acts as the only thing keeping the mist within the defined space...and separating me from the object of my desire.

He's facing away from me beneath the spray, and my eyes greedily devour his naked form, tracking the water as it carves paths down his skin before disappearing down the drain at his feet. My dick stirs, thickening between my legs at the sight of him.

He's a walking, talking wet dream. An aphrodisiac that's as sinful as it is addictive.

And right now, I'm in desperate need of another fix.

My want for him is making me brash. Reckless. But the more time I spend with him, the more I realize I don't care. Not when being with him feels as good as it does. Which is why, without thinking or talking myself out of it, I slip out of my clothes and step through the opening between the panes of glass.

His shoulders are taut and drawn up as he wets the dark waves of his hair, and I find myself unexpectedly entranced by the freckles dotting his shoulders; ones I noticed on our first night together. They're so innocent and unexpected, and I find myself reaching out to run my fingers over them, connecting them with invisible lines.

He must not have heard me join him over the spray pelting down over his body, because his muscles tense beneath my touch before relaxing again. And then, like he always seems to do, he presses back, creating a tighter seal of my skin against his.

Even if it's only the diameter of my fingertips, it's enough to ground him—and me too.

Leaning in, I swipe my tongue over the side of his neck, lapping at the residual salt on his skin. It mixes with his natural, musky taste, and the combination goes straight to my already aching cock.

A low moan slips from him, and his head falls back against my shoulder. "What are you doing?"

Smiling against his skin, I trace my palms up and down his sides. Goosebumps break out over his flesh where my skin coasts over his, even under the heated spray of water.

"You aren't the only one needing to wash off the ocean. Figured I might as well join you."

My lips glide over his pulse point, a spot I've discovered is highly sensitive over the past few days. Brushing over the thin patch of skin has the desired effect, and he lets out a harsh breath, one of his many tell-tale signs of being turned-on.

I've never felt so attuned to another person or been able to read them with a look alone.

That all changed the moment I laid eyes on him in that bar earlier this week.

Another soft groan rumbles out of his mouth as my hands roam his body, teasing over his heated skin. They map his chest and abs, skittering down his happy trail to where I'm dying to touch him most, yet I don't.

I want to draw this out, keep him on edge—burning with lust and anticipation—as long as I can before our time together is over. Before reality and responsibility creep in, effectively bursting the bubble of sex and freedom we've settled into.

A low, appreciative hum leaves Pierce's throat as I continue my torment. Kiss after kiss carve over his skin as my hands take their time trailing over his body. He's on fire beneath my touch, and the water pouring from the showerhead above us has no hope of dampening the flames.

"Fuck," he mutters, arching into the contact. "You're barely touching me and already driving me mad."

"Believe me, you do a damn fine job of making me insane too."

Lust licks at my veins, creating an aching want that I feel down to the marrow of my bones. I can't seem to ignore it any longer, so rather than fighting it, I lean into recklessness…and act.

I kiss along his shoulders and down his back as I sink to my knees until they collide with the tile floor beneath us. Grasping his hips, I hold him in place when he attempts to spin around and face me. As much as I love tormenting him with my mouth on his cock, there's another piece of him I'm dying to taste.

"What are you—"

"Stay right there for me," I tell him, fingers digging into his flesh. When he doesn't make a move to continue turning, I release him. "Good. Now, hands on the wall."

Obeying my request, Pierce places both palms against the shower wall in front of him, but it doesn't stop him from glancing at me beneath one arm, unchecked lust swirling in his blue irises.

Grinning, I lean forward and flick my tongue against one cheek.

"Fucking hell," he mutters, his head slumping forward at the first brush of my tongue over his skin. The sound draws out a devious chuckle from me.

Oh, baby. You haven't seen anything yet.

Shifting focus, my tongue glides across the base of his spine before reaching one of the dimples in his lower back. I swirl around them before dipping inside, not missing the way he presses back against my face.

"I'm thoroughly obsessed with these." I lap at the divot, collecting the water cascading over his skin. "They'd look so fucking good filled with my cum."

Pierce lets out a nervous yet turned-on laugh that quickly turns to a gasp when my hands grip the tight globes of his ass and spread them. He jerks forward the moment my tongue brushes against his hole, an abysmal attempt to wriggle free of my hold.

Little does he realize, there's not a chance in hell of him escaping me now. Not until he's left a breathless, panting mess.

"Wha—"

"Where the hell do you think you're going?" I ask, my grip on him tightening. My teeth nip at one cheek hard enough to leave a mark, only for me to soothe the bite with gentle flicks of my tongue. "I said stay there, didn't I?"

"I didn't think you were planning to…" He trails off when I sink my teeth into his flesh again, leaving the thought hanging thickly in the air between us.

Water pours over us as my lips move back to their destination, taking his silence as permission to proceed. My palms spread his cheeks again, yet the tip of my tongue barely slides down his crease before he attempts to pull away for the second time—effectively denying me the very thing I crave.

And it's then I'm hit with a realization.

"Question for you, Pierce," I mutter darkly before lashing my tongue against him again, only to smile when he jerks at the contact. "Has anyone done this to you before? Or is this something we need to check off that little list of yours?"

Glancing up, I find his hooded, ocean eyes already pinned on me from beneath his arm again. The desire in them is unmistakable. So is the hesitation.

"I, uh…yeah. It is."

A possessiveness surges through me at his admission, and if possible, my cock hardens even more at the thought of being the first person to pleasure him this way. To own and claim this part of him, the way no one has before.

I let out a low, appreciative hum that turns to a groan as the flat of my tongue swipes over his rim again. "Perfect. Because our nights together are running out, and I'm planning to make the most of them. Devour you in every sense of the word. And that starts with your deliciously tight ass."

Kneading his cheeks in my palms, I cover him with my mouth again and do exactly as I said.

I fucking devour him.

I swipe the flat of my tongue over the sensitive bud, loving the way it clenches beneath my tongue. To his credit, he doesn't shy away this time. In fact, after a few minutes of thorough attention on his hole, I'm surprised to find him pushing back against my face. Leaning into the pleasure my body is feeding him.

And if I thought there was any way I'd leave this place without craving him, I was so wrong.

Pierce is a drug created just for me.

An intoxicating concoction of sweetness and sin, capable of bringing me to my fucking knees.

He reaches around, fingers clawing at my scalp before knotting in the short strands of hair at the top of my head. His touch edges on forceful as he drags my face in closer and holds me exactly where he needs me most.

And I'm loving every moment of it.

"Oh my fucking God," Pierce groans, his head dropping back. "Don't stop, Will."

Stopping isn't an option. Never fucking was, and I make damn sure to let him know it.

I put everything I have into bringing him to the brink of ecstasy, burying my face between his cheeks until I can't breathe. But it's not enough for me to just have my mouth on him. I want to touch him too. *Need* to wrap my hand around him, to feel just how much he's enjoying the wicked way my tongue caresses him.

My hand taps the back of his thigh, urging him to lift it onto the built-in bench to his left.

"Up," I command roughly, and he's quick to obey. "Good. Keep leaning forward."

His new position allows me to easily slip my hand between his legs and grasp his cock in my palm. My own throbs as I give him a firm stroke, begging for some attention in return, but this isn't about me. The only thing I'm focused on right now is him and how my touch causes him to fall apart at the seams.

My tongue returns to his hole, taking a long, languid swipe over the puckered rim while I pump him in my fist. The dual sensation elicits a moan from Pierce, and I don't miss the way his ass and thighs clench as he pushes back against me.

Feeling him use me as a tool for his own pleasure—to find his release—might be the most potent part of this connection. How his inhibitions disappear entirely at a single brush of his skin against mine.

It's fucking electrifying.

Pre-cum leaks from his dick as I pay extra attention to his crown, rolling my thumb over the sensitive spot below the head. Another throaty gasp leaves him, and his fingers tighten in my hair to a point of near pain.

"Oh shit," he pants, hips rocking into my touch. "That feels so fucking good."

I grin before sinking my teeth into one firm cheek, the nip earning me yet another delicious sound that goes straight to my dick.

"That's it, baby. Get there. Use me. I wanna feel your ass clamp around my tongue when you come."

My wishes known, I dive back in like a man starved. This time, with no intention of stopping until his release spills through my fingers and washes down the drain between his feet.

He jolts forward when my tongue spears past his rim, the movement causing him to thrust into my palm again. His cock twitches in my grip as my tongue swirls around inside him, and I tighten the hand wrapped around his length. More pre-cum seeps from the head as I stroke him faster, taking him closer and closer to the place we both want him to be.

I push a finger on my free hand inside him beside my tongue, pressing the tip against the spot that lights him up like fireworks on Independence Day. It has the desired effect, drawing a sharp inhale before a soft chain of expletives falls from those sinful lips.

The sound of him unraveling because of me is potent, as exhilarating as it is intoxicating, and I don't think I've ever been more turned on in my damn life.

I continue tormenting him with my hands and tongue, drawing pleasure from him with every touch. His dick twitches and pulses with his impending orgasm as I slowly massage his prostate with the tip of my finger some more, and it's not long before he's vibrating. Shaking with desire and pent-up lust. Dangling right on the edge of release.

And when he nearly rips my hair out from the root, I know he's there.

"Will. Fuck, I—"

He doesn't have a chance to finish the thought before a strangled sound comes from him—some mixture of a moan and a sigh—and cum spills from his dick. It coats my fingers and the shower tiles while his ass clamps down on my tongue, and I'm quick to withdraw the finger lodged beside it to feel the full effect.

I continue stroking and licking him through his climax, both with my palm and mouth, and it's only when his grip loosens in my hair and he slumps forward against the shower wall that I pull from his body and release my hold on him.

My gaze traces over his backside, and I smile at the clear evidence of my teeth sinking into his flesh in the form of a couple crescent-shaped indents. I lean forward and swipe my tongue over them like I did before, acting on impulse and lust alone, while my brain fixates on a single word.

Mine.

But the second it crashes into my consciousness, I stumble over the possessiveness—no matter how errant the thought might be. Because I know, while this man might be mine for the rest of the week…that's where it ends.

I do my best to shove it down, ignoring the unwarranted sting that has no business ruining the little time we have left.

"I…" He pauses and shakes his head, chest heaving as his sapphire gaze collides with mine from beneath his arm.

The sight of him all flushed and out of breath has the desire and tension coiled in my stomach knotting further. But it's the way his legs tremble as I move my lips and teeth across his ass cheek that make me downright feral for him.

"Now that we've checked that off the list, get out of the shower and on that fucking bed," I growl against skin. "I'm nowhere close to being done with you."

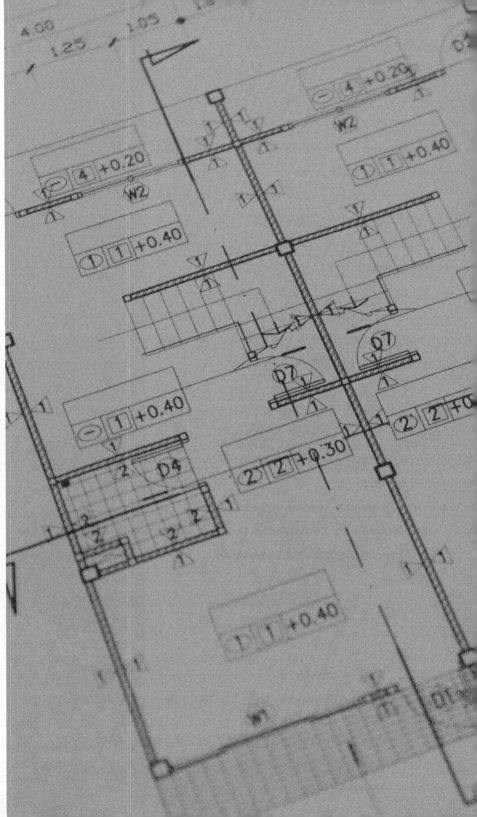

ELEVEN

Pierce

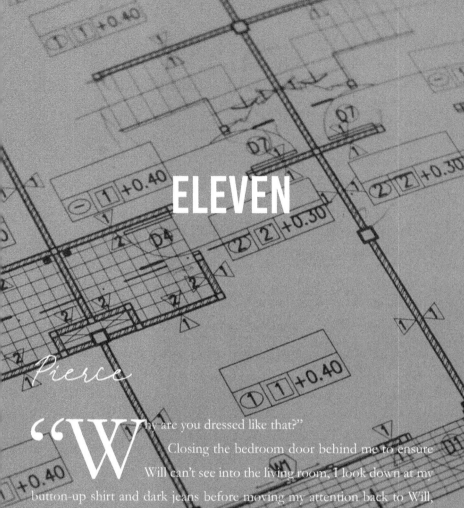

"Why are you dressed like that?"

Closing the bedroom door behind me to ensure Will can't see into the living room, I look down at my button-up shirt and dark jeans before moving my attention back to Will, who's as edible as ever, freshly showered and wearing nothing but a towel.

"What? You don't like what I'm wearing?"

"For the record, I will always prefer you naked." He takes a few steps toward me. "But I didn't think we were doing anything tonight. Plus, I haven't seen you in anything but a t-shirt since the night we met."

It's on the tip of my tongue to say how full circle it's all come since this is our last night together, but I don't need the reminder, and something tells me neither does he. Ignoring the foreboding that has felt like an unwanted companion since I opened my eyes this morning, I reach for him, tugging at his towel and closing the distance between us.

"I'm taking you out tonight." I press my lips to his—unable, or refusing, to stop touching him, I can't be sure. I just know that in twenty-four hours this will not be my life, and the thought alone makes me wish for a different one.

"You're taking me out," he muses, a little smirk on his lips. "Like on a date?"

"Like on a date," I confirm confidently, despite the tide of insecurity rolling in whenever I think of what I have planned for tonight.

"I've never been on a date," he reveals, a hint of excitement in his voice.

"Neither have I."

It's both a lie and the truth, because while I've been on a few dates, I've never been on a date quite like this—a date that is somehow akin to hello and goodbye. Where the moment is both fleeting and forever, the end and not the beginning.

Bittersweet.

Will's gaze darts between my shirt and my face. "Where are we going? Because I didn't really bring anything that could be deemed date-worthy."

Bringing my hands up to his biceps, I give them a quick squeeze. "It might be a little too tight because of these, but I think I've got something you can wear."

Dropping my arms, I take a few steps back before turning toward the closet. I reach for my black button-up, smiling to myself, because who would've thought that my uptight wardrobe would be of any use to anyone but me.

"Are you going to dress me in your clothes, baby?"

His voice is nothing more than a soft whisper, warm breath skating across the nape of my neck, the unexpected closeness of him behind me sending a shiver down my spine.

Taking the shirt off the hanger, I shift my body till we're back facing one another.

"Turn around, soldier" I command, my voice low and husky.

The side of his mouth twitches, fighting a smirk. It's not often that I assert myself with Will, quite enjoying the dynamic between us that allows me to loosen the tight grip I have on every aspect of my life. He turns, listening to my instructions, and my gaze wanders over the pits and scars on his back and shoulder.

On instinct, like it does every time, my mouth gravitates to the blemishes, kissing each painful reminder. Once, twice. A kiss full of empathy, a kiss full of respect. It's a moment of shared silence.

Thank you for your service.

I hold up the shirt, and Will wordlessly threads his arms through the sleeves, his muscles fitting through better than I expected. My gaze travels a path up the length of his exposed chest, past the hollow of his throat, over his lips, and finally settles on his hazel eyes that look more forest-green tonight. The air is thick between us as my hands attentively do up each button on the shirt, his skin vanishing inch by inch.

He swallows hard, bringing my attention to the bob of his throat before I meet his eyes once again. I don't expect to see the longing and sadness that are sitting like an anvil on my chest, staring right back at me.

I'm past the point of imagining that this *thing* between us is one sided. I'm past the point of wondering whether my honesty is more embarrassing than it is refreshing. I don't have a single rational thought left when it comes to this man, and at this point, I really have nothing to lose.

Soon enough, it'll be like it never happened—him, me, and my overzealous heart.

My hands pause at the last button and I lower my mouth to his collarbone, kissing across it and up his neck.

"Pierce." My name comes out like an anguished breath.

"I know."

Feeling the weight of every emotion between us, I continue kissing him until my lips are on his, and the kiss shifts from subtle to aching. Our mouths move against one another with a desperation that will never be satisfied. A thirst that'll never be quenched.

"We need to get out of here," I say, groaning as I pull away from him.

Will runs his teeth across his bottom lip, and I can read enough of his expression to know the last thing he wants is to leave this room.

"Trust me," I assure him, securing the last button on the shirt. "We'll be back here before you know it."

He straightens his spine and holds out his arms. "And how do I look in your clothes?"

The words leave my lips before I can reel them back in.

"You'll always look better out of them."

Smirking, he shakes his head. "If you really want me to leave this room, you're not helping your case."

"I'll leave," I tell him, raking my gaze over his body. "Meet me out front when you've finished getting dressed."

His face scrunches up in confusion. "What?"

"Trust me," I repeat while stepping back. "We'll get back here quicker if I go now."

Without another word or any more of an explanation, I leave a perplexed Will behind, convincing myself my idea for tonight won't end up being an epic fail.

Glancing around at the place that has become our makeshift sanctuary for the last seven days, I hope the quick DIY transformation is enough to make this night unforgettable.

The rental is spacious; its open plan has both the living area and kitchen flowing into one another, with a small square table placed in between, almost like it's trying to separate the two.

There's a chair on either side of the table, and I've covered the top with a white flat sheet I happened to stumble upon in the closet also containing a box that had a first aid kit, candles, matches, and a flashlight. Assuming it was their emergency plan in case the power ever went out or someone injured themselves, I took it upon myself to use them as the life savers in *my* emergency plan.

Surrounded by two plates, two sets of utensils, and two wine glasses, I placed a handful of tealight candles in the middle of the table. It's not an elaborate candelabra or a memorable centerpiece by any means, but it does the job.

At least, I hope.

Switching off the main light, there's a glow that still remains from the range hood in the kitchen that complements the flicker of the candles, enhancing the romance of it all.

My cell vibrates in my pocket, letting me know our food is on its way, just as I hear the bedroom door open.

"What's all this?"

Inhaling, I slowly release my anxiety-ridden breath and turn to face Will. "It's our date. Well, it will be when dinner arrives."

"So, we're not going out?"

"No."

If I was worried he would be disappointed, the immediate drop of his shoulders has me brimming with pride. I knew he was as conflicted as I was on how we should spend our last night together.

"I didn't really want to share you with anyone else tonight," I confess softly. "And hopefully this still constitutes a first date."

Without a word, he walks toward me with slow and steady steps, his expression indecipherable. I can feel my chest tightening the closer he gets, the anticipation of whatever he's about to say making it almost impossible to breathe.

Standing in front of me, he raises a hand to my cheek, the pad of his thumb gently caressing my bottom lip.

"Tell me," he muses. "How attached are you to the idea of dinner before dessert, because I don't know how long I can keep my hands off you for."

His mossy gaze never leaves mine, his soft touch on my face a complete contradiction to the desperation of his words. I don't want him to keep his hands to himself, and yet there's something about being the one to make a man like Will wait. To be the decision-maker when he's so used to handling the reins. I have the power to draw the night out and let dinner be our foreplay. But the truth is, the whole week has been foreplay, edging us to unimaginable heights, both physically and emotionally while preparing us for our inevitable fall.

Tonight is my way of doing something special for him, to give him something to remember our week together. But who am I kidding? There isn't a single thing on this earth that could supersede the memories of his kiss, his touch…*him*.

"Kiss me," I say, giving him the permission he doesn't need but I know he wants.

I anticipate eager, desperate lips, but I'm met with a gentle, patient kiss instead. Neither are things familiar to Will.

Despite his mouth on mine, I can't help the smile that spreads across my face.

He leans back to look at me, his face mirroring mine. "Your smile is beautiful, but is there a reason I'm kissing teeth?"

I laugh, causing my smile to widen. "I'm sorry."

Cupping my cheek, he shakes his head, the golden brown in his eyes shimmering in the dim light. "Don't ever apologize for smiling."

My pulse quickens at the softness in his expression; his transformation from impulsive to intentional, turning my insides into jelly. "You're being awfully sweet."

He lowers his mouth to mine, stopping just before they meet. "I'm a sweet kinda guy."

My tongue slips out to wet my lips, his eyes darting down to the movement. "I beg to differ."

"Really?"

Nodding, my breath hitches at his close proximity, anticipating the unknown, while loving that even in our final hours there's still so much to learn about one another. And I have a feeling I'm about to experience a whole different kind of seduction.

"Let me change your mind."

"Please d—"

The words are silenced by Will's lips pressed firmly against mine. He curls his arm around my waist, and I hold his face between my hands as he slowly guides us into the bedroom, until the backs of my knees hit the mattress.

He slowly breaks the kiss, his fingers reaching for my shirt. With the same attentiveness I used to button up his, he carefully undoes mine. His mouth follows the same path, pressing soft, open-mouthed kisses down my neck and across my collarbone.

His hands glide over my shoulders, slipping between my skin and the cotton material before pushing the shirt down my arms until it's falling onto the floor. He presses his palm to the middle of my chest, a clear prompt for me to sit down.

Shifting myself farther away from the edge of the bed, I widen my legs. Will raises a knee between them, and I find myself leaning back till I'm flush with the mattress. He places a hand on either side of my head, caging me in with his body hovering over mine. Our eyes lock; the desire I'm so used to seeing within them is missing, yearning filling his irises instead.

I lift my hand to his face, my thumb brushing over his cheekbone. "What is it?"

His tongue swipes across his lower lip. "It almost feels like a crime that I've never taken my time with you."

"Is that what you're doing now?"

"I'm fucking trying, but…" He shakes his head, the rest of the words held captive on his tongue as his gaze hungrily darts down my chest and back up to my face, finishing off the sentence for him.

I slide my hand to the back of his neck. "There's no wrong or right way to do this," I say, alluding to our last night together. "As long as you're touching me, it's already perfect."

The truth has gotten easier to disclose with Will in recent days. My mind and heart have begun dangerously running on the same wavelength, and my mouth is losing its filter.

Bringing his head down, I close the distance between us, my lips back on his, determined to have him here with me, in the present, and not lose him to thoughts of tomorrow.

His mouth travels across my jaw and down my neck to my chest. Over the span of a week, this man has touched me and kissed me *everywhere,* made me come over and over again—more times than I can even count—and yet the reverent way his lips make their descent down my body is enough to have my heart beat right out of my chest and bring me to my knees.

My cock strains against the zipper of my jeans as goosebumps erupt all over my skin. When Will's hand reaches the waistband, he skillfully unbuckles my belt, dislodges the button, and slips his hand inside.

He tuts, raising his head, that familiar smirk spreading across his face. "No underwear. You're going to surprise me right till the very end, aren't you, baby?"

Wrapping his fingers around my bare cock, he squeezes my rock-hard length, causing me to groan. He strokes me a few times as he kisses his way back up my body. When his lips finally return to mine, there's a sense of rightness in the world that we're both exactly where we're meant to be.

His tongue caresses mine, slow and languid, exploring and tasting in a way that feels like it's the first time our lips have ever touched. My blood simmers in my veins, a low and yet powerful heat coursing through me as his touch ignites me.

My hand tugs at the collar of his shirt. "Take this off," I murmur against his lips.

The kiss stops as he shakes his head while peering down at me. "No."

"What do you mean no?" He straightens to his full height. I push myself up and reach for him, but he takes a step back. "What are you doing?"

He places a protective hand on his chest, over the shirt, where his heart is. "I loved the way you dressed me."

I bite the inside of my cheek to stop myself from smiling. I have no idea who this man is and what he's done with Will, but I'll keep him.

This version and the next and the next after that.

Tonight, Will is peeling back each and every single layer—the ones I've only dreamed he'd let me see—each one revealing more about him than the one before. It's what I've craved this whole week. I've wanted nothing more than every morsel and crumb of who he is.

But as I keep my gaze locked on his, I'm starting to realize there isn't enough time tonight for me to handle Will's vulnerability. It makes every second that passes feel like a double-edged sword I have to swallow.

I need to regain my equilibrium, return us to a place that is both familiar and safe. Even for a moment, I need *my* rough and greedy Will back. Rising up and gripping his shirt in my hands, I roughly yank the material apart, the buttons popping free and pinging to the floor.

Taking us back to that very first night, when he did this to me.

"And how about the way I undress you?"

TWELVE

Will

He's baiting me. And on any other night this week I would've risen to the challenge and made him pay for even thinking he had the upper hand. It was the dynamic we had settled into, one we both enjoyed thoroughly.

But it's already been established that tonight isn't like every other night. The mood, the date that I all but railroaded...*everything* is different. And I don't wear my heart on my sleeve like Pierce does. The declarations, so real and vulnerable, that sound so effortless coming out of his mouth, are not my forte. The only thing I can do is worship his body with my own.

And I intend to.

From sunset to sunrise, I don't wanna be anywhere else but buried inside him. The only difference is I want to take my time getting there.

Memorize the scent of his skin, the muscles in his back, the curve of his hips…his Venus dimples. The way his body melds to mine.

The way he looks when he comes, my name on his lips.

In a life where I've lived nothing more than a series of events and moments that have transitioned me from one place to the other, I knew this week with Pierce was anything but that. By our second night together, I knew he would be someone I would look back on fondly. So by the time I leave tomorrow, I want every part of him permanently etched into every fiber of my being.

Standing only a breath apart, the heat and tension between us rises, but I ignore it. I ignore the familiar flames of desire burning in Pierce's blue eyes and resist the urge to forcefully throw him onto the bed and sink myself deep inside of him.

In a complete contradiction, I raise my hand, brushing my knuckles down his cheek. "I know what you're trying to do."

He yanks at the waistband of my jeans, dragging the zipper down. "You mean besides getting you naked?"

When he lowers himself to his knees, I literally have to bite my fist to stifle the groan that wants to leave my mouth. Roughly, my hand holds on to his head, my fingers tugging on the strands of his hair till he's looking up at me. "You're not fighting fair."

He licks his lips. "I learned from the best."

Bending at the waist, I capture his mouth with mine, the angle not ideal, but as always, the kiss leaves me wanting more. Keeping our lips sealed together, I guide him to stand and back him to the edge of the mattress.

"Let's start this again, shall we?"

He falls willingly when I push him, and I reach for the waistband of his jeans before dragging them down the length of his body. My gaze follows the motion, taking in the light hairs that guide me down his abs and toward his dick. It rests proudly against his stomach, thick and long, veins running up and down the underside, his crown a perfect shade of pink.

He drops his legs open, and I find myself kneeling between them. I hook my arm underneath one of his knees, spreading him wider and giving myself better access as I press my lips to the inside of his leg. Enjoying the sharp intake of his breath, I skate my mouth across his skin, traveling to the apex of his thigh. Kissing close to his cock, but not close enough.

"Will," he breathes out. "Are you trying to kill me?"

"Just the opposite, baby," I say in between kisses.

My heart beats wildly inside my chest, every one of my nerve endings feeling alive and wired in the most unfamiliar way. I know adrenaline. I've *lived* adrenaline. But as my mouth explores his body and tastes his skin, I feel as if my only purpose in life is to be here, right now, with him. As if the life I lived before Pierce ceases to exist, and everything else will be referred to as "after."

Letting his leg go, I move up the length of his lean body, mapping each rib with my mouth and running my tongue over one nipple, giving it a quick bite before moving on to the other. Pressing my free hand to his heart and feeling it pounding out the same frantic rhythm as my own, I'm comforted to know that I'm not alone in this.

Traveling back down his torso, I guide myself to the head of his eager cock that is stretched and glistening with pre-cum. Wrapping my hand around him, I give him one languid stroke before slipping him between my lips, his length thick and heavy on my tongue.

"Fuck, Will," he pants.

He cups the back of my head, keeping me in place as I start to bob up and down his shaft. I work him over, taking him as deep as my throat will allow me, wanting to devour him and drive him crazy simultaneously.

I return my arm around his knee, pressing his leg farther into his chest, giving myself more access as I pull off him and make my way down to his balls. They're heavy as I suck each one into my mouth, rolling them around with my tongue, loving the way I can hear Pierce's voice echo around the room. Cursing, calling my name, panting, and whimpering.

"I love those sounds you make for me, baby," I mutter, gliding my tongue back up his shaft, swiping it over his crown again. "They might as well be branded into my brain."

Covering his cock with my mouth again, I hollow my cheeks as I move up and down, bringing him to the edge over and over again.

"I'm gonna come," he pants. "Fuck, Will. Please."

The desperation in his voice is music to my ears, a soundtrack that I know I'll play on my loneliest nights I have ahead of me.

A plan in mind, I drag my mouth off of him and slowly jack his length. I smear his sticky pre-cum up and down his shaft before skating my fingers down his taint and then tapping them against his hole.

"I can't wait to get inside of you, baby."

He groans at my words, and my own cock throbs, neglected and aching to slide into the paradise of his body. I give myself a quick stroke and squeeze before climbing up off the bed, hastily rolling a condom on and grabbing the lube.

When I return, Pierce looks picture perfect with his head thrown back and hand dutifully stroking up and down his dick. His legs are spread wide, bent at the knees and feet flat on the mattress, every part of him calling to me. Inviting me in.

On my haunches, I settle between his legs, the dip of the mattress announcing my presence. His eyes lock with mine as I squeeze lube onto one hand and use the other to take over stroking him.

I paint the sticky substance around his hole, and he gasps at the cool sensation. My movements are slow and leisurely, like I have all the time in the world. Like he's not on the edge of a cliff, desperate to fall.

I slip two fingers inside him and feel his loud groan right down to my dick.

"You look so fucking beautiful with my hands all over you."

I work him over with my fingers and hand in tandem, moving in and out and up and down. His cock thickens in my fist while his hole tightens deliciously around my fingers.

"Fuck, Will. Need to come. Please," he begs, voice raspy with need.

I move faster and deeper, hitting all the right spots, wanting to bring him to the edge but wanting to be inside him that much more.

The lust between us elevates to new heights as I watch Pierce completely at my mercy, morphing and shifting into something that almost feels out of my reach. It's something new and unfamiliar. Something I'll miss, but something I never really had.

"Fuck, I'm coming," he shouts, his whole body tensing as it arches off the bed, cum coating my hand and his stomach, his ass pulsating around my digits.

In a quick movement, I release my hold on his dick and slip my fingers from his ass. He whimpers at the loss, his body still coming down from the high of his climax.

I collect the remnants of his release off his stomach and coat my fingers. Bringing them to his hole and pushing as much of it as I can into him, I curl and pump my fingers inside him, stretching and loosening him to take me until I can't fight the need to be inside him anymore.

Pulling my fingers free, I line myself up with his entrance, gliding the head of my cock up and down his taint before sliding past the rim.

Between the lube and cum, I slip right in to the hilt, his body sucking me in with ease.

We're the perfect fit, like the last two missing pieces in a puzzle.

My body hovers over him, looking down into his eyes as I rock in and out of him. Pierce wraps his legs around me, heels digging into my ass, while his blue eyes bore into mine, brimming with so much emotion it almost makes me want to turn away.

Because it unexpectedly hurts.

It hurts to want and to have and to let go.

It hurts to want *him* and have *him* and let *him* go.

Lowering my head, Pierce captures my mouth, and the feel of his lips on mine ignites something inside me. It makes me feel unprepared and off-kilter, like a version of myself I've never met before. There's a deep-seated need to claim and own him. To consume him in his entirety until there's no him and me, only *us*.

I feel his cock begin to harden again between us, and everything seems to speed up. We get messy and desperate. He sucks on my tongue as I relentlessly pound into him, feeling feral and unhinged as he takes all of me.

"You feel so fucking good," I murmur against his mouth. "Like all my fucking Christmases came at once."

We're nothing but teeth and tongues as my body tries to wreck and ruin him. I'm unraveling—bullets and IEDs have nothing on what this man is doing to me.

I can feel my muscles tightening in anticipation, my orgasm inevitable. But the idea of this being over, slows me right back down. My strokes become long and slow and measured, hitting his prostate with purpose and precision. And because he's so attuned to me and my body, Pierce matches my pace, slowly rolling his hips.

We hold on to one another, his touch a different type of desperation now. I cling to him, kissing every inch of skin within my reach.

I press my mouth to his neck, licking and sucking, branding him with memories I hope last him a lifetime.

"Will." My name falls from his lips as his head drops back, like both a plea and prayer, and I feel them both, deeply.

The *want* to slow down, the *need* for more.

"I got you, baby," I whisper.

And I do. I have him for every second between now and tomorrow, and come hell or highwater, I'm not going to let him go.

Morning comes far sooner than I'd like, and with it, my alarm to get my ass up and move if I'm gonna make it to the bus stop to hitch my ride home. Unfortunately, there's no part of me that wants to leave after I'm showered, dressed, and packed, especially since Pierce is still lounging in the bed alone.

"Ready to grab breakfast?" he asks, glancing up from his phone when I exit the bathroom with my toiletry bag. "I can just throw something on and shower when we get back."

"I actually gotta get a move on," I say, dropping to the edge of the bed beside him, only to immediately regret the words when his face falls.

"Oh. Yeah. Okay," he says, words short and clipped before his brows furrow. "I just realized… How are you even getting back to Seattle?"

I smirk, knowing damn well Pierce is going to lose his shit when I tell him. "The bus."

As expected, his eyes widen comically. "Is that how you got here?"

"Sure is. Though, that feels like a lifetime ago, if I'm being honest."

He gapes at me like I've completely lost it, and to be fair, I'd probably think the same thing if I were in his shoes. "Well, shit. Do you just want a ride back up? I mean, we're both going to the same city."

The offer is appealing, especially if it means getting one more meal with him at the cafe. Hell, maybe one last quick round of mind-blowing sex too. Yet I know all of that is just delaying the inevitability of us going our separate ways.

And after last night; the slow and sensual sex. The way he reheated the takeout he bought for our date at midnight. Eating it together, and talking to one another, the moonlight so beautifully morphing into a sunrise as our backdrop...I don't think I have it in me to drag this out.

My smirk turns soft. "I'm going to base, actually, but I appreciate the offer. Already got my ticket and everything," I tell him, waving my phone.

"At least let me take you to the bus stop, then?"

I arch a brow. "I have a feeling you wouldn't let me say no even if I wanted to."

"You'd be right," he muses with a grin, sliding out of bed and quickly dressing in the first clothes he can find.

We're out the door and in his car five minutes later, me directing him to the bus stop near the other end of town. The drive is a quick one in a town as small as Cannon Beach, and I can tell from the way Pierce's expression falters, he was hoping for more time.

He pulls off the road, parking in a mostly vacant lot about fifteen yards from where I'll be picked up. His eyes stay fixed out the windshield, staring at nothing, and for the first time in days, things between us feel awkward. Forced, even.

"I don't really know how to do this," he murmurs finally, breaking the silence.

My lips quirk into a small grin. "Say goodbye?"

He makes a non-committal sound in his throat, almost like he's in disagreement with my assessment of the situation, and I laugh.

"Is that not what we're doing?"

"I guess, but…" Trailing off, he releases a long sigh and finally turns to look at me. "Saying goodbye feels weird. Wrong."

I shrug despite the way my body thrums from knowing I'm not alone in that feeling. "Then we don't. We can go with *see you later*."

This earns me an exasperated look, bordering on annoyance.

"See you later? You're going halfway around the world soon. It's not like we can FaceTime while you're in an active combat zone."

He does make a point there. And more importantly, the turn of this conversation is making me realize saying goodbye—or anything remotely similar—is the last thing I want too.

Rather than linger on it, though, I make light of the situation. If only to shove aside some of the heaviness growing in my chest.

"You could always write to me," I say, smirk on my face. "I could be your very own *Dear John*."

I earn an eye roll with that comment, and he playfully shoves my shoulder. "Okay, fine. You've officially ruined an entire week of memories in a single second, so you can go now."

Chuckling, I grab him by the wrist, using the leverage to reel him toward me in the passenger seat, and press my mouth to his. He hums, the vibration traveling through his lips and into mine as he kisses me again is slow and languid.

"What was that about ruining your week?" I murmur before stealing another kiss, this one more chaste in nature.

His laugh is low and husky. "Yeah, yeah. You made your point."

My fingers trail through his short, black waves, memorizing the texture of the soft strands against my skin. Mapping his face with my gaze, I do my best to memorize *all* of him. Everything I can, I file away in a little box labeled *Pierce* I know I'll reopen many times after we part ways.

"Will," he whispers, fingers tracing my jaw. "Are you being serious? About me writing to you, I mean."

My brow furrows, and I cant my head. "Yeah, if you want to."

"Well, then I kinda need an address to send it to." An innocent little grin forms on his lips. "You know, unless the Army prefers carrier pigeons."

It's on the tip of my tongue to tell him that emails would work just fine where I'm headed, but part of me is intrigued by the idea of having an old-fashioned pen pal while I'm deployed.

I hold out my hand for his phone, and though he has a quizzical look drawing down his brows, he pulls it out and unlocks it before handing it over. Pulling up his notes app, I tap out the information he'll need to write to me, then place it back in his palm.

"There you go. Problem solved."

Looking down at the screen, he smirks, reading what I typed out.

"William Thompson," he murmurs before meeting my eyes. "Now I finally know your last name."

A laugh slips from me, noting the irony that, in the week we've been together, we've shared plenty of deep and intimate conversations between sessions of learning each other's bodies, but we never exchanged last names.

"I can't believe *that's* the thing I never told you."

Another low hum. "I have a feeling there's plenty you still haven't told me. And mine is Evans."

I smile, loving the way his name suits him. "I'm glad to have met you, Pierce Evans."

The bus chooses that moment to pull up to the stop, effectively cutting our goodbye off at the knees. But not before Pierce's fingers wrap around the back of my neck and he presses his mouth to mine in a kiss that I wish could last an eternity.

Breaking free is the last thing I want, but I do it anyway, far sooner than I'd like. Duffel in hand, I climb from the passenger seat, only to stop before letting the door close behind me.

I can't keep the somberness out of my voice any more than I can force this ache in my chest to go away as I look at him for what might be the last time.

"Take care, Pierce."

His teeth dig into his bottom lip, and I see all the things he wants to say written all over his face. They're sitting on the tip of his tongue, and he's fighting the urge to wear his heart on his sleeve, knowing how much harder this goodbye would be if he did.

Throat bobbing, he gives me a small nod, and I know he's managed to swallow it all down or put it in a box and lock it with a key. Instead, I'm met with a two-finger salute and a watery, heartbreaking smile.

"Stay safe, soldier."

part two

the letters

September 15

Will—

I've started and stopped this letter no fewer than ten times, wondering if you really meant it when you said I could write to you.

I'll be honest, when you mentioned it, I thought nothing of it at first. It seemed like a nice enough offer to appease the guy whose bed you'd been sleeping in. I didn't think I'd be here weeks later, struggling to get you out of my head.

It's been torture. Embarrassing even.

I think about our week a lot. I think about you a lot. Trying to imagine what you're doing halfway across the world.

I hope you're safe.

—Pierce

September 27

Pierce—

I'm as safe as I can be in a war zone, but I appreciate the sentiment regardless.

I absolutely meant it when I offered you to write to me, and I'm glad you decided to take me up on it. Even if it did take you ten plus times to get through it.

Truthfully, reading it, only to find your name penned at the bottom, has been the best thing to happen to me in the weeks since leaving the States. How's that for embarrassing? If it's not enough, I can do you one better.

You haven't left my mind since we said goodbye. Okay, maybe you shift from the forefront to somewhere in my recesses at times.

But you're always there.

Something as small as your incessant questions or how you'd arch into my hands when I'd touch you will come back to me at random, and I'd be a liar if I said I don't let my thoughts linger on those moments with you.

Reliving them in my mind might be the only thing getting me through this tour at the moment.

Hope to hear from you again soon.

—Will

October 6

Will—

I've been smiling so much. I hardly recognize myself. It doesn't feel as silly to admit that your letters are a highlight for me now that you've given me a little bit of insight into your own thoughts.

You're a lot more forthcoming on paper. I like it. Had I known before, I might've handed you a pen and notebook whenever I wanted you to answer one of my questions.

We're still doing that, right? Since I'm not going to get an answer off you instantly, I'm going to make an executive decision and say yes. Truth is, there are so many questions I wanted to ask you when we were together, but I didn't want to come off as too intense or invasive.

But this way I can't see your reaction if I ask the wrong thing or touch upon a topic you don't want to talk about. And the worst-case scenario is that you ignore my question or don't write back—please don't do that. If I ask something you don't want to answer, just change the conversation. I can handle that.

Now, if I recall, it's my turn to ask you a question. I'm going to shoot my shot and ask about the one thing I'm certain you don't want to write about. Why'd you join the Army?

—Pierce

October 19

Pierce—

We're jumping off the deep end right away, are we?

My relationship with the military is a long and pretty sordid tale. I grew up an Army brat, my father having been a lifer before he passed in combat overseas when I was a teenager. Mom and my baby sister took his death pretty hard, but all it did for me was show me where I'd dedicate my life. He taught me so much about what it means to be a good man: to put honor and family above all else, protecting them at any cost. And in my mind, the best way I could do that was to follow in his footsteps, and pray I was worthy.

His passing was actually the reason I chose my MOS (Military Occupation Specialty: the military's fancy term for a career) of a combat flight medic—so I could help save people in situations like his, hopefully giving them a better outcome. A chance to make it home alive, rather than in a flag-covered casket. It's something I've accomplished with my medevac team more times than I can count, and each of them brings me a bit more peace and closure from his loss.

All of this is much to the dismay of my mother and sister, of course. They don't understand any of it, and I don't expect them to, but it doesn't make the loneliness this lifestyle can bring any easier to handle. I guess the only downside of becoming a lifer like my dad is the strain it's put on my relationships with the two of them. Every time I reenlist or go on another deployment, it only causes another argument or bout of silence between us. I think that might be my only regret when it comes to why I joined the Army.

Damn, I just realized that was a lot more than you asked for. Seems like you're right, putting that onto paper wasn't nearly as difficult as it would've been to tell you in person. Don't let that give you any ideas, though. Your incessant love for our game of twenty questions might be the death of me, but I'll keep playing along if it means I keep getting letters back from you.

And if we're getting deeply personal, what made you decide you needed a change of scenery from Colorado?

—Will

October 30

Will—

Hold up. You have a sister? Why didn't I see that coming? You're so sure of yourself. I thought for sure you were an only child. Now I'm trying to picture the version of you that you've described—the loyal and devoted son and brother—and it actually suits you. I'm so sorry you lost your father at such a young age. Even as a grown man, the thought of losing either of my parents makes my chest ache, so I can't imagine dealing with that as a teen.

Not that you need my consolation or there's any weight in my approval, but I think he would be so proud of the man you've become. I'm sure he left you big shoes to fill, and I'm certain you're managing to do that just fine.

It's understandable that your mother and your sister are concerned for your safety, especially after the loss of your father it would be beyond incomprehensible to lose you that way too. We may have only spent a week together, but the idea of living in a world with you no longer in it makes me feel sick to my stomach. In fact, every time I receive a letter from you, the tension throughout my body loosens for a few days, and then it's rinse and repeat.

Now my turn. Why did I leave Colorado?

It's such a loaded question, because there isn't one single specific answer. The easiest way to explain the

move is to admit I didn't like the man I was in
Colorado.
 I was uptight and unhappy, working for my father
and living the life he wanted for me.
 Unlike you, I didn't want to be the same man as my
father... I just wanted to be me.
—Pierce

November 12

Pierce—

I do have a sister, and I love her dearly. I often joke and say she's my better half, and despite our currently strained relationship, I'd still do just about anything for her. I think you'd like her, actually. Or at least get along well enough. You have this same air of seriousness on the surface level, but just beneath, there are layers of surprises.

I know for certain both she and my mom take issue with my career path because of what happened to my dad, and you're right, I can't fault them for it, nor can I fault you for worrying either.

I guess I wish I had just a bit more support from the people who are meant to love me the most.

While I might have chosen to actively follow my father, I can understand not wanting to be weighed down by expectations or living in the shadows of what they've built. It takes a lot of guts to branch out on your own and become your own person, and I hope he doesn't think less of you for that.

When it comes to simply wanting to be yourself, can I just say, I like who you are. Or at least, I like the version of you I met in Cannon Beach, though your statement makes me wonder how much of who you are in my memories (and filthy fantasies) is the real version of you.

Which begs the question... Just who are you, Pierce Evans?

—Will

November 23

Will—

I've spent days trying to work out how to answer
this. If I say I don't know, is it a cop out?

It's not that I don't want to tell you, it's just I don't
know what to tell you. I'm boring, in every sense of
the word (much like you claim to be).

I went to a private school—never skipped. I was
class valedictorian and voted most likely to stick
to their ten year plan. I lost my virginity when I was
eighteen and realized I was bisexual at twenty.
There is no elaborate coming out story, and sleeping
with Hannah Sweeny was far from memorable.

Like I said, boring.

Cannon Beach is probably the most spontaneous
thing I've ever done, and to admit that to a guy who
is so worldly and experienced has my cheeks
burning with embarrassment, but it's the truth—and I
find with you, I can only tell the truth.

I think I might like to get married and have a
family of my own one day, but then I don't know if
I've just been conditioned to want those things or if
I actually do.

My parents are high school sweethearts who have
this perfect life together, and if marriage and
children isn't in the cards, I can deal, but I at
least want to feel a love like theirs. Even just once.

—Pierce

December 3,

Pierce—

As I recall, I told you you were anything but old and uninteresting, and I stand by that. Regardless, I would hardly call these details about who you are "boring" since I find them insightful.

I suppose I'll return the favor since I so rudely forced you to bare your soul (and embarrassment) for me to see—as if I haven't already seen all of you plenty of times before.

I knew I was gay pretty early into puberty, so that made for a much more interesting coming out with my mother, seeing as Dad was gone so much. Then again, I think she might've been glad I interrupted the infamous "birds and bees" talk she was stumbling through to tell her there was no chance I'd be getting anyone pregnant in this lifetime—an idea both of us were mortified with for entirely different reasons.

I didn't have much of a public coming out besides that, and I didn't end up losing my virginity until I was nineteen from the world's worst app hookup with a guy, I'm ashamed to say, whose name I don't even remember.

After my dad died, Mom made sure we stayed put in Seattle. That allowed me to make friends who I would know for more than a couple years at a time, and I threw myself into athletics to help cope with losing my dad.

But back to you.

In regard to marriage and kids, I can understand the appeal, though if I were in your shoes, I'd also wonder if it was my own desire to have these things or just the result of conditioning.

Cannon Beach was spontaneous for me too, but I have to say, I'm glad you made it your destination for your little pit stop. Something about our whole meeting feels a bit like kismet to me, wouldn't you agree?

And if we're talking about love, I'll admit, the idea is enticing. The way I remember my parents being when Dad was alive is like you describe your mother and father's relationship, and it's something I wouldn't mind having for myself.

The only worry that lingers is if my future partner will resent my career as much as the rest of my family does.

Hope things in Seattle are going well and no ice storms hit on your first winter there.

—Will

December 14

Will—

Things in Seattle are well. It's been a slow start being the new guy, but I'm finding my feet. I'm pushing myself out of my comfort zone and forcing myself to be more extroverted—a complete opposite to the Pierce who lived in Colorado.

For reference. I used to watch the sunrise and sunset from my office window every day. I stared out at that amazing mountain view, multiple times a day, without ever truly looking and appreciating what was on the other side of the glass.

It didn't really hit me until we were sitting on the beach after our surfing lesson, the sun beaming down on us. The sound of the waves, the smell of salt in the air...and you.

I've never been more grateful to the universe that I didn't miss out on you.

Our week together made it a little easier to take the leap into this new life, to ensure I don't repeat those mistakes and fall into the same underwhelming routine from before.

I joined a gym and a basketball team. I go out with friends from work and I leave the office at 5 pm. every day. A few times, I even flew home and spontaneously surprised my parents.

It's all baby steps but they're because of you.

Excuse the different colored ink but I wasn't able to finish the letter in one sitting and the only thing around is this blue pen.

I reread your letter and how you'd be worried your partner would resent your career like your family does. I'd be lying if I said I understood the draw to the military but I'm grateful for you and all the other men and women who feel called to it.

I don't know with certainty that your partner will or won't resent you but I do know the physical and emotional distance could surely take a toll. It's a unique type of love, a not for everyone type of love, if I'm honest.

But I'm certain a man like you will find Mr. Right someday, and he will love you more for the life you've chosen for yourself, not despite it.

I hope you're eating and sleeping as much as you can. Stay safe.

—Pierce

December 28

Pierce—

It's funny you mention the sun rising and setting, because I find myself watching both each day on this side of the world. They cast a stunning glow over the desert landscape, and lately, it's the only two times of day where a sense of peace settles over me, and I'm able to forget the reason why I'm here in the first place.

Even choosing this lifestyle isn't easy. The things I've seen, they're sure to haunt me for the rest of my days. It's not something civilians often understand, and yet another reason why the idea of bringing someone romantically into this life feels like a bad idea—no matter how much I might want to. The last thing anyone needs is to fall in love with me, only for me to leave and come back less of who I used to be.

I'm glad to hear Seattle is becoming home to you and you've integrated who you are and who you want to be into this singular, new life. I know I've said it before, but it takes a lot of guts to start fresh with no familiarity, and for whatever it's worth, I'm proud of you for doing it anyway.

You've taught me some lessons about myself too, and have caused me to use my free time here to reflect on the things that matter most. To determine if the man I am, sitting in this tent writing by lamplight, is the person I truly want to be.

Whether it be fate or happenstance that brought us together, I'm glad it did. As weird as it might sound, I can't imagine not knowing you, even if we only did have a single week together.

No new question from you, though? I have to say, I'm definitely

surprised and almost disappointed, but I guess I'll take another turn if
you're leaving it open.
   Have you been back to Cannon Beach?
   —Will

January 9

Will—

You're right, it's so unlike me not to ask you a
question. I guess I've just had a lot on my mind lately,
or maybe I chickened out on what I really wanted to
ask you.

Have you ever considered leaving the military? Or
rather, would you? If the right person came along?

That's definitely more than one question. I bet you
regret bringing up how I missed one now.

And no, I haven't been back to Cannon Beach. I
don't think I'll ever go back there—too many
memories I want to preserve. I don't need to make
new ones.

How long until you're stateside again?

I'm sorry, the reminder of Cannon Beach just has my
mind running wild. I don't even know why I asked
that, it's not like you can tell me anyway, right?

—Pierce

January 21

Pierce—

Asking if I've considered leaving the military is such a loaded question with an equally complicated answer.

On one hand, yes. There were moments when the loss of life I've witnessed or distance between my loved ones and I would feel far too great, and for the briefest of moments, I imagined getting out once my contract was up. Returning to civilian life and finding a new calling. But that's all they were: moments in the grand scheme of years dedicating my life to a purpose far greater than just myself. On the other hand, no. I can't see myself leaving, simply because I wouldn't be me if I did, even for the right person.

I'll admit, even though Cannon Beach is one of my favorite places on this planet, I find myself agreeing with you. Imagining myself there without you after our week together feels very dissatisfying, like I'd be tainting it somehow.

As for when I'll return stateside, you're correct when I say I'm not sure. The deployment is only meant to last into the summer, but if I've learned anything from my time in the military, it's that things can change in the blink of an eye.

I hope it's not too much for me to say, when the time does come and I return to Washington, I'd love to see you. If that's something you'd be up for.

—Will

February 11

Pierce—

Three weeks, and still no response from you? Damn, I guess I mistook your question about when I'd be returning as you wanting to see me.

Not a whole lot is new here—at least that I'm able to talk about. But as they say, no news is good news, and I often tend to agree when it comes to a warzone.

I'm mostly teasing about your silence, though. I'm sure you've just been busy living your best life in Seattle, and that's why you haven't written yet. Admittedly, there's a part of me that's quite jealous you're getting to experience such a vibrant (when it's not raining) and lively city for the first time. If I can make any recommendation, you need to try the pizza place on the corner of Denny and Cedar, right by the Space Needle. It's quite literally to die for.

Hope you find a break in all your fun adventures and write back soon.
—Will

February 22

Will—

I can't apologize enough for the unanswered letters. Firstly, you didn't misread my question. If you're in Seattle, I wouldn't turn down an opportunity to see you.

Secondly, I got a promotion at work, which is the main reason I've been radio silent. I didn't think I wanted the job until I put my hat in the ring, but I love it far more than expected.

I'm a project manager now, which is exactly what the title suggests: organizing and delegating from within, in addition to what I was doing before. It's a busy role and, thankfully, most people are happy to work under me so the transition has been smooth.

I'm nervous about falling into bad habits because of this but my new friends seem to keep me in line for the most part. I think you'd like them.

Hopefully by my next letter, I can report back on the pizza.

—Pierce

March 6

Pierce—

No need to apologize for not writing back immediately. I know things get busy and hectic, and sometimes communication slips through the cracks. It's more noticeable on my end because there isn't much to keep my mind occupied at night, and I find myself rereading some of your old letters while waiting for a new one.

Congratulations on the promotion! While I know next to nothing about engineering, it sounds like the perfect job for you, so long as you still make the effort to leave work at work.

I'm glad you've found people to hold you accountable to the whole "new city, new you" thing you've got going. The last thing you'd want is to backslide into the same place you were in Colorado, especially before I have the chance to get back and see you again.

A pizza update is a must. Just promise you won't go ruining it by adding pineapple.

—Will

March 17

Will—

You dont like pineapple on pizza? How did I not know this?

I feel like I need a moment of silence to commiserate our friendship because it's surely over now. What other foods dont you like? If you say tacos, consider this my last letter.

Im sorry to hear the nights are hard. I know how easy it is to get lost in your own thoughts, and just how dangerous it can be. The constant reel playing on rotation in your mind. All the things you did or didnt do, things you did and didnt say.

It's safe to say Pierce the Overthinker is still here, and here to stay.

I can hear you laughing from wherever you are. I guess some things about me havent changed.

—Pierce

Pierce—

Warm pineapple is disgusting, and I will forever stand by that statement. Tacos, on the other hand, are to die for—especially authentic ones, so I guess our friendship is saved.

I'm not sure if I should be glad to hear overthinker-Pierce is around for good, considering I worked damn hard to get him out of his head that week on the coast. I do understand where you're coming from more than I care to admit, though.

Since we're on the subject of laughs, I've thought quite a bit about yours as well. About you in general, actually.

Embarrassing truth time: You're pretty much the only thing getting me through these lonely nights. My thoughts become lost in the memories of you and us and our little bubble of Cannon Beach, and you're right when you say it can be dangerous. It starts making me wish for more time, more moments to turn into memories.

I guess what I'm trying to say is, though it might not make a whole lot of sense... I miss you.

—Will

Pierce—

Paging my favorite overthinker! I think you're starting to rub off on
me—and no, not in the fun way either.

It's been weeks and weeks since sending my last letter, and while we
never promised these exchanges would last forever, my own overthinking
brain is telling me I probably said something wrong. Maybe I came on
a bit too strong with the whole "I miss you" thing, and if that's the case,
I apologize. I don't want to step out of bounds or make you feel
uncomfortable.

We've been pretty openly forthcoming through these exchanges over the
past months, and I suppose I didn't want to water down how I was
feeling. I honestly didn't see you having an issue with it, especially
when you've always been the person who wanted to know those things
more than anyone else.

Or maybe the last letter got lost in the mail, and now I'm just making
a complete ass of myself.

Anyway, I'm not really sure how to end this.

I hope you're well and that I hear from you soon.

—Will

May 4

Pierce—

I'm really starting to wonder if you've turned into Casper, because it feels an awful lot like you've ghosted me. The only thing is, I'm not sure why, and I'm left with so many questions I know I might never get the answers to, but I guess I'll ask them anyway.

What happened? Was it something I said? Did I completely misread the intention behind your words? Was everything from that week together one-sided, and was I simply a way for you to pass time and feel a little less lonely?

Why, now, when I've finally cracked open to show you everything on the inside, have you decided to close off and pull away? Why did you allow yourself to become a place of safety and refuge if you weren't intending to stick around?

So many questions, so little closure.

The more I try to shove thoughts of you from my head, the harder they are to ignore. The laughter and happiness become more vivid and vibrant in my memory until they're blaring in technicolor so bright, it's impossible to drown out. And, God, how I've tried.

So here I am, vomiting words on a page you may never read, writing to you when I know I should just let it go. Because if you've made anything clear in your deafening silence, it's that whatever this thing between us was, it's over.

I know I should have more self-respect than to send this. After all, I will never be the type of man to beg for someone's attention. But I also know this one will end up in the mail, just like all the others before it.

Even when I know you won't respond.

—Will

May 15

Will.

I miss you too. sometimes.

Love always.

Pierce

part three

the city

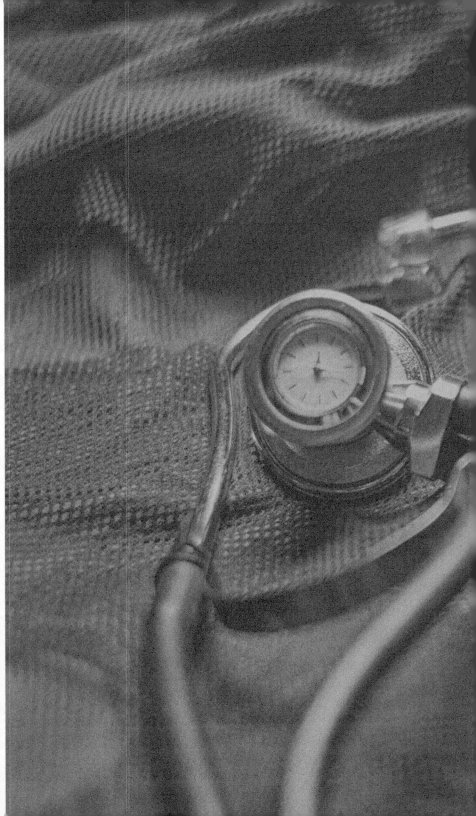

THIRTEEN

August

Will

I knew my sister would get married one day, or at least, I'd hoped she would find someone she could envision spending her life with. But in all the instances where I pictured her wedding, it never included me rushing through the doors of the church, late and unannounced.

My eyes frantically search for a familiar face, like I need someone here to acknowledge that I belong here. That I'm *welcome* here, despite the distance between myself and the rest of my family since—

"You made it," a familiar feminine voice says from behind me.

My pulse pounds beneath the collar of my dress blues, and I impulsively reach up to adjust the tie I know is already perfectly in place before turning to the woman who brought me into this world.

Her hazel eyes are shrewd when my gaze collides with hers, but there's also a hint of tiredness in them that's impossible to miss. Even if it's been nearly a year since I've looked into them.

"I wouldn't have missed it," I say in way of greeting, stepping toward her.

"You and I both know that isn't true."

My teeth sink into the fleshy wall of my cheek, digesting her comment. The accuracy in it, as much as I wish she were wrong.

Truthfully, the only reason I made it home for this is pure lucky timing. If Emily had chosen a date any earlier, I'd never have made it—despite always wanting to be the one to walk her down the aisle. There's no way my request for leave would have been approved, not when my buddy, Jared, wasn't even able to take leave for his first child being born last month.

It's one of the many things we're required to give up for the honor of serving this country.

"You look well," my mother says, cutting through my thoughts. Those judicious eyes flick down the length of my body before returning to my face. "So much like your father in that uniform."

Most people would think the statement was a compliment. I almost wish I could trick myself into hearing it as one, but I know our history, so I can hear the underlying tone of disapproval snaking its way through her words.

And damn, if it doesn't cut me to the core just as much as it did the last time I saw her. But I shove it away and paint on a smile.

"And you look absolutely beautiful, Mom. The move to Florida seems to suit you."

I step forward, ready to kiss her on the cheek the way I always do, but before I have the chance, she steps out of reach. The clear rejection slices at my composure, causing my smile to falter briefly before settling back in place.

"I know you're still upset with me—"

"Is that what we're calling it now?" she asks, eyes narrowing on me. "Because from where I'm standing, *upset* doesn't even begin to cover half of it."

My jaw tics as I grapple for a hold on my confidence, but it's difficult at best.

I knew coming back wouldn't be the warm, happy homecoming people imagine when a soldier returns from a deployment. After all, my mother contacting me out of the blue while overseas to tell me Emmy is getting married was a shock in itself. Expecting her to welcome me with open arms would have caused me to think I'd entered *The Matrix*.

Still doesn't make reality any less sobering.

"It's my life, and I—"

"A life you seem hell-bent on ending prematurely by willingly sending yourself into a *warzone*," she snaps, and the harshness in her tone could send the Devil himself into hiding.

"Mom—"

"William Auden Thompson, we are *not* going to discuss this now. Not on your sister's big day."

Her pink lips press into a flat line, and it's a look I know well, having received it plenty of times growing up. It's the one that tells me the matter isn't up for debate, so I might as well drop it and walk away with my tail tucked between my legs. So that's exactly what I do.

Sighing in concession, I shift my attention around the now-empty corridor we've been occupying. "Where is she, then? I'm assuming we're wanting to get this show on the road." I pause, my gaze colliding with hers again before adding, "And don't even think for one second that I'm not going to be the one walking her down that aisle, because we both know that's the only reason you even bothered to tell me she was getting married in the first place."

I wait silently for a rebuttal from her, knowing if there's anything I'm willing to go toe-to-toe with my mother on, it's this. Since the day Dad died, I knew I'd be the one taking his place in moments like these. He'd want it that way—of that, I'm certain.

Angry with me or not, I'll be damned if I let our mother take this away from Emily…or from me.

Thankfully, I catch her eyes softening just the faintest bit before she nods. "Wait there, just around the corner, and I'll go get her."

A sigh of relief slips past my lips, and I nod.

She doesn't wait, heading off toward a set of double doors at the end of the hall where my sister must be hidden from view. I follow her instructions, moving to slip into a small alcove out of sight, but not before I hear her call my name.

"Auden." Turning, I catch her gaze trained on me from where she's halfway down the hall…and I swear, there's a hint of a smile teasing her lips. "Angry with you or not, I truly am glad you're here."

Something inside me cracks, fissuring at the seams, and I have to clear my throat a couple times to grind out a soft *me too* before she disappears from sight entirely.

My career in the military has been a point of contention from the very beginning, something I assumed with time would dissipate and eventually morph into acceptance and understanding. But it's been years, and the argument has now become a family staple.

It has grown and festered like a cancer, spreading slowly, contaminating the very best parts of my life, tainting every good moment.

Shaking my head, I push down the memories and the painful words I scribbled across a page, which threaten to surface at the reminder of just how much I've let the Army take from me.

Retracing my mother's footsteps, my gaze reaches the door she disappeared through just as she reopens it. My heart nearly stops at the first sight of my sister in that dress, and I'm glad to have a moment unobserved to appreciate the weight of this momentous occasion.

"Mom, c'mon," Emily says in a flurry as they approach where I'm hidden.

"Just relax, darling."

"I really don't want to keep everyone—" Her words die on those burgundy painted lips when she catches me step toward her in her periphery, and she gives out a long sigh. The same one she gives when she's reining in her annoyance before coating her words with sugary sweetness. "I'm sorry, sir, but you have to—"

"Walk the bride down the aisle?" I finish for her. A grin stretches across my face when she turns fully toward me, and I watch the gears in her brain as she processes what she's seeing.

"*Auden?*"

I lift my arms out to the sides. "In the flesh."

"Oh my God!" she squeals before closing the space between us and launching herself into my open arms. I catch her on instinct and spin her around in a circle like she's a little girl, holding her tightly against my chest. As tight as I can. The scent of her perfume envelops me the instant her arms fling around my neck, and the familiarity causes my eyes to flood with unshed tears that don't quite spill over.

I catch my mother's gaze over Emily's shoulder, and she gives me a soft smile before entering the chapel to give us some privacy, for which I'm more than grateful. Keeping my composure is already proving difficult, so the last thing I want is an audience.

The door separating us from the rest of the guests closes again with a soft *click,* and I press a kiss to the side of Emily's head and whisper, "Hey, Emmy."

She leans back, equal parts surprise and excitement in those mossy green eyes I've known my whole life while they trace over my face. "Is this even real, or are you some sort of mirage?"

I chuckle softly before setting her down and releasing her from my hold. "You try to take over being the funny twin while I was gone?"

"I've always been the funny one," she rebuts. "How are you here right now?"

Her words tug at my heart more than I ever thought possible. "I'd do anything in my power not to miss this."

Tears well at the corners of her eyes, threatening to spill over, but I'm quick to wipe them away with my thumbs, careful not to smudge the black lining her bottom lids.

"C'mon now, no crying yet. You'll ruin your makeup before the ceremony even starts."

She lets out a watery laugh and shakes her head. "It's waterproof."

"Regardless," I murmur, my lips curling up in a smirk. "I don't want that new husband of yours to come kick my ass for making you cry before the wedding. Even if you are my little sister."

Her hand playfully swats at my shoulder, but there's a giant smile on her face now. "You would find a way to slip in a dig about being three minutes older."

"Every chance I get, Emmy. I don't make the rules, I just follow them. And speaking of rules, apparently you don't abide by them. What gives you the right to up and decide to get married in the few months I've been out of the country?"

The apples of her cheeks redden as she looks up at me sheepishly. "I'll be the first to admit, it was a bit of a whirlwind. But it wouldn't be nearly as shocking if you made a little effort to keep in touch, you know." She arches a subtle brow, begging me to disagree.

A twinge of guilt hits me, as I'm sure it's meant to. "We didn't exactly leave things on the best of terms last time we spoke. I wasn't sure you wanted to hear from me."

In true Emily fashion, she rolls her eyes dramatically. "Of course I wanted to, Auden. Don't be ridiculous. Voicing our concerns was meant to make you look at things from another perspective, but I will always support you and your choices." Her hand lands on my arm, and she gives my tricep a gentle squeeze. "I want you to be happy, you know? And if going off to war and saving people's lives makes you happy, then you should do it. Even if I don't understand it or agree with it, I always want you to follow your heart."

More emotion clogs my throat, and I quickly divert the conversation to anything that doesn't directly involve me.

"Well, speaking of following hearts, you gonna tell me how you met the guy who stole yours? Or why I didn't get a damn invite to this thing?"

Her smile falters before she whispers, "I didn't want you to feel bad if you couldn't make it, and I knew it was a possibility with how quickly everything came together." She pauses, clearing the emotion from her throat. "But you know my friend Julian from work?"

When I nod in reference to one of her fellow high school teachers, she continues, "Well, he'd met him in their rec basketball league and introduced us. We hit it off instantly." A dreamy expression crosses her face. "It was so easy and natural, Aud. I don't know how else to describe it."

"You just knew," I murmur, and I can't help the way my brain shifts to a pair of blue eyes and dark, wavy hair.

"Exactly." The glowing grin on her face shifts after a moment, like she's suddenly realized where we are and what's about to happen all over again. "As much as I want to catch you up on everything you've missed, we really should get moving. I don't want to keep everyone waiting longer than they already have."

I'm about to point out that if anyone gets to be fashionably late at a wedding, it's the bride, but I choose to keep the thought to myself. Instead, I go the route of getting one more laugh to ease whatever might be left of her nerves.

"One more question first," I tell her, a single brow arched. "How much was your dowry? Must've been pretty hefty for Mom to finally get you married off so quickly."

That earns me a light-hearted gasp and another smack on the shoulder. "Oh my God, Auden. And here I thought I actually missed you."

"I'm kidding, I'm kidding." I meet her bright, unfiltered smile with one of my own. "I really am happy for you, Emmy. You deserve the world."

Tears well in the corners of her eyes again, and she rapidly blinks in an effort to keep them from spilling over.

"Oh, damnit. Now you've got me ready to cry all over again."

"Don't you dare," I tell her, taking hold of her hand and leading her to the double doors. "Get it together, Thompson. You're about to get married."

She nods, letting out a deep breath and knocking against the wooden doors leading to the nave, signaling the usher or whoever is on the other side to let us in.

Music swells as the doors part in front of us, and Emmy gives me a warm smile as we step through them. All eyes are glued to my sister as we make our way down the aisle, and I can't say I blame them. She's a vision— an absolute goddess donned in lace and silk.

My own gaze drifts around the room, smiling at familiar faces, friends and family I haven't seen or spoken to in years. Happiness blossoms inside my chest with every single step, a feeling I so often don't feel when my reality barely aligns with everybody else's. The possibility that I could've missed my sister's wedding day and the privilege to be by her side down this aisle has my eyes stinging with unshed tears yet again.

Leaning into her, I subtly shift my head and murmur under my breath, "I'm so happy I made it."

She squeezes my bicep, and I can't wipe the smile off my face as we reach the end of the aisle. Lifting my head, my gaze finally lands on the man who's captured my sister's heart, the man I'll have to kill if he ever hurts a hair on her head.

The man who—

Time seems to slow to a screeching halt and move into hyper-speed all at once as my brain registers what's happening. Comprehends just *who* is standing mere feet away from me while I take Emily's hand and lead her up the steps to the altar.

And just like that, the best day of my sister's life becomes the worst of mine.

Because the man I'm about to hand my sister to, I already know. Emotionally, physically…intimately.

I met him in a bar on the Oregon coast, dressed in a suit not at all unlike the one he's wearing right now.

My brain halts, causing my steps to falter for the briefest moment as my gaze collides with a cobalt blue one I'd know anywhere. The same ones that have entrapped me since the first time I saw them.

This can't be happening.

Only it clearly is. I know it has to be the moment recognition takes over his features too.

We're in the middle of a cosmic joke, and I'm the fucking punchline.

Swallowing hard, I try to rid myself of the bile trying to climb up and out of my throat and catch my falling smile.

I can do this, I can play the part of the doting brother giving away his sister. The stoic soldier, never shaken under any circumstance.

Staff Sergeant Thompson, reporting for duty.

"You're going to love Pierce," she whispers before kissing me on the cheek. "You'll see."

She pulls back, giving me one final smile before turning to slowly make her way up the stairs to meet her groom.

Only, instead of gazing lovingly at his bride, Pierce is still staring at me, a million questions swirling in his irises.

But I do the only thing a good soldier can do.

I ignore the stabbing pain in my chest and sit quietly through the ceremony, all while my sister's words echo loudly through my head.

You're going to love Pierce.

Little does she know…I already do.

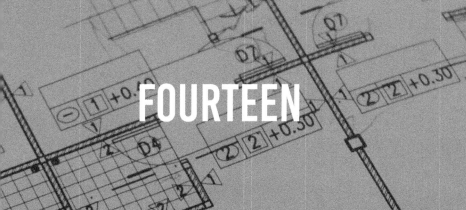

FOURTEEN

Pierce

Will.

That single word has been the only thing in my brain for the past few hours. Truthfully, he's never far from my thoughts—hasn't been even with Emily coming into the picture and quickly stealing what was left of my heart after he and I went our separate ways.

Now, though?

He's front and center, taking up all the space inside my brain since the second I saw the name badge on his uniform as he led my bride down the aisle.

Thompson.

I've somehow ended up in some fucked-up version of *The Twilight Zone*, only there's no waking up from this nightmare.

Photos and cocktail hour are a complete blur, and part of me wonders if I'm simply functioning on autopilot by the time Emily and I cut our cake and step out for our first dance as husband and wife at the reception. I sweep her around the dance floor with skill and ease, and I realize it's a damn good thing Emily can't see my face while I do. Otherwise she'd be sure to notice me unable to look away from where Will stands near the edge of the dance floor.

I do my best to ignore him and his presence, but I can't seem to for more than a few minutes at a time. Even in the moments when there's hundreds of feet and dozens of people separating us, I feel him. Like the heat of the sun burning into my skin on a summer day.

It's set me on edge—makes me jittery and anxious as Emily and I make our rounds to thank all the friends and family who made it to celebrate what is meant to be the happiest day of our lives. Instead, it's only become a day I can't wait to see the end of—if only to find a moment where I can breathe again.

Running a hand through my hair, I fight the urge to pull at the strands in frustration and scream. Guilt begins to creep its way into the forefront of my mind, while the break in my heart that Emily had all but sewn back together is quickly beginning to fray, again.

How the fuck did we get here?

This isn't how I envisioned our wedding day. This isn't how I envisioned the beginning of our life together, or what was supposed to be the best day of our lives.

The entire situation is less than ideal, and yet it's impossible to change the circumstance Will and I have found ourselves in.

I'm a married man.

And there's not much either of us can do about it now—especially here, at *my wedding*.

"I suppose congratulations are in order."

I wouldn't need to know the soft timbre of his voice to realize he's snuck up beside me, his shoulder only inches away from my own. As attuned to him as I am, I felt him closing the distance between us the second Emily parted ways to rejoin her girlfriends on the dance floor.

His close proximity makes me want to hide my gaze, worried every single guest will be able to see the history of intimacy between us. See the shock at being up close to him and the relief of knowing he's alive. Not even as I clear my throat and force out a response far more put together than I feel.

"Thank you."

A quiet chuckle comes from him—a sound I've dreamed of more times than I can count—but it's humorless at best, and I catch him shaking his head out of my periphery.

"'Thank you,'" he echoes, incredulity laced in his tone. "That's all you have to say right now?"

"What more would you have me say?" I reply as calmly as I can possibly manage.

He scoffs. "I think the obvious thing would be some sort of explanation."

"It would be, if I had one," I hiss, finally turning to look at him. Only, the second I do, I realize my mistake. Because he might be even more beautiful than I remember, especially when he's right there, just within my reach.

His gaze draws over to mine, and it's like I'm sent right back to that week on the coast. To the very first time I got lost in those two mossy pools, or how I'd memorized the way they were dispersed with dashes of golden brown.

To the way they always seemed to see right through me, like I was little more than cellophane.

His brows pull down at the center, but I don't miss the way his eyes soften at the edges—almost as if he's recalling something similar—before looking away. Yet the glutton I am when it comes to him can't stand to have his gaze anywhere but on me. Not after having gone months without it.

Especially when I thought I'd never feel the weight of it again.

"Look, Will—"

"You can't call me that anymore," he says quickly, gaze darting around the room filled with people. Anxiety mixes in with his irritation, and it's almost as surprising as him grabbing my forearm and all but dragging me toward the edge of the ballroom. An action to presumably gain more privacy, but all it does is set my nerve endings on fire more than they've already been all evening.

I yank my arm out of his hold. "What the hell are you talking about?"

"Will," he grits out. "You can't call me Will anymore."

With a fair amount of distance between us and the remaining guests, I look at him in confusion. "So, what? You lied to me about your name?"

His lips curl back in some semblance of a sneer. "Will *is* my name, but it was also my father's," he explains. "Which is why my whole family—basically everyone in my personal life—calls me Auden."

And with a single, two syllable name, all the pieces fall into place.

I blink, trying to garner some equilibrium within the circumstance we've found ourselves in. The one where the man I pined and ached for like a missing limb for months happens to be…

Fuck, I can't even bring myself to think it.

"Oh my God," I mutter, fingers raking absently through my hair before sinking back against the wall.

Will matches my pose, leaning against the wall to my left. I hate how my body is hyperaware of his proximity or the way I can feel his body heat radiating toward me until it sinks through the layers of fabric and straight into my skin.

"How did this happen?" he whispers.

If that isn't the question of the fucking year.

I don't know anything right now. My brain might as well have been tossed in a blender and made into a smoothie the second it registered him walking Emily down the aisle, and there's no chance of it solidifying while I'm within his proximity.

"Jesus, Pierce. You didn't think something was off when she told you her last name? Or were those details you skipped over before planning this little shotgun wedding?"

Frustration comes to a boiling point, spilling over at his insinuations, and my fists clench at my sides...only for the new piece of jewelry on my left hand to feel a little too tight.

"Of course it took me aback," I snap, shooting him a glare. "But in case you weren't aware, Thompson is a pretty common last name in the States. Shared by you, Emily, and over half a million other people. And yes, I did fucking check that statistic."

A humorless chuckle leaves his mouth. "Well, thank heavens for that."

My jaw tics as I attempt to rein my temper back in, infuriated by his sarcasm and judgment. I know that going off on him—here of all places—isn't going to make this any better.

"Emily told me she had a twin brother named Auden. I obviously only knew you as Will, and that you said you had a *younger* sister." A set of expletives slips from him, realization dawning before I continue. "You never mentioned her name or being a twin, so besides the same last name, there wasn't any reason for me to connect the two of you."

Daring to be brave despite the anxiety coursing through me, I cast my gaze to him again.

He really is as beautiful as I remember. Tanner than he was at the coast, and his light brown hair almost seems to edge on blond with the shorter military-approved cut. But the thing that steals my breath as I look at him is the newfound jaggedness to his edges. Ones I'm sure are invisible to most, yet I can see them clear as day.

If he feels my stare, he doesn't show it. In fact, his eyes close in defeat before he tips his head back toward the ceiling, as if in silent prayer.

"Emmy's not the sentimental type to keep photos of me around her place either, and I've been deployed or stationed elsewhere for so long prior to getting back here, I doubt she even has any recent photos of us together," he explains, and I feel a little bit of reprieve that, even if it's the smallest amount, he is slowly starting to see it all from my point of view. "Shit, the only one I remember ever seeing was—"

"The two of you in matching onesies on Christmas when you were eight," I finish for him. It's a photo I've seen countless times at Emily's, along with one of the many stories she'd shared with me over the months since we met. Stories of a childhood I know too much and not enough about, now I know there's Will's point of view. My mind picturing that same little boy, with the goofy smile, and my chest aching at the loss I feel of not knowing it was him all along.

"Right," he whispers, the word coming out a bit ragged.

The silence between us is painfully loud and accusing. How could we have shared so much, only for it to feel like I knew so little.

"It's not like I knew your mom or dad's names to compare the two either. That'd have been the only give away. But you and me…" I blow out a breath and let my head fall back against the wall. "I dunno, we never got that far."

Will is pensive beside me, processing the information, while the reception continues unfolding before us. The lively music filling the ballroom and the happiness and fun being had on the dance floor only twenty yards away are a complete juxtaposition to the sight he and I must be.

Like we're both holding a live grenade in our palms and we have to decide what the fuck we're gonna do with it.

"We should probably—"

I don't have a chance to finish the thought, because Will pushes off the wall beside me and makes a beeline toward the exit. My eyes stay locked on his retreating form as he slips out the double doors leading outside, and it's not until I'm through them myself that I realize I'm following him. Drawn to him, to wherever he is, just like I was all those months ago. Like no time has passed. Like nothing has changed.

Except we'd both be fools to not realize this changes everything.

Him running away only proves it.

He's halfway down the path to the parking lot when the fresh air hits me, and though I know it's stupid and I shouldn't, no amount of self-control can stop me from calling out after him.

"Wi—*Auden*."

His shoulders stiffen, the sound of that name from my mouth as foreign to him as it is for me to speak. It's not enough to have him stop, though. If anything, he picks up his pace before reaching a jet-black Challenger, yanking open the driver's side door, and climbing in.

I come to a halt in front of him as he starts the vehicle, and I place my hands on the hood, like that alone is enough to keep him from plowing me over to make his escape. At this point, I could hardly blame him if he did.

The hood rumbles and vibrates against my skin, matching the anxiety wreaking havoc on my nervous system as we stare each other down through the windshield.

His jaw clenches in the glow of the dashboard as he rolls down the window and utters a single word over the roaring engine.

"Move."

The demand is emphasized by the engine revving beneath my palms.

"Please, just wait. Talk to—"

A sardonic sort of laugh slips free, and he shakes his head. "We're long past the point of *talking,* don't you think, Pierce?"

He's right—I know he is. The time for talking would've been months ago. In the countless pages of those goddamn letters, where we spilled our secrets and innermost thoughts to each other without batting an eye. Where safety lay in the fact that thousands and thousands of miles separated us, and the words were only ink on a page, rather than ones spoken aloud face-to-face through a simple pane of glass.

"I swear to you, I didn't know. You have to believe that. God, if I had, I'd…" I trail off, not knowing where my thoughts are trying to lead me.

In all the time that I've studied his face, I've never seen an expression quite like this. Quite literally torn in half between rage and regret. Hatred and—

Don't go there. Not now.

His eyes might as well be on fire as he half glares, half pleads with me through the windshield.

"Pierce, I swear to God…" he says, voice coming out strained between gritted teeth. "If you don't get out of the way willingly, I will fucking *make* you."

His pain and anguish cut through me like a knife; the closed-off soldier, exposed and bleeding before me. It's enough to have me stepping around the hood, slowly making my way toward his open window like I'm approaching a cornered animal.

"You have to know," I tell him, trying to salvage whatever this is. "When I asked her to marry me, I never thought I'd see you again."

I catch the tensing of his jaw, the muscle popping out as he shakes his head. Over and over and over again before he shifts the car into drive. His attention stays locked straight ahead, staring out the windshield when he speaks.

"Don't worry, Pierce," he says, his voice cold and detached. "After today, you never have to."

And while I know that statement should bring me some amount of relief, all it does is slice through those remaining threads and break my fucking heart.

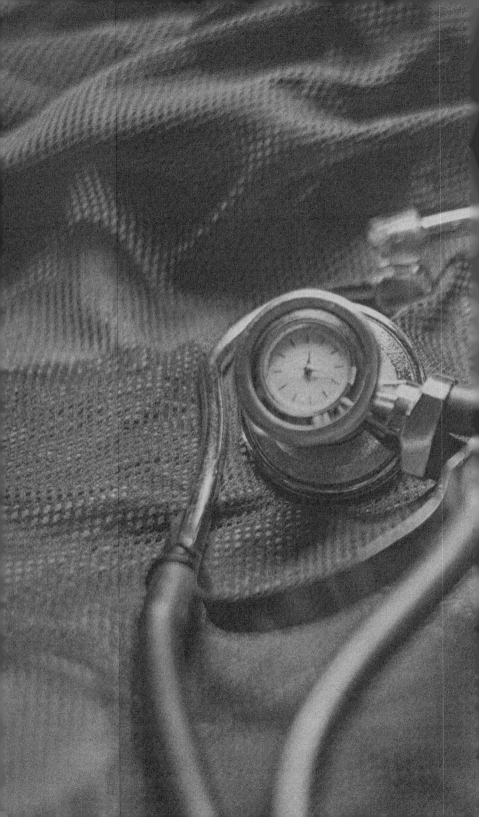

FIFTEEN

Will

I don't remember the drive back to my new apartment between Seattle and Tacoma—off base living being one of the new perks of moving up to staff sergeant on deployment. Escaping from that wedding was my only form of self-preservation, and I'm glad I did. There was no way I could spend another second hearing Pierce talk about how I slipped from his mind long enough for him to fall in love with someone else, let alone my fucking sister.

Okay, maybe that's not exactly what he said, but being as I was at *his* wedding, it's all I heard.

He's *married.*

And if for just a single moment I can ignore the fact that it's to my sister, I still have to reconcile him moving on from us and choosing forever with someone else. Meanwhile, I've spent the last ten months living and breathing for a single week spent with him in Cannon Beach.

Fuck.

The collar of my dress blues feels too tight around my throat as visions of our week together begin flashing in my mind, and I instinctively reach up to rip the tie free. But it's not enough. The whole uniform feels stiff, and the white shirt I've worn plenty of times before is scratchy against my skin.

For the first time in my life, I loathe it. The look, the feel, the weight of it.

The weight of what it's cost me.

I strip out of the uniform as quickly as I can, my movements frantic as I exchange it for a pair of sweats and a hoodie.

I'd be a bald-faced liar if I said I hadn't thought of the two of us finding each other again once I returned stateside. It was one of the few things that helped time pass. The idea of running into one another at a random coffee shop or bar somewhere in Seattle turned me inside out like some kind of lovesick fool.

Writing to him and telling him of my return, only for him to ask to pick up where we left off. It was as ambitious as it was improbable, but never in my wildest imagination did I envision *this* becoming our reality.

No part of me wants to be alone tonight, knowing all I'll do is wonder and obsess and fill in the blanks left from the bomb dropped on my lap by Pierce's unexpected reappearance.

And yet, alone seems like all I ever will be.

Grabbing the bottle of whiskey the realtor left—a gift for my service— off the kitchen counter, I unscrew the lid and stare at the amber liquid, my only company for the night.

It's a bad decision, the wrong one even, but as I raise the bottle to my mouth, ignoring the shot glass on the counter, I realize I don't even care. The whiskey is like fire roaring down my throat, but it's nothing compared to the complete desolation I feel inside my chest.

Emotions clog my throat and flood my brain as I take swig after swig, the sting and burn on the way down almost non-existent. I'm numb to it. Numb to fucking everything, yet feeling so much at the same time.

Betrayal. Anger. Hurt. Resentment.

Things I have no fucking right to feel.

And I'm suffocating beneath it all.

They're married. He's moved on, I remind myself. *He was never really yours in the first place.*

But that's just it, isn't it? Even if the words were never spoken—even if there was never a definition to what we were to each other—there was no part of me that doubted he was mine. I didn't even truly need the words. I didn't need declarations, because in my heart of hearts, I knew the truth. I *felt* it to my core. Every part of him was mine.

And I was his.

Wasn't I?

That's how it felt between the shared glances and touches and secrets and letters.

The letters.

My race to finish the bottle of whiskey means the alcohol is hitting me hard and fast, distorting my thoughts, impeding on all logic and rationale.

"He was fucking mine!" I shout into the empty void, tempted to throw the bottle across the room at the wall. But I know I'd feel no satisfaction watching it shatter into a million little pieces, mirroring my heart.

It's just pure agony.

As if I need to add fuel to the fire, desperation for the truth—for some sort of fucking answers—slams into me like hurricane force winds, and I tighten my fingers around the long neck of the whiskey bottle. Dragging it off the counter, I take another swig before heading to my bedroom.

Toward where I'll hopefully find what I seek.

My gaze darts around all the closed boxes. Unpacking them was the last thing on my mind when I arrived in the knick of time for Emily's wedding. I start with one box and then the next, and before I know it, I'm ripping the place apart, leaving a mess of chaos and destruction in my wake, desperate for proof he was mine first. Clothes, bags, and books tossed on the floor, over and over again, until my hand curls around the very thing I'm looking for.

I stare at them, a bomb ready to detonate.

Searching for the whiskey in the mess, I take a long pull, needing my new best friend to dull the ache. I don't know if I have the strength for this, if I can handle finding something within their pages that shows me anything other than him feeling the same things I did. Yet I can't bring myself to put them back either.

I scan the room for anything else I might need, landing on a pack of smokes and my lighter. Opting to forgo the cigarettes, I grab the lighter and stash it in the pocket of my hoodie along with the stack of letters. Grasping the bottle of whiskey by the neck, I head over to where one of the windows overlooks the hazy Seattle skyline off in the distance.

Shoving open the window to the fire escape, I climb through haphazardly—bottle in one hand, the other on the sill. The metal creaks beneath my weight as I sink down into a seated position, pressing my back to the brick exterior of the building.

Mist hits my face with the wind, the only remnants of a passing storm, as I slowly pull the letters free from my pocket. I've read them enough times over the past months to know what they say by heart—and all the things unwritten and unsaid between the lines.

Tears I've been holding on to since I first saw him earlier today freely stream down my face, mixing with the spray of mist in the cool night as my gaze glides over the pages, painfully reciting his words of hope and secrets and broken promises.

All of which are completely fucking meaningless now.

Useless and abandoned.

The masochist in me continues to drown my sorrows in liquor and read, but it does nothing to ease the betrayal caused by the ink and paper in my hands.

So I take the lighter and set it ablaze instead.

I watch the flames as they take over the page, first slowly and then spreading more rapidly until I'm forced to drop it or be burned myself. The ink disappears before my eyes, the paper turning to nothing but ash on the metal before falling through the grates or being blown away in the wind.

And it's freeing. Even if only for a moment.

So I do it again.

I rip another letter from the envelope and scan over the page in search for the clues or lies within the words, only to find nothing. And then I take another drink before turning that one to ash too.

I keep going, over and over again.

Sinking into a cycle of pain and regret, I drown my sorrows in liquor as I read the words written by the man who felt like forever, just at the wrong time.

My hands shake when I reach the last letter, the one that serves to do nothing but break my heart all over again each time I read it. My vision blurs, not even seeing the last lines he'd ever penned to me—the only one where more words are left off the page than on it. They're all there now, though, even through the tears streaming down my face. They were written in bright, invisible ink, drawn in the portrait of a woman who happens to be my sister.

It all makes sense now. Even if I wish it didn't.

The whiskey does nothing to take away the stinging pain in my chest anymore, but I pour it down my throat regardless, and pray it'll be enough.

More tears stream down my face as I raise the flame to the final part of him still in my possession—the last piece of evidence that what we had was reality and not a fantasy I'd conjured out of loneliness.

And as ink and paper are consumed by fire, disappearing into nothing, I let go of all the what-ifs and could've-beens. The dream that there could be more to me than just a soldier, living his life in his father's footsteps.

I let go of all the memories. His touch, his taste. His body, his mind.

His heart that I thought I had.

My soul that will never be anyone else's to take.

I let go of all of him—and who I was with him; of the version of me he once said he misses.

Because that person doesn't exist anymore.

Will must vanish in the night, only for Auden to take his place.

Vanish he does as I release everything we had and wait for that feeling of freedom to hit me. For the ache in my chest to lessen, for the hurt and anguish to disappear just like the ash did in the wind.

It never comes, and instead, I feel nothing.

Yet, I feel fucking everything.

SIXTEEN

Auden

Dread fills the pit of my stomach, and I might as well be walking into my own goddamn funeral when I pull open the door to my and Emily's favorite brunch spot near the heart of Seattle. *God, this is a terrible fucking idea.*

When Emmy texted from her honeymoon, asking if I'd be available today to grab brunch with her and Pierce when they returned, I almost didn't respond. I hate that the horrible thought even crossed my mind, but I'm remaining firmly in self-preservation mode. To the point where I'd honestly rather be back in the Middle East than spend the next hour sitting at a table with my sister and her new husband.

Also known as my ex-lover.

But since I've still got leave time, there's no real reason for me to deny her request…and she knows that. Hence the way my stomach turns again when I catch sight of the two of them seated at a table near the corner of the restaurant. Emily spots me before I can reach the hostess stand and immediately waves me over to join them.

Here goes nothing.

I have to mentally steel myself as I approach, noting my twin sister is the embodiment of sunshine and happiness; sporting a green knee-length sundress, a tanned glow from their time south of the border, and those innocent freckles that always pop out on her nose during the summer months.

"You look beautiful as ever, Emmy," I tell her as I place a gentle kiss on her cheek and seat myself beside her. "Married life suits you."

"Or maybe it was all the newly-married sex from our honeymoon," she counters playfully.

I know it's meant to be a lighthearted way to break the ice, but the joke doesn't quite land, and I damn near choke on my spit before catching Pierce's slight wince of discomfort out of my periphery.

The image of them together crashes in my mind like the ocean during a storm, causing chaos and turmoil, but I shove it down and force a smile.

"Oh, yeah? Safe to assume this brunch is to tell me I'm gonna be an uncle already, then?"

Emily's soft lilt of laughter fills my ears. "Not quite yet. We're gonna enjoy just being married for a bit first."

Small fucking miracles.

"Understandable, considering how quickly things came together for the two of you."

Keeping the suspicion out of my tone is nearly impossible, but I manage. Or at least, I think I do. Emmy doesn't seem to think anything of it, probably because I've never been one to question her life choices. Even if neither she or our mother will return the favor.

Pierce stiffens before murmuring," I guess we were what everyone means when they say 'when you know, you know.'"

"Apparently so." My smile is tight and forced when my attention shifts back to my sister. "Then if we aren't here to celebrate a bun in the oven, why'd you ask to meet for brunch?"

"Do I need a reason to spend time with my brother now?"

"Laying it on a little thick there, don't you think?" My voice sounds completely foreign and fake as I try to hide my discomfort with humor. "You forget I spent the first eighteen years of our lives together? Plus the nine months in the womb?"

"Fine, you caught me. My intentions aren't entirely selfless," she reveals. "I really just wanted to properly introduce the two of you in a little less…chaotic environment."

"We chatted a bit at the reception," Pierce chimes in, recovering before I have the chance to speak.

Emmy beams at her new husband before pinning me with a look of suspicion. "You mean before Auden here disappeared out of thin air?"

"I was tired," I lie. "Traveling ain't easy when you're racing against the clock."

The reminder morphs her expression from suspicious to soft. She reaches over the table and places her hand over mine. "Thank you. I can't believe you swooped in like that. It was the best kind of surprise." She turns to face Pierce. "And now that Auden is home from overseas, the two of you can really get to know each other. He used to play basketball with Julian and Deacon, too, actually."

"I can make my own friends, Em—Julian and Deacon being proof of that. You don't need to set up playdates for me," Pierce interjects with an awkward laugh.

"Oh, c'mon," Emily chides with a laugh, not at all put off by Pierce's tone. "Is it a crime for me to want my two favorite men to love each other as much as I love them?"

Fuck.

If Emmy's goal was to take the blunt butter knife currently sitting on the table and drive it between my ribs until she pierced my heart, she's doing a damn good job of it.

I can't stop my gaze from shifting to Pierce, and when he does the same, I'm immediately drawn into the depths of his eyes. Drowning in the countless shades of blue. But what stuns me to silence is the pain residing in them, lingering just below the surface.

It takes far more willpower than it should to break away.

"I guess not," I say, recovering as much as I can.

Thankfully, the waitress comes over to take our order, halting any and all conversation of Pierce and I having some *quality time*, especially when the person suggesting it is the only one blissfully unaware of just how much time we've already spent together. A fact that I'm reminded of the second Pierce orders pancakes from their all-day breakfast menu; the same thing we ate together in Cannon Beach.

I can't contain my smirk, which he catches, and then—because I'm not above being a petty asshole—I go out of my way to order corn and zucchini fritters, with a side of crispy bacon, just to throw him off balance.

And from the subtle arch of his brow as I hand the waitress my menu, I've succeeded.

As expected, Emily shifts right back into chattering the second the server leaves, and fortunately for me, she's moved on to an entirely different topic. I'll take any small miracle I can get if it means surviving this brunch with my sanity intact.

She dives into informing me all about their honeymoon, scooting her chair closer to show me all the photos from their time down in Mexico. She's animated in the way she talks, explaining the funny moment behind the photo of Pierce looking absolutely terrified with a monkey on his shoulder or telling me about the kayaking excursion they did where she tipped into the water, only to pull Pierce in too when he'd tried to help her back into hers.

Pierce stays quiet through most of the exchange, only adding in commentary or details when prompted by Emmy. The heat of his gaze never leaves the side of my face, though. Not for a single fucking second, and I know he's silently searching for some clue as to what I'm thinking or feeling.

But those are two things he's no longer privy to.

"I'm gonna wash up quick before our food comes," Emmy says after concluding her honeymoon tales. "Baby, can you order us another round of mimosas if the waitress comes back while I'm gone?"

Pierce gives her a gentle smile, and for the first time since seeing the two of them together, I find limitless, unfiltered affection in it. "Sure thing, sweetheart."

The term of endearment cuts like a blade to the heart, only to be slightly eased by the way her smile lights up when she hears it.

If anything is clear to me from the twenty minutes I've spent with them, it's that she's happier than I've ever seen her—absolutely fucking glowing. And truthfully, I couldn't be more thrilled for her. After all, she's my sister. I want everything for her. Nothing but the absolute best.

I just wish her happiness wasn't at the cost of my own.

My gaze trails after her as she disappears from view, and I breathe out a sigh of relief. The silent tension between Pierce and me has knotted and coiled my intestines, and I'm hoping that will ease in the moments when we no longer have to put on a show for her. Yet it seems to build higher when my gaze shifts back to him now that we're alone.

His deep blue eyes are already waiting to lock with mine, and for what might be the first time since I've known him, his expression is entirely unreadable. I'm not sure how I feel about that.

"This is..."

"Fucking awkward?" I supply.

Pierce leans back in his chair and sighs. "Understatement of a lifetime. But I couldn't exactly tell her I didn't want to join the two of you for brunch without giving her a reason."

"You could've just lied."

Lord knows you've been doing enough of it.

He must read the unspoken words on my face, because his brows crash together at the center. "I didn't plan for this to happen, Will."

"*Auden*," I correct him with a bite of irritation. "I told you, my name is Auden."

He lets out a soft curse under his breath before leaning forward again and resting his elbows on the table. Frustration and unease ripple beneath the carefully constructed mask he's set in place, the only sign that he's as uncomfortable as I am.

"This whole fucking situation is impossible," he says.

"Clearly not, because here we are."

"Okay, jackass. I meant knowing how to navigate it," he snaps before scrubbing a hand over his face. His gaze drifts to where Emmy disappeared, only to return to me, looking more lost than before. "Do we just tell her?"

My brows shoot up, floored by his suggestion.

Sure, the thought has crossed my mind about a thousand times since staring at him down that church aisle. Yet knowing it's what should happen and actually following through on it are two entirely different things, especially when I know the only thing it would do is hurt one of the only people on this planet I'd do anything to protect.

"Tell her what, exactly? That we've met before? That we have history?" I lean forward, mirroring his pose, and drop my voice to barely more than a whisper. "Tell her that I've fucked you six ways to Sunday and still remember the way you say my name as you come?"

His nostrils flare and eyes heat with unmistakable desire before they drop to my lips, clearly remembering those moments in vivid, explicit detail for himself.

"I wouldn't go that far with it. Saying we've met before wouldn't be out of the question, though. Should be more than enough to save us from pretending our way through every interaction we have from here on out."

"If you think it would be that simple, you clearly don't know your *wife* as well as you think you do," I hiss, unable to disguise the bite of venom on the word "wife" as it leaves my lips. "She'd want to know where, how, and when. And what would we say then? Lie through our teeth and hope she doesn't figure it out? Because Emmy isn't one to drop things."

"So then what would you suggest we do?"

"We stay the course we're on. We don't tell her. There's no point."

His eyes are hard as he stares at me, and I can tell he wants to fight me on this. But deep down, he knows that if there's any right move when it comes to this situation, this is it. If I need to do a little more to convince him of it, then fine.

"Telling her the truth, hashing out all the details of our past together... it would only hurt her. And for what? What good could possibly come from it?" A somber smile curls the side of my mouth, and I don't bother trying to hide it. "Everyone has a past before they meet their person, you know? The two of you are clearly together and happy, and the events leading up to that aren't important. Especially one as trivial as a week-long sexcapade with the wrong person."

It rips me apart to reduce what we were to nothing more than a fling of little importance—just a way to pass time and enjoy the small amount of freedom our stint away from reality offered. But in the cold light of day, it's the truth.

We were simply a moment in time.

A blip in the grand scheme of a lifetime.

A lifetime he's chosen to spend with my sister.

Pierce's gaze continues searching mine briefly, and I think I see a flicker of pain there before he looks away and concedes. "Fine. We'll do this your way. But if this comes crashing down around us and everything unravels, remember I was the one who wanted to come clean and tell her."

I sink back in my chair and cross my arms over my chest, not quite sure I believe what I'm hearing. As if he has a leg to stand on here when *he's* the catalyst for this whole fucking disaster.

"Where do you get off?" The question comes out in a snarl as I cock my head. "You've known her for, what, a few months? I've known her for twenty-six *years*, Pierce. If we're going to trust anyone's judgment on how this will all shake out, it's damn well gonna be mine. I don't care how deep your connection is or if you are her fucking husband."

He huffs out a sigh and shakes his head, clearly wanting to say more, but by the grace of God, Emily chooses that moment to reappear. Truthfully, I'm thrilled with his annoyance at having to yield.

Emily's none the wiser as she slips back into both her seat and the conversation like she never left, effectively breaking our stalemate. "So now that you've heard all about us and the honeymoon, it's your turn to fill me in. How've you been, Auden?"

My fingers wrap around the stem of my glass before I lift it to my lips and take a swig of the liquid courage, if only to give myself a moment to think of an answer that'd be both safe and satisfactory enough for my sister.

Unfortunately for me, I come up with nothing.

"You know me. Not a whole lot to update on." I pause, then add, "Unless you're wanting to hear all about the gory details of being a medic at war before we eat."

"I think I'll pass on that tempting offer," she says with a slight grimace before moving into a more teasing tone. "But c'mon. It's been months since I've seen you, even before the deployment. You're telling me nothing has changed? No special guy has decided to finally make an honest man outta you?"

My smile falters, and I can't help my gaze from darting over to Pierce for the briefest moment, only to find him already staring intently at me. Like he's just as curious about my answer as she is.

Maybe even more.

I shift my attention back to my sister and force my smile to even out again. "Like I said, Emmy, you know me. I love my life, I love my career. It'd take someone pretty fucking special to come in and change all that around."

"Surely, the right one will come along eventually."

This comes from Pierce, and I allow my gaze to float back to him.

"I used to believe that. Even found one who came close." I give him a smile tainted with calamity. "But now I'm starting to think that guy doesn't even exist."

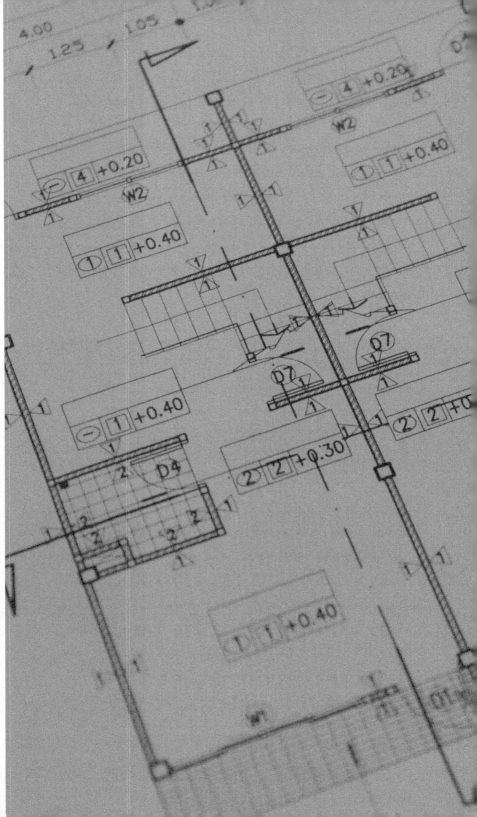

SEVENTEEN

Pierce

"Look what the cat dragged in," a familiar voice calls from behind me in the locker room of our local gym.

A hand lands on my shoulder, and when I glance up from where I'm lacing up my shoes on one of the benches, I find my friend Parker smiling down at me.

"What the hell is that supposed to mean?" I ask, grinning. "Because the way I see it, there's only one stray in here, and that's you."

Parker clutches his chest, taking mock offense. "Damn, is that the way you talk to the only person here who missed your insufferable ass?"

"Don't let him lie to you," Julian calls from where he and his husband, Deacon, are shoving their bags into lockers. "I missed you plenty."

Deacon glances over his shoulder and shrugs. "I'm not getting involved."

"You gonna be able to keep up after all that time away?" Parker teases. "What has it been, three weeks since you showed up?"

"Give the man a break," Julian chides. "He was too busy getting married and then sipping margaritas on the beach with his wife to show up to the gym."

"Mojitos, actually," I correct, rising to my full height. "Tequila and I aren't known to be friends, so I stuck to rum."

"Tomato, potato."

Deacon shakes his head fondly at Julian before glancing over at me. "You guys had a good time?"

I think of the clusterfuck of a mess I've found myself in and settle on a response that is completely inadequate. "Yeah, it was nice to get away after all the…stress."

Well, Emily certainly had a good time. I did to the best of my ability, seeing as every time I'd look at her, I couldn't stop searching for similarities between her and her brother. Any sign or indication that I might've missed in the time since knowing the Thompson twins.

Yet every time, I came up empty-handed. It should've been expected, what with them being fraternal twins, but it was frustrating nonetheless. And it made it difficult to enjoy what our all-inclusive resort had to offer.

Grabbing my gym towel, I hang it around my neck before shoving my bag into one of the lockers, waiting for the rest of the guys to finish getting ready.

"We're still waiting on one more to fill in for Brandon," Julian says, checking his phone. "He should be here any minute."

"I'm here now, actually."

Ice shards fill my veins at the familiar, low timbre, and my eyes sink closed in prayer that I'm just imagining his voice. Except, when I steel myself and turn toward the door, I find I'm thrown right back in the midst of this inescapable nightmare while staring into a pair of green-hazel eyes.

Will.

Fuck. No, it's Auden.

Even though I can't afford any slip-ups when there are other people around, retraining my brain is clearly proving to be more difficult than I originally thought. It's almost like I'm subconsciously refusing to merge the two, because when I finally submit to calling him Auden, just like everyone else, it'll be like Will doesn't exist.

Like *my* Will doesn't exist.

I shake my head, as if I can physically rid myself of the thought, because who am I kidding? He hasn't been mine since the second I chose to marry his sister.

"You know him?" I ask.

Deacon nods, but Julian is the one who replies. "You forget that we're the reason you even met that wife of yours?" he reminds me. "Why wouldn't we know her brother?"

It makes sense, obviously, but I'm still in denial that my decision to join a gym and make new friends has landed me in my very own nightmare.

I was supposed to be in the honeymoon phase of my marriage; instead it feels like I've been banished to purgatory—a life stuck between the pinnacle of what happiness should look like and the hell I'm currently in.

"I used to come here and play ball with them before I was shipped out," Auden says.

"More like whoop all of our asses," Julian says.

I arch a brow. "Really?"

"From the way Emily tells it, he probably could've played in college," Julian informs me, unknowingly handing me another piece of the puzzle that is Auden. "If he wasn't so dead set on turning the military into his entire personality."

"That's a mild exaggeration," Auden mutters, but from the way color tints the tips of his ears, I have a feeling there's more truth to it than he'd care to admit.

His discomfort at being the center of attention has me rushing to claim the spotlight.

"Hey, I didn't come here to get the 411 on my brother-in-law." The words taste sour on my tongue, but I keep my expression neutral. "Are we going to play ball or not?"

We're all sitting at the front of this new juice bar that opened up a few doors down from the gym, cooling down after our workout and celebrating our win. Julian was right about Auden and his basketball skills; our original team was solid and we didn't often lose, but with Auden, it was as if the other team didn't even show up to play.

"How long are you here, Auden?" Julian asks, just as the waiter finishes handing us all of our drinks.

Using my straw to stir my juice, I keep my gaze averted and pretend I'm uninterested, hating that my curiosity is piqued by a question I already know the answer to.

"I have another week or so of leave time," he answers. "After that, I'll be back to work."

Julian arches a brow. "Another deployment already?"

Auden's gaze shifts to me for the briefest moment before flicking back to Julian. "No, there's no way I'd be going back so soon," he explains. "I'll just be working on base like I was before deployment."

"No more playing war hero for you, huh?" Parker says.

I wince at the bold and slightly intrusive question, knowing Auden— despite saving many lives—would never describe himself that way. A fact made more obvious from the way his jaw clenches before he forces a smile.

"Not till they need me to."

Parker opens his mouth to ask another question, but Deacon— perceptive as he is—must sense Auden's unease and interjects with a question of his own about work and other idle bullshit, dragging Parker's attention, and the conversation, from Auden. Julian is quick to swoop in too, changing the subject on our end to something else entirely.

Unfortunately for me, that subject is…well, me.

"So when's the big move?"

Auden's head pops up, curiosity piqued by the question, as his gaze darts between Julian and me. "Move?"

"Yeah, your sister and Pierce are about to close on a house in the 'burbs between Tacoma and Seattle, officially becoming one of those gross married couples."

Julian innocently spills all the things I don't want to discuss with Auden, especially with an audience.

"You and Deacon are married," I counter.

"Yeah, but we haven't settled into suburban hell yet," Julian counters right back before looking at Auden again. "I'm surprised you didn't know."

The steel in his voice is unmissable. "I guess I have a lot more to catch up on than I thought."

Shit, shit, shit.

I have nothing to feel guilty for. Logically, I know that.

After all, Emily's my wife. She's the person I've promised to spend the rest of my life with, and the only natural step is for us to truly merge our lives together; this house is just one example of that.

So why the fuck is the way Auden's expression slowly closing off so gutting to me? I thought my choice to move on and leave him in the recesses of my mind was only damaging to me. A life with him was unattainable—out of my grasp—and yet, it feels like remaining alone and single might've been better than bearing witness to his heartbreak.

My eyes land on Will's—fuck, *Auden's*—shoulder, fixating on the pale scars visible beneath the edge of his cut-off. Ones I know the history behind. Ones I've traced with my fingers, and lips, more times than I can count.

Unfortunately for me, Auden chooses that moment to lift his gaze, only to find me staring like a goddamn deer in headlights.

Shit, shit, shit.

Caught red-handed, I quickly divert my eyes to anywhere but him and rise up off my seat.

"I gotta get going. I'm going to head back to the gym and grab my bag, but I'll catch you guys next time," I say to no one in particular, doing my best to ignore the way Auden's gaze is searing the side of my face.

"Pierce."

I've only taken a handful of steps when the sound of my name has me pausing. I glance over my shoulder to see Deacon coming up behind me, staring at me curiously.

"Yeah, what's up?

"You good?"

Ah, fucking hell.

The thing about Deacon is, while he might be the more silent and broody between him and Julian, he's also observant as hell. A lot more than he lets on. Which is why I feel like I'm an ant under a magnifying glass as he stares at me, waiting for an answer.

I try for nonchalant, giving him a one-shoulder shrug. "Of course.

Why wouldn't I be?"

His lips twitch, like he knows I'm full of shit. He doesn't call me on it, though, instead offering a shrug of his own before uttering, "No reason. But let's catch up for drinks soon. You free this weekend? After the move, I mean?"

"Yeah," I say a little too brightly. "That should work."

Once I make my way into the locker room, my body sags onto the bench and I bury my head in my hands, needing a moment of reprieve away from Auden's stare, his judgment...*him*.

A thought that would've never crossed my mind when I said goodbye to him all those months ago.

Eventually, I drag myself off the bench and pluck my gym bag out of the locker. I rummage through my backpack in search of my cell, checking for any messages from Emily when I find it. Stepping out of the locker room, I round the corner and slam into a hard wall of muscle.

"Shit, sorry."

The phone falls, clattering on the floor, and the stranger bends over, rushing to pick it up. As he straightens to my height, I come face-to-face with an exasperated Auden.

"Just go," he says, irritation laced in his tone as he holds my cell out to me.

Taking it from him, I quickly brush past while trying my best to ignore the sinful mix of his familiar cedarwood scent and sweat. Things I never would've noticed if it weren't for our week on the coast.

Against my better judgment, I exit the gym and wait for Auden. When he finally bursts through the doors, I'm quick on his heels.

"Can we talk?"

He keeps walking. "I don't have anything to say, Pierce."

"Will," I say sternly, and the use of the wrong name, *our* name, has him whirling around, his jaw clenched, his eyes filled with fury.

"Don't. Call. Me. That," he seethes, shaking his head. "You don't get to call me that when we're alone, not anymore."

"Auden, please," I plead.

"Go home to your wife, Pierce."

"I do love her," I blurt out. "I know it's not something you want to hear or even believe, but I do. She makes me incredibly happy, and she fits in the life I want for myself."

"She deserves more than to be some puzzle piece that just so happens to fit," he bites back.

I shove my hands in my hair, frustrated. "That's not what I meant and you know it."

A humorless laugh leaves his mouth, sending chills down my spine. "Of course. That's your MO, isn't it? Saying things you don't mean."

"Auden." His name comes out like a strangled sigh. "That's not true."

Hazel-green eyes hold my stare. "Isn't it?"

The defense dies on my tongue, because what does it matter? I'm married now. I made a commitment. I took vows. There's a line between us that can't be crossed, backward or forward.

"Auden," I breathe out almost inaudibly. "I'm so sorry."

He turns his head, robbing me of the truth always present in his eyes. "Yeah, me too."

EIGHTEEN

September

Pierce

A sharp knock on Emily's apartment door pulls me from where I'm taking apart her bed frame, and I glance up to where she's fastening her earrings in the bathroom with a frown. There's no reason for anyone to be at her apartment at barely seven in the morning on a Monday.

Unless…

I narrow my gaze on her. "I thought I told you we didn't need movers?"

She glances at me, her familiar green eyes taking on a mischievous glimmer, before heading down the hall without answering.

"Emily," I say, a small amount of bite in my tone at being ignored. "We agreed to no movers."

"Yes, but you never said anything about reinforcements!"

Oh, Jesus Christ.

Shaking my head, I reroute my focus back to the task at hand as the faint sound of a masculine voice drifts down the hallway, paired with the familiar sound of Emily's. They converse for while, and irritation settles in when I hear her mentioning items that will be moved to the new house.

"Not movers, my ass," I mutter under my breath as I continue removing the forty million screws holding this damn bed frame together. Though, I have to admit, a small part of me wishes I'd have agreed to have professionals do this shit about ten minutes into taking this fucking thing apart. And my irritation only grows when one of the metal bars for the base drops on my foot after loosening the final screw holding it in place.

"Goddamnit," I curse sharply before letting out a huff of frustration.

"Need a hand?"

The question startles me, but not nearly as much as glancing up to see Will—*Auden*—leaning against the door frame, just…staring at me. Stoic and unreadable.

After the last time we saw one another, I'm not surprised by his apathy.

"What are you doing here?"

The words are out before I can stop them, and from the subtle arch of his brow, he can tell it wasn't a question I'd meant to let slip. Of course, from the athletic shorts he's wearing and the tee clinging to his muscled biceps, I'm pretty sure I know the reason for his presence. Still doesn't keep my heart from stuttering when he confirms it.

"Emily asked me to come help you load the moving truck."

Fuck.

God love her, but she's one of the most meddlesome people I know. And with her pushing for the two of us to spend time together ever since returning from our honeymoon, I should have seen this coming from a mile away. Yet, somehow, I'm still shocked to see him standing here, wishing he denied his sister's request when I can't seem to. And looking far more delicious than he has the right to on top of it.

Emily appears in the doorway behind her brother, and this time as I stare at them side-by-side, I'm floored I didn't see it sooner. It isn't just about physical similarities, but it's their mannerisms and facial expressions. The way they both bite the corner of their mouth anticipating my reaction to Auden's presence, for two very different reasons.

"As a form of compromise," Emily starts as her gaze moves from her brother to me, "Auden offered to help you get the things we're taking to the new house from here and your apartment. Then we can hire one of those moving places to take the rest for donations. Okay?"

All I can do is nod at her silently, not finding a reason to object, no matter how much I might want to. At this point, it would only cause unnecessary friction and raise questions I'd rather not answer concerning my history with her brother.

"Perfect. Then I'm off to work," Emily chirps. "You have a key to the house, right, baby?"

I don't miss the way Auden's jaw tics at the endearment—the same one he whispered in my ear on countless occasions only months ago. It's nearly imperceptible, as is the flash of hurt in his eyes, only to be gone a moment later.

"Pierce?" Emily asks, and I realize I've been staring at her brother, completely oblivious that she's been talking to me.

"Yeah, sorry. I have a key." I offer her a gentle, yet forced, smile. "Have a good day at work."

She offers me another one of her radiant, genuine smiles before squeezing her brother's bicep and spinning on her heel. Their clicking on the laminate echoes down the hall, growing fainter until the sound of the front door opening and closing again signals her departure.

My gaze falls to my hands in an attempt to ignore the heat of Will's— *fuck, Auden's*—gaze on me, but I know it's in vain. I can feel all of it, like he's in the air surrounding me. Suffocating me with his mere presence.

"So…where do you want me?"

Anywhere but here.

"You don't have to do this."

"If you honestly believe that, you don't know my sister well enough to be married to her."

He has a point; not about me *not* knowing her, but that Emily is relentless. There's no untying the complicated knot we've found ourselves in, so instead of trying, I just nod at him in resignation.

"Just let me finish pulling this apart and we can start loading the truck."

Thankfully, the universe is on my side and it takes me less than fifteen minutes to get Emily's bed into easy-to-maneuver pieces and begin taking each of them down the stairs.

Auden and I work in an amicable silence, exchanging a few words here and there, directing one another from room to room and grabbing everything Emily wants to take to the new place.

"I'm surprised the two of you don't already live together," Auden says, pushing another box into the box truck. "Then again, it seems like it was a bit of a shotgun wedding to begin with."

My teeth grind together as I drop my box on top of the one he just loaded.

"When you know, you know," I bite back, using the same words I did at brunch the other week. Only, this time, the flash of hurt on his face has me regretting it almost immediately. "Will—"

"I told you to stop calling me that," he snaps, and there's a flare of fury in his eyes. "No one in my family calls me that, and if one of them—especially Emily—catches you when I've only ever been Auden to you, then this whole fucking ruse will start to fray and fall apart at the seams."

"You're right," I murmur, casting my eyes to the ground. "I'm sorry."

This isn't the guy I spent a week wrapped up with, naked and sweating and completely oblivious to the world around us. Not the soldier I exchanged countless letters with, falling deeper into familiarity with every time I read his words on a page. Not the person whose body I know better than my own—the one I still find myself dreaming of.

No.

The man standing in front of me is a complete fucking stranger. The time that's passed since we last spoke—not to mention the wedding band currently feeling far too tight on my finger—has made sure of that.

My thumb absently reaches over to where it rests on my ring finger, rolling over the cool metal and spinning it in place.

Auden scoffs, and when my gaze lifts to his face again, I realize he's caught my fidgeting. Is fixated on it, actually, his tongue poking at his cheek, before he shakes his head and glares at me.

"Whatever. Let's just get this shit over with."

The whole moving process goes rather smoothly for most of the day, and for that, I'm entirely grateful. Spending the day with Auden in near silence has been painful in itself, but add in having to see the way his muscles move and flex when he lifts boxes and furniture, and it's downright fucking torturous. And since mother nature had to throw another wrench in the plans by starting to downpour in the past hour since we made it to my apartment across the city, his shirt is now soaked and sticking to his body like cling wrap.

I'm starting to think the universe has it out for me.

We're on the last set of boxes now—a good thing, seeing as these last few have to sit between us in the cab of the truck—and at this point, I'm desperate for a reprieve.

Which is the exact opposite thing I get when we're in the elevator and halfway down the building, only for the lights to start flickering…and the elevator to come to a halt.

We're enveloped in darkness moments later before the dim emergency light flicks on overhead, illuminating us with a hazy, yellow glow.

"Oh, you've gotta be fucking kidding me," Auden curses, back colliding with the wall of the metal deathtrap we're currently locked in. "Please tell me there's a backup generator or something to get us out of here."

"I'm not sure," I mutter, eyes sliding closed as I mirror his position across from him.

"How aren't you sure?"

"Because I don't exactly make a habit of getting trapped in an elevator during power outages," I bite out, my eyes snapping open to glare at him. "But seeing as it's an old building and storms have knocked out the power for hours before, I'd say it probably doesn't."

I catch Auden's glower through the yellow haze as I slam my hand on the emergency call button and pray for a fucking answer. Thankfully, the operator is on moments later, letting us know that half the city is experiencing a blackout, and they'll send someone to get us out as soon as possible.

He slams his hand into the elevator wall. "Un-fucking-believable."

Well, shit.

Plucking my cell out of my pocket, I pull up my message thread with Emily and send her a text.

Me: Might be a while. We're stuck in the elevator at the apartment. Blackout on this side of town.

My phone buzzes moments later, Emily's name and photo popping up on the screen, and I swipe to answer.

"Hey, you okay?" she says the second I lift the speaker to my ear.

"We're fine," I tell her before glancing at Auden, who is staring at the ground like he'd rather be anywhere else than here. "Are you okay? Where are you?"

"I'm good, thankfully I just made it to the house. Power's out here too, though. I have my phone light, and I'll see if one of the neighbors has any spare candles or flashlights I can borrow, since you two have ours in the moving truck."

Fuck.

"Just don't drive anywhere," I tell her. "I'll be there as soon as I can."

"Be safe, okay? I love you."

A knot forms in my throat, and I'm acutely aware of Auden's presence when I whisper back, "You too, sweetheart."

We hang up and I keep my eyes trained on my cell phone screen, the tension between myself and Auden thick with absolutely no way to assuage it.

"Is she safe?" he asks some time later, breaking through the quiet.

"Yeah," I answer. "Power is out at the new house too, but she's staying put."

Nodding, Auden tilts his head back, arching his neck to look up at the ceiling, or more accurately to look anywhere else but at me.

Logically, I know his feelings toward me are valid and warranted, but the man who occasionally lets his mind drift back to Cannon Beach is gutted that Auden can just switch on and off whenever he feels like it.

I know that makes me a hypocrite of the worst kind, and obviously I have no intentions of making things any more uncomfortable than they already are, but he won't even acknowledge my existence, and that makes the silence between us suffocating.

A long, slow sigh leaves me as I try to get comfortable on the floor, pushing the box of liquor I was carrying out of the way. The bottles rattle and clink together, and I reach over to still them, ensuring none of them break.

Noticing a half empty bottle of Jim Beam, I grab it by the neck and unscrew the lid. Overwhelmed by our proximity and Auden's disdain for me, I take a long pull of the room-temperature liquid, and figure this is as good a time as any to start drinking.

"That's one way to pass the time," Auden mutters, and they're the first words he's spoken in what feels like hours.

Wordlessly, I pluck another bottle out and hand it to him, all the while trying to ignore the heat of his fingers brushing against mine. Or the look in his eyes when he glances down at the bottle, realizing it's the same kind of whiskey we shared while naked in the hot tub months ago.

Closing my eyes, I lean my head against the elevator wall as the quiet continues, the tension dissipating to resignation with every quiet sip. The juxtaposition of old and new feelings between us, simmering just beneath the surface.

"What else do you have in these boxes?" Auden asks some time later. "Any food? Because I'm fucking starving."

He starts ripping the tape off the next box labeled *Kitchen* in search of anything edible. I know the feeling, with the liquor now swimming through my veins, creating a hunger in the deepest pit of my stomach.

If only the hunger I'm feeling was for food alone.

Unfortunately for Auden, there's no food he can actually eat, unless he intends to start scarfing down uncooked pasta and cold marinara, instant mashed potato powder, or pancake mix.

"Leave it to you to not have a single bag of chips or some fucking trail mix in your pantry," he mutters and moves to the second box after folding the top flaps of cardboard over themselves to close the first again.

"Sorry, I didn't realize I'd need my doomsday survival kit to load a fucking U-Haul in the middle of Seattle."

He grumbles something incoherent under his breath as he rips tape off the next box, but my heart crawls into my throat when, even in the dim lighting, I can see the word written on the side.

Open.

It's a meaningless word to most, but I only wrote it on a single box. One that I know the exact contents of: my college diploma rests on top of a box of files. And on top of that, a large, flat black box—

I drop the bottle, the clanking sound echoing against the metal walls, and lunge forward, desperation oozing out of my pores as I grab for it. But even in his slightly intoxicated state, Auden's too quick.

Which is why I feel like I might vomit on the spot when his hand lifts a stack of envelopes, analyzing them before meeting my pleading stare.

Like he's just seen a ghost, he's pale, his eyes haunted, his expression pained.

"You still have my letters."

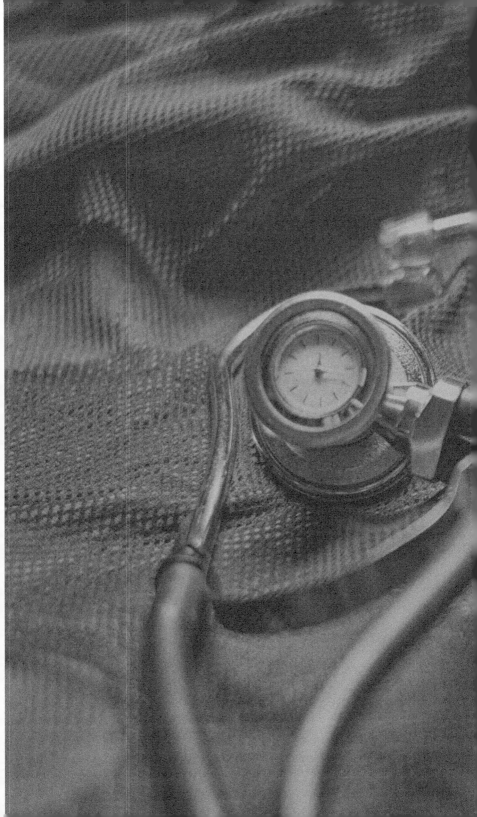

NINETEEN

Auden

It feels like the floor just dropped out from under me as I stare down at my own handwriting on countless opened envelopes, and the feeling only grows when I look up at Pierce to see the agony on his face.

And all I can do is keep looking between the two, like they're puzzle pieces that don't fit together right. Because they don't. None of this makes any sense, no matter how I try wrapping my head around it.

"Why?"

It's the only thing I can think to ask, but I can tell from the way Pierce's mouth screws up in pain that it's the wrong thing to say.

"Just…put them away. Please."

I raise them in the air. "Tell me why you still have them."

He shakes his head, his face still the picture of torture, but he remains silent.

"*Pierce.*"

"Leave it alone, Auden."

I can hear the pain in his voice, the unmistakable shake, all his hurt and vulnerabilities. Undeniable proof that underneath all his bravado, he still remembers.

"I'm not gonna leave it alone," I say honestly. "So you might as well explain."

He leans into my space, going to grab them from my grasp, but even with the amount of liquor I've consumed, I'm faster than him. I yank my arm out to the side, keeping my words out of reach.

Irritation floods his features. "I kept them. So what?"

"Nothing," I say coolly, downplaying my interest. "I guess you're just still full of surprises."

Echoing the exact words said on Crescent Beach, I anticipate—even hope for—a reaction, and when his eyes flare with rage, I feel a sliver of victory. But there's something else in them too. An intimacy I've seen before, flashing in his blue irises. Yet the moment his jaw tics as he holds out his hand, waiting for me to give the letters back to him, it disappears.

His impenetrable wall, thrown back up before my very eyes.

"Can you just give them back, please?"

I should respect his wishes. Hand over the words I'd written to him in the time I'd been deployed. Every lonely thought inked on sleepless nights, and each piece of me I'd shared with the man I'd started to fall—

I clear my throat, as if it will be enough to push the errant line of thinking back into the recesses of my brain. But the problem with shoving those emotions down is all that's left is my anger. The resentment and rage that've been fueling me since the moment I realized it was him standing at that altar.

And they've made me petty. Defiant. Even a little vindictive.

He must realize it too, because rather than following through on his threat, he sighs and slumps against the wall beside me. His shoulder brushes mine as he does, and I feel the heat of his body radiating toward me like a furnace.

It might be more intoxicating than the liquor in my veins.

My fingers shake slightly as I pull the first letter from its envelope and unfold it, finding my familiar scrawl inked on the page. But the second I see his name written at the top, I drop them to my lap and grab the bottle of whiskey at my side to take a long pull instead.

"I take it you don't still have mine." He says it so softly, I almost don't hear him. Part of me almost wishes I didn't, if only to prevent the truth from slipping out unguarded.

"I did. Even after you went radio silent, I still kept them."

My eyes stay trained on the bottle of whiskey in my hand, picking at the label before taking another swig. It burns my throat and heats my stomach, all the while chipping at the walls I've desperately built to keep him at bay.

"*Did,*" he muses, a sardonic sort of laugh leaving him when he realizes my use of the past tense. "So where are they now?"

"Where they've belonged since the moment you said *I do.*" My gaze shifts, colliding with his. "Burned to nothing but ash."

It should make me feel better, seeing the way his face falls. Empowered or liberated, even, to know I have even an ounce of power to hurt him the way he has me.

Instead, all I feel is empty.

His fingers tap absently against his own bottle of whiskey, and he nods a couple times. "I guess I deserve that."

"Probably more, if we're being honest," I murmur more to myself than him.

He scoffs and lifts the bottle to his lips, taking two long pulls of the liquor before he hisses and slams it to the floor between us. "Then lay it on me, Auden. It's the only way we're gonna get past this."

My head snaps toward him, irritation and bewilderment fighting to take over. Because there's no way the man sitting beside me can be this dense. No fucking way he can't see the gravity of where we are.

"Get past this?" I repeat, unable to keep my tone neutral. "Are you fucking delusional? There *is* no getting past this."

"There has to be. Don't you get it? There's *no* other option." His fingers rake through his hair as another disbelieving sound leaves him. "Your sister is my wife, so that means our holidays, birthdays, vacations, and futures are linked now. And they'll be that way for the rest of our fucking lives." He releases a long, slow breath. "For the sake of our sanity, we have to find a way to leave the past in the past."

How the fuck can I do that when I thought you'd be my future?

The thought has my throat clogging with emotion, and no matter how many times I attempt clearing it, my words still come out dragged over gravel. "Well, then maybe I'll make it easy for you and disappear. We'd all be a helluva lot better off that way."

"Emily wouldn't, and you know that."

"She's survived before. Surely she can do it again."

He shakes his head. "She needs you. More than you realize."

Guilt hits me square in the chest, as I'm sure it was meant to, and God, I try to push it down. Attempt to bat it away before it swallows me whole, consuming me in regrets.

"Well, you're the one who put us in the middle of a chess game," I mutter, trying my best for an air of indifference. "Sometimes you have to sacrifice the queen to win the game."

A sudden bout of fury rages in his eyes, my comment stoking a fire that I should've known better than to light in the first place. "Except this isn't a fucking game we're playing. This is my life, your *sister's* life, and everything in that goddamn box only serves to complicate it."

"You're the one who kept it all."

"Which was clearly a mistake," he snarls, tone sharp and cold as he glares over at me. "So just put the letters back, close the lid, and pretend you never saw them."

The request is clear, leaving little room for debate. But what cuts me deepest is how easy it is for him to shove me—*us*—in a nameless box to be forgotten. Tossed aside.

Meaningless.

Swallowing hard, I glance down at the letters in my hand—the only tangible piece of our past that's left. My eyes skim over the words on the page, seeing but not reading them. I don't think I have it in me to try anymore. Not when he's hell-bent on erasing it from existence.

Clenching my jaw, my thumb traces over my messy scrawl, and I find myself taking a page out of the Pierce I met at the beach by whispering words I have no business speaking.

"I was fucking crazy for you."

I'm not sure why I give voice to the thought, especially now, when it doesn't matter. Not when I have no choice but to build a bridge and get the fuck over it the way he clearly has already.

He blows out a breath, and I hear the tell-tale sound of him taking another swig of whiskey. I follow suit, wishing I'd been smart enough to keep the errant thought to myself.

The last thing I expect him to do is respond.

"You weren't alone in that."

A scoff leaves me, and it's my turn to drink. The liquor burns as I attempt to douse the pain and irritation his claim causes. Because if there was any truth to his statement, he wouldn't have dropped me like a bad habit the moment—

Don't go there. Not right now.

Rerouting my way of thinking, my lip curls up in a snarl as I mutter, "I sincerely doubt that, considering you didn't care one fucking iota—"

"Of course I fucking cared, Auden." His words come out in a harsh bite, eyes hardening as he glares at me. "I still do, even when I should know better. When I'm smart enough to realize that caring for you makes this harder on both of us. But it's not enough to make me stop."

He takes a deep, calming breath. "I know I've hurt you, that every interaction we have seems to *keep* hurting you. And I'm sorry for it."

"You're sorry," I repeat blandly, tasting the bitterness the sentiment holds as I tip my head back against the wall.

"More than you know."

His head rolls back so he's staring up at the ceiling of the prison we've found ourselves in. Like he might somehow find an escape route written in the metal there.

Silence thickens the air between us, and it's stifling. Like a cloud of poison threatening to fill my lungs and choke the life out of me if I'm stuck in here much longer.

A feeling that's confirmed when Pierce's voice shatters the quiet, and I might as well asphyxiate on his words.

"I never wanted to hurt you. All I ever wanted was the opposite."

My eyes slam closed for a moment, and I try to keep my composure.

It's a difficult feat when all I want to do is scream at him that *he's* the one who did this. Who ended things before they could ever truly begin. Who crushed my heart into finely ground powder with his bare hands.

Who made a choice…and chose the wrong fucking twin.

But when my lids lift and I look over at him, I know I can't say it.

Because, despite my intentions earlier, and even with how badly he's hurt me, I never want to hurt him. Never want his heart to be a casualty in this war we've been fighting, despite him already decimating mine.

"Then why do you still have these, Pierce?" I whisper, lifting the stack of letters in my hand. "'Cause seeing them? Knowing you have them? It *hurts* me. It's a fucking blade to the gut, over and over again."

"Because I'm selfish, all right? Have you ever thought about that? Is that what you need to hear?" His head rolls against the elevator wall to look at me, eyes a mixture of rage and regret swirling together beneath the surface. "I'm selfish, and I wanted to keep you. To keep *us*, even when I have no right to do so. Even if it had to stay hidden like some dirty little secret, I needed a piece of reality where you were still mine."

For the second time tonight, it's as if the floor has dropped out from under me. I'm in freefall, ready to crash to the earth at a thousand miles per hour.

And once I hit the ground, I know I'll explode. Combust into a million fragments.

What's more jarring is that, from the look on Pierce's face, he's in the same boat.

His lips part slightly, probably in shock at the truths he let spill from his mouth. The deep, dark secrets buried in the recesses of his mind that he's tried to keep hidden like the letters kept in that fucking box.

Yet, thanks to the alcohol wreaking havoc on our inhibitions, they've been brought to light…and no matter how much he may want to try, it's a bell that can't be unrung.

"You're right. That's really fucking selfish," I mutter, fingers dancing around the mouth of the bottle in my lap. Because I have to do *something* with my hands, or I'll risk reaching over to touch him.

If that happens, I don't think I'd ever be able to stop.

"I know." He swallows roughly, Adam's apple bobbing with effort while his focus dances between my eyes and mouth. "But not as selfish as some of the other things I'm thinking right now."

His expression hides nothing, and I swear I can pluck every thought from his brain as if it were my own. Every memory whirling through his mind. Reliving each kiss or touch or sigh as if they'd happened only yesterday.

I watch them all replay in the blue depths of his eyes, those stolen moments entrancing me as well. To the point where I'm leaning toward him, desperate for a closer look.

To feel those things, even just one more time.

"Thinking them is one thing," I hear myself say, my breath hitching as our mouths draw nearer. "It's not selfish until you act on it."

Pierce wets his bottom lip, and we're close enough now that I feel the faintest brush of his tongue. The heat from his breath sends my heart crawling to my throat, and when his fingers somehow find their way to my jaw, skating lightly toward my ear, it might've stopped entirely.

"Then call me fucking selfish."

My response dies in my throat when the sliver of space between our mouths disappears entirely, and I get my first taste of him in what feels like a lifetime.

It's a jolt of electricity, the initial brush of his lips, but when they mold more firmly to mine, it turns to a simmer. A constant and familiar humming between us as we lose ourselves in the intoxicating taste of each other.

Whiskey and sin, like that very first night.

The liquor bottles and letters are long forgotten, no longer acting as a distraction from the thing we truly crave: each other.

My fingers thread into his hair, fisting the onyx waves that never fail to drive me mad with uncontrollable want. He's pliable, like putty in my hands, as I tug at them, and the small bite of pain causes his lips to part in a gasp. I slip my tongue into his mouth, taking full advantage of him opening, and his slides with mine in a slow, seductive dance.

It's like coming home. As easy as breathing.

But that's just it.

With his lips on mine, it feels like I can finally breathe again. Like I hadn't realized I've been starving for oxygen every moment since our last kiss.

Pierce's hand glides down my throat before curling around the back of my neck, anchoring there like it's the only thing keeping him grounded. His skin on mine lights me on fire, flames of lust and want licking at my every nerve ending.

And I burn for him.

Desire takes over, and before I think better of it, I snake my arm around his waist and haul him to me. He comes willingly and settles on my lap, ass nestled snugly over my aching length already tenting my athletic shorts. Strong thighs bracket mine, and the ridge of his own erection grinds against my stomach in the most erotic, sinful way.

It's everything I want but still not nearly enough. When it comes to him, I doubt anything ever would be.

My arm stays locked around Pierce's waist, holding him against me with no intention of ever letting him go again, all the while the hand threaded through his hair controls the kiss. Angles his head and mouth for better access so I can completely devour him.

"Will," he groans.

That name on his lips, that sound from his throat, has my cock aching, needing and searching for more friction.

The elevator jolts beneath us suddenly, and I hear the faint hum of electricity that causes me to break away from him. There's a glassy look in his eyes—a mixture of liquor and lust—and all I want is to pull him back in for more. Anything and everything he's willing to give me.

Yet, as he catches his breath, the fog seems to lift until he's barely more than a deer in headlights, absolutely terrified of what's happened.

He scrambles off my lap and to his feet, panic and regret taking over.

"Shit, shit, shit," he mutters, his fingers clawing through his hair. "God fucking damnit."

I can't help it; I fucking laugh. The kind that's more unhinged than it is funny, because there's nothing comical about this. A fact made only more evident when Pierce's eyes land on me like I'm deranged.

Ignoring the question in his gaze, I rise to my feet and adjust myself, anticipating the inevitable.

"Look, what just—"

"Save it. I already know what you're gonna say," I mutter, the tone of my voice purposefully ambivalent. "And don't worry, it won't happen again."

The elevator doors choose that moment to open, and I grab a box and rush to exit, almost running to the truck. A single second longer in there with him, and I know he's going to decimate the little piece of my heart that's left.

The sound of his footsteps eventually close in behind me.

"I'm sorry."

"I said save it," I snap as I put the last box in the truck. "I really don't wanna fucking hear it."

Pierce's eyes soften, and I hate the look in them. One that speaks of pity or charity.

Rather than getting in the truck, I slam the door and start out in the rain, no destination in mind. At this point, it doesn't matter where I go. Anywhere is better than here.

"Where are you going?" Pierce shouts, and I hate the tinge of worry in his voice.

"Don't worry about it."

I hear the telltale sounds of him coming after me, and when his hand wraps around my forearm, I quickly shake him off to keep going. "Auden, stop. Let me at least call you a cab."

"I'd rather walk," I bite back.

The rain falls harder, the cold, wet feeling a welcome relief after the undiluted anger coursing through my veins.

"I'm sorry!" he calls after me, asking me to come back, to stop, to talk, but I don't. Without turning to hear what else he could possibly have to say, I keep going, putting as much distance between myself and the man I'd give anything to call mine—knowing he never will be.

And God knows I can't hear him say that fucking word one more time.

Because *sorry* doesn't fix the heart he keeps breaking.

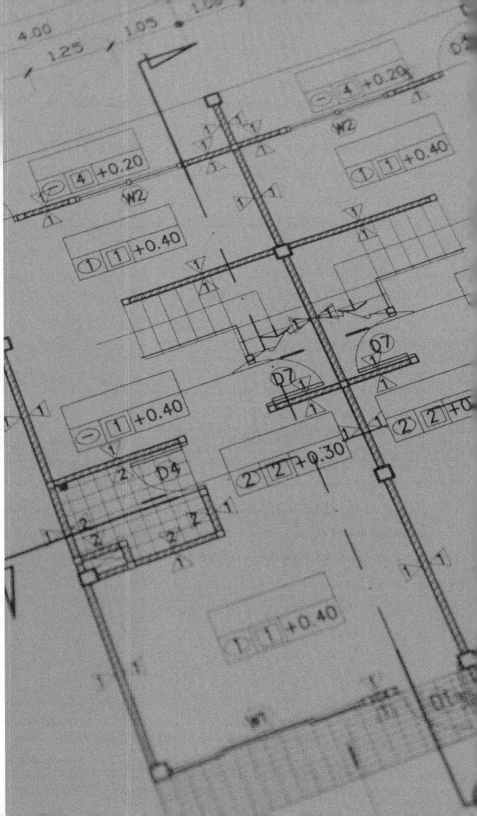

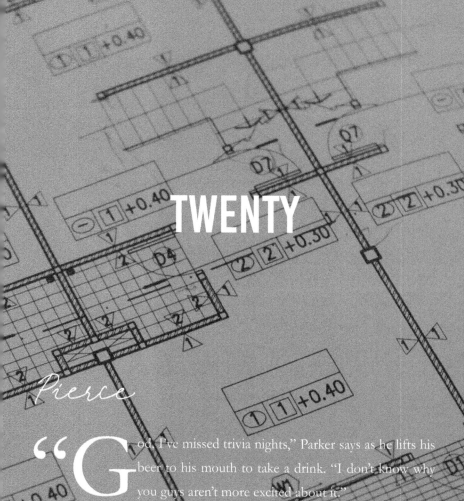

TWENTY

Pierce

"**G**od, I've missed trivia nights," Parker says as he lifts his beer to his mouth to take a drink. "I don't know why you guys aren't more excited about it."

Parker's best friend, Cohen, snorts. "Maybe because you're such an insufferable know-it-all and we aren't even needed?"

I let out a sharp laugh and shake my head, always enjoying the way the two of them go back and forth when we all go out. It's all in good fun, though, because Cohen is damn near attached to Parker's hip unless Parker is at the gym with the rest of us. Not that any of us mind, enjoying him becoming a permanent addition to the group of friends I never thought I'd find when I left Colorado.

"Hey, you made it!"

I glance up, catching Julian's line of sight, only for my entire body to feel like it's been tossed in a furnace when I find Auden at the other end of it.

Shit.

Auden scans the table, his gaze stumbling when he sees me before it continues back to where Julian is standing to greet him. He says hello to the group, handshakes and back slaps being exchanged, which is a complete contradiction to the quick tip of the chin he offers me.

The snub should be expected, especially after the way we left things last week. I keep hurting him over and over again, and to expect him to be anything more than civil toward me is truly above what I deserve.

As karma would have it, Parker pulls up a chair beside me, naturally assuming my brother-in-law and I would have no problem sitting next to one another for the evening. My whole body recoils at my errant thought; the truth of what we are to each other, still something I refuse to become accustomed to.

"I didn't know you'd be here," Auden murmurs, eyes locked straight ahead as he says it. "Emily's been on my ass about getting out and seeing people now that I'm stateside again. I should've assumed you'd be here. Had I known, I wouldn't have come."

"They're your friends too," I tell him, stating the obvious. The visible ease in which he's slipped back into the group is proof of that. "I don't expect you to isolate yourself because of me."

"Still," is all he says.

Silence settles between us, lingering thickly in the air as the rest of the guys chat and mingle around the table. I'm painfully aware of just how close his thigh is to mine, and visions of the other night invade my thoughts as the heat of his skin emanates through both our jeans.

"Maybe we should talk—"

"There's no point." Auden's voice is low and firm as he cuts in, and for the first time since he got here, he allows his gaze to shift to me. There's frustration in his eyes, but also a small flicker of something else I can't quite place. "Let's just…get through the night without any of them catching on, okay? Then I'll head out so you guys can enjoy the rest of the night."

Swallowing hard, I nod, having nothing else to offer him. "Okay."

He doesn't respond, instead slipping on a mask as he smoothly inserts himself in the heated debate Julian and Cohen are having about nature versus nurture. I know I should keep my attention away from him—and I should definitely move myself away from him physically—but instead, I find myself ensnared by him until the MC calls over the microphone for the first round to start.

The tension eases as our concentration is on the game, and, unsurprisingly, our team comes in first, thanks to our well-oiled machine, aka Parker's know-it-all nature and Cohen's competitiveness.

As we finish and win the third round, Auden surprises me, and everyone else, by rising from his seat. "I'm gonna go close out my tab. Anyone else need anything while I'm up there?"

I take in everyone's confused expressions at his abrupt departure and am quickly reminded that everything between us is fabricated. The shitty attempt we make to coexist around Emily, around our friends, it's all fake.

My laughs. His smiles.

They're nothing but polite and strained; communication between strangers. Because that's what my denial of him is reducing us to.

My eyes stay locked on Auden as he heads toward the bar, catching on the way his jeans hug his ass when he walks. That is, until I'm smacked in the shoulder by Julian, who I turn to find giving me a disapproving look.

"What the hell are you doing?" he says under his breath.

"What?"

He arches a brow. "You're looking at your brother-in-law like he's a fucking snack and you haven't eaten in a month."

Shit.

These two might've become my best friends since moving here—and I might trust them implicitly in the short time we've known each other—but I don't need them seeing me look at him that way.

So I do the only thing I can. I fucking deny it. "I don't know what you're talking about."

"Nice try, but you can't bullshit a high school teacher, Evans." Julian glances toward the bar discreetly before returning his gaze to me. "Now, spill before he comes back here."

Deacon snorts and shakes his head. "You're such a fucking gossip sometimes."

"And I'm gonna need a lot more alcohol to spill those kinda details," I counter, only to regret the words the moment they leave my lips when Julian's mouth drops open at my confession.

Deacon raises his hand to Julian's chin and closes his mouth. "Excuse my husband's nosiness, but I think you've rendered him speechless."

"Not speechless, just..." He shakes his head. "I was only giving you a hard time. I had no idea..."

"No idea what? That I'm bisexual?" I blurt my business out as a deflection, but of course it doesn't work, and tipsy Julian has turned into Detective Sutton, determined to unlock all my secrets.

He taps his finger to his chin. "You know, I noticed Auden was very hot and cold toward you, but I assumed he just didn't like you because you married his sister."

Deacon nudges Julian's shoulder. "I told you it was weird between them at the gym the other day."

Fucking hell.

"Look." My eyes catch on Auden returning back to the table. "There's nothing to tell. Can we drop it?"

"I believe that as much as I believe in Bigfoot," Julian murmurs beneath his breath, and thankfully, by the time Auden reaches us, the conversation has moved on to something else.

He places a tray of drinks we didn't order on the table, and distributes them accordingly, a bottle of beer landing right in front of me.

"Where's your drink?" I manage to ask.

Straightening his spine, he slips his hands into his pockets. "I'm actually gonna head out."

"Already?"

Play it fucking cool, Pierce.

If I thought they all missed my outburst, Deacon's eyes boring into the side of my skull say otherwise. I take a long swig of my beer to appear casual and unaffected, but I know I'm failing miserably.

"Yeah, I've got PT in the morning," he explains, a tight smile on his lips. "And that's no fun to do hungover or running on no sleep."

While PT is likely, my gut knows he's leaving because of me. I expect to feel guilty, but all I feel is needy and desperate.

For *him.*

It takes every ounce of strength I have to not demand he stay, and it's obvious Julian and Deacon notice. And this time, instead of the jovial questioning from before, they're both looking at me with something akin to pity.

"What?" I blurt out, unable to keep the defensiveness from my tone.

"Nothing." Julian raises his hands in surrender. "But I think you might need to get that"—he points in the direction of Auden walking out—"all off your chest."

An hour later and a switch from beer to whiskey, Julian and Deacon have me spilling my guts to them in what can only be described as a spectacular display of word vomit. The time in Cannon Beach, the agreement to keep things quiet about our past…the elevator…everything. I didn't realize until it was all out in the open, but I've never told *anyone* a single detail about Auden. Or rather, *Will.*

Not my best friends.

Not Emily.

Nobody.

Ironically, the most I mentioned of him to anyone was Emily, but never by name, only that there was someone I was still moving on from before her. A guy I thought could've been it for me, but it just didn't work out. Besides that, though, I could almost convince myself he never existed if the feel of his lips and taste of his tongue weren't ingrained into my memory.

Maybe because I thought it'd be tainted. Take away from how real and special and *ours* it was.

Taking a long swig of my whiskey, I let the sliver of relief at sharing my burden run through me. Parker and Cohen left shortly after Auden did, leaving me alone with the two men I trust most. Even if this means they now think the worst of me, I still know they will never spill my secrets.

Deacon leans back in his chair and lets out a long sigh. "Damn. I was not expecting that."

"It makes our whole situation look like child's play, honestly," Julian supplies before looking at his husband.

I let out a low snort at the reminder of the unconventional conception of their relationship and lift my drink to my lips, barely noticing the burn of the liquor at this point.

"Thanks for the rousing show of support, guys."

Julian raises his own drink and shrugs. "I'm just saying, if I thought what Deacon and I went through to get here was shit, I think you've got us beat."

I roll my eyes and push back in my chair. "Well, if I'm done being tonight's source of entertainment, I think I'll see myself out."

"We didn't mean it like that, man," Deacon says, catching my arm. "It's a tough situation to be in, you know? And it's not exactly something that has an easy solution either."

He's right, as much as I wish he wasn't. If there was a way to flip off whatever lingering emotions I have when it comes to Auden, I would. In a fucking heartbeat.

It would be even easier to wish the whole week never happened, but the mere thought of it fills me with an overwhelming sense of sadness. This *thing* between us is hard and complicated now, and has real, agonizing consequences. And yet the thought of never ever meeting him, touching him...*fuck*...loving him. It isn't even a possibility, and it still hurts like a fucking blade through my chest.

Feeling both defeated and depleted, I run a hand over my face. I'm not used to having such conflicting emotions simultaneously. Both light and heavy. Hurt and yet strangely hopeful.

"Look," Julian says, drawing my attention back to him. "Obviously I care deeply about Emily—"

"As do I," I remind him, my tone clipped. "You know, since she is my *wife*."

Julian arches a brow. "I'm not insinuating you don't. I was only gonna say that I like you too, and I don't want to see anyone get hurt in this."

That's the last thing I want either, but...

"I think it's inevitable," I say honestly. "Auden's hurting every day."

So am I, but I know I don't have the right to voice that thought aloud, even when I know they'd understand. Whether it's Auden's sister or not, I chose someone else. Of sound body and mind, I made the decision to move on. Move forward.

It's too late to tell him I broke my own heart getting over him well before I ever broke his. I thought I could put him in a box with his letters, but everything we shared was too big and too beautiful to ever be sized down to something so inconsequential.

Now, I'm reaping the consequences for trying.

"Your best option is to stay far away from him," Deacon says, eyeing his husband. "Easier said than done, I know, though I think you've already figured that out the hard way."

"And the times when it's literally impossible to not be in the same room?" I ask, genuinely wanting answers, wanting help. Fucking something other than unknowns and a head full of contradictions.

"Don't make eye contact."

The incredulity of this makes me laugh. "Wouldn't that just make it more awkward?"

"No," Deacon says firmly. "What's gonna make shit more awkward is the way you two eye-fuck each other when you think the other isn't looking. Or anyone else, for that matter."

Blue eyes bore into mine, and I feel the guilt of his words before I even hear them. "Because what are you going to do if your wife catches you looking at her brother the way we did tonight?"

TWENTY-ONE

Pierce

I don't even realize where I am until I'm standing at the door, fist raised and pounding against it. But I'm not in the right state of mind to give a damn. About breaking the stupid thing down or about the noise I'm making at nearly one in the morning.

Coming here, especially while my inhibitions are lowered, is the last thing I should be doing. After what happened in the elevator a few days ago, and given our history, I should be putting as much distance between Auden Thompson and myself as humanly possible.

Hell, I was in the cab, set to go home and sleep off the drinks Deacon and Julian kept feeding me—the same drinks that also made me miss Auden. The alcohol had my mind mixing up memories and reality, making me *ache* for him.

So, here I am. Like a moth to a flame, the liquor swimming through my veins, not giving a single flying fuck about anything other than seeing the man on the other side of this door.

"Auden, I know you're in there," I hear myself growling, though my voice sounds foreign to even my own ears. Too feral and full of desperation.

A minute goes by without an answer, and the urgency within me amplifies. My fist meets the wood again and the door rattles within the frame at the contact, the same way it does in my chest at the hollow sound.

"Open the fucking door, Auden."

I'm about to slam my fist against the wood again when I hear the faint sound of the lock sliding out of place. There's a moment where I think I imagined it—that my intoxication has started creating hallucinations—before the door swings open to reveal one very confused Auden.

Who happens to be shirtless and in a pair of jeans hanging low off his hips.

His brows crash together when he sees me before his eyes dart past me into the hall, as if looking for someone else.

"Pierce. What's going—"

I push past him before he can get the rest of the question out, walking into the apartment without waiting for him to invite me inside. Probably because, deep down, I know he has every right and reason to slam the door in my face if given the chance.

I run my fingers through my hair, brushing back the damp strands currently weighed down by the rain water. My attention quickly shifts around the apartment before falling on him again.

His bare back is to me as he flips the lock in place, and my eyes quickly dart away before I get sucked into the perfection that is his body.

The only issue with this not-so-thought-out idea of mine to just show up here unannounced is, now that I'm here in front of him, I have no idea what to say.

I do another sweep of my surroundings, noting the bottle of whiskey on the coffee table with a tumbler glass half-full of the amber liquid. A wry laugh leaves me as I cross the space to grab it and swirl the liquor around the glass.

"Thought you skipped out early tonight because you had PT in the morning?"

And because I haven't already done enough damage tonight, I down the contents of the glass in two swallows, any amount of common sense still left in my body completely vanishing in an instant.

More liquor. Right. That'll do the trick.

"You know why I really left, Pierce."

That I do. He all but told me his intentions the moment he arrived earlier tonight, ready to make some excuse and slip out of the evening before any further damage was done.

But then my inebriated self decided to show up soaking wet at his door, effectively soiling that plan.

Yep, brilliant fucking move, Pierce.

My gaze lifts to find Auden, only to see he's still standing across the room, back pressed against the front door, just…watching me. The wary, guarded expression on his face when he turns to me serves as a dagger to the heart.

Though I can't tell if the obvious distrust is for me or himself.

"What are you doing here?"

The question is barely more than a whisper, and if I hadn't been intently staring at his lips as they formed the words, I'd have thought I imagined them altogether. And, God, I can't stop myself from staring at his mouth.

"I don't know. I just...ended up here."

Nothing makes sense anymore, not even in my own head.

All I'm certain of is our moment in the elevator has been living in my mind on repeat, spinning like a broken record since spilling the details to Julian and Deacon. Truthfully, it's consumed my thoughts since it happened, and no matter how hard I've tried to push the memory away, it's been driving me to the brink of insanity.

That's when I realize maybe the reason I've found myself here is because the fresh, vivid memory of his lips on mine have pushed me over the edge entirely.

And now I'm in freefall, ready to take him down with me.

"How did you even know where I live?"

"Emily." We lock eyes again, and I catch his harden slightly. "When she shared your contact with me, your address was there too."

He shakes his head before a soft, exasperated laugh leaves him. "Figures."

I don't respond and instead reach for the bottle of whiskey on the coffee table, refilling the tumbler with a finger or two of the liquor.

"I think you've had enough for one night."

"That's something we can agree to disagree on, soldier" I tell him, raising the glass in mock salute as the old nickname sneaks past from my loose lips.

He's up in my face a second later, snatching the glass from my fingers before throwing it against the wall across the room. It shatters on impact, shards falling to the floor as alcohol cascades down the wall in tiny rivulets.

Never in my life did I think I'd see someone ordinarily as cool and collected as Auden Thompson absolutely lose his shit.

Then again, the circumstances we've found ourselves in are anything but ordinary.

"What the fuck is your problem right now?" he snarls, wheeling back on me.

And he's right there. Right *fucking* there, his breath coasting over my lips and chest brushing mine when we inhale at the same time.

"You are, Auden. You're my fucking problem. You and those perfect fucking lips I can't get out of my head." I blink, my eyes dancing back and forth between his, and whisper, "Why can't I get you out of my head?"

A row of perfect, white teeth sink into his plush lower lip, and my God, I'm tempted to pull it free and take it between mine instead.

"You need to go home. I..."

"You what?"

Some sick, masochistic part of me can't help shifting my attention back to his eyes, taking in their moss green depths and being hypnotized by the amber flecks. Of course, the second I catch sight of the agony within them, I instantly regret looking in the first place.

Or maybe it's regret for being the reason he's hurting to begin with.

Either way, it's too much for my intoxicated brain to unpack right now.

"I don't think we should be alone together." His Adam's apple bobs as he swallows, and his eyes shift away from mine. "Not after what happened..."

He doesn't finish the rest of his thought, but he doesn't need to. I know exactly where his mind went. After all, it's where mine has been living since it happened.

The elevator.

"No."

His brow lifts slightly. "No?"

"No, I don't think we should be alone together." My tongue darts out, wetting my lips. "But it's a little too late for that. I'm already here, and we're already alone."

Liquid confidence has me stepping in closer than I'd ever dare sober, drawn into the intoxicating allure that is him. Only a sliver of space separates us now, and I know I'm playing a dangerous game. And I doubt I'll make it out unscathed.

But I don't have it in me to care.

"Pierce…"

"I want you," I mutter, my breath whispering against his lips.

His jaw tics. "You're drunk."

"But we're supposed to be…" *How did Emily put it? Oh, right.* "…'getting to know each other.'"

The words disgust me as they leave my mouth, knowing full well there's not a person on this planet who knows me better than the man standing in front of me.

Not even Emily.

A sharp, unamused laugh leaves Auden. "Not like that."

"Mmm, no. You're right." I lick my lips, my tongue lightly grazing his too, we're so close. "Except we already *do* know each other like that. Don't we, *Will?*"

The name feels foreign and familiar leaving my mouth all at the same time. Like coming home after being away for far, *far* too long.

His eyes sink closed, but I see the war etched into his features. The battle raging within him as he clenches his fists at his sides.

"Don't do that."

"Do what?"

I sink my teeth into the side of his neck, eliciting a throaty gasp that does everything for me. His cock is hard against me, a clear sign that, while he may be fighting this, he's enjoying it too. A boldness takes over me, and I slide my hands between our bodies and cup him over his jeans.

"*Fuck*," he hisses.

I don't miss the way he arches into my touch as my hand and mouth continue tormenting him the same way he has me for *months* now.

But all too soon, he comes to his senses, uttering another plea.

"Pierce, stop. You have to stop."

But I don't listen. Instead, I squeeze his dick through the denim before moving to the button, flicking it open. And though he's asking me to stop, he doesn't do a damn thing to actually make me.

"Why?"

"Because..." He trails off as my tongue slides down the column of his neck, tasting the hint of his body wash against his skin. "Because—"

"That's not a reason, Will," I mutter. My mouth moves up his throat until I reach his ear, and I whisper a question I'm not sure I really want the answer to. "Don't you want me too?"

"Pierce, you're drunk. You don't know what you're saying. Think about—"

"I don't want to think." My teeth graze over his pulse point, nipping at his flushed skin before bringing my forehead to rest against his. I breathe him in, the familiarity of his touch and presence fogging my mind more than the alcohol swimming in my veins. "I want to *feel*."

More than anything.

"Pierce," he utters, it coming out rough and ragged, and I know he's fraying at the edges too. Coming apart at the seams every time we keep denying this—*us*.

My hand leaves his cock, sliding up his body until it wraps around the back of his neck. Our lips are so close together, we're sharing the same breath, but the distance still feels like the thousands of miles that tore us apart.

It shreds any thread of sanity I have left, causing a plea to leave my lips.

"Please."

He wavers, but doesn't fold, no matter how much I can tell he wants to. No matter how much I'm *praying* he will.

I make a final attempt, his name falling from my lips—the name he's told me time and time again not to speak—and it's that one, single word that has his control snapping.

And then his lips land on mine.

TWENTY-TWO

Auden

The moment our lips meet, I'm lost to the world.

Every rational thought of getting him out of my apartment, into a cab, and safely home fly right out the damn window, only to be replaced by a white-hot need that's as consuming as it is addictive.

My hand slides around to the back of his neck, fusing us closer, needing more as I ignore the panicked voice in the back of my mind telling me we shouldn't be doing this.

I shove his damp shirt over his head, quickly filling with the same desperation and desire clearly clouding his judgment. But it doesn't seem to matter. I don't fucking care where this leads or how poor of a decision it might be to entertain whatever this is with him.

My heart might be ripped to shreds by the end of whatever this is, and our world will undoubtedly go up in flames, but it's not enough to stop me from wanting him.

Needing him.

I crush my mouth to his again, tasting the liquor and lust on his tongue as it duels with mine. His hands trace and map over my bare back and shoulders, leaving goosebumps in their wake.

"God, Will. Need you," he mutters, his breath coming out in harsh pants. "I need you so much, it fucking hurts."

Raw emotion claws through my chest at the desperation in his voice. Maybe because it mirrors my own. Maybe because his need for me diminishes the heartache of his easy dismissal of us all those months ago.

Either way, I'm committed to our destruction as we continue stripping each other to nothing, our hands grappling for purchase on any bare skin we can find, all while our mouths fuse together at the molecular level.

We move deeper into my apartment, stumbling to my bedroom in a way that reminds me of that first night we spent together on the coast. And the stabbing pain it causes in my heart fuels me as much as it hurts.

My hand wraps around his hard length, stroking him firmly as I continue devouring his mouth. He lets out a soft gasp against my lips when I roll my fist over the head, collecting the pre-cum and spreading it down his shaft.

"Oh, shit," he gasps, and I'm quick to swallow it down with my lips and tongue. But there's a niggling in the back of my mind as we bite and nip and tear each other apart that causes me to falter and break away.

"Are you gonna regret this?"

He stills before pulling back in confusion. "What? Why—"

"Answer the question, Pierce," I demand, leaving no room for debate.

A frown takes over his features, and I can tell he wants to bite back from the way his brows draw down. But he reels it in almost immediately before murmuring, "I'm not that drunk, if that's what you're asking."

"Good," I mutter, my lip curling back in a wicked smirk. "Then get on the fucking bed."

Not waiting for his obedience, I push him onto the mattress, and I'm hit with a sense of euphoria as I stare down at his naked form splayed out before me. Almost like he should've been there all along.

Quickly grabbing a condom and the lube from my nightstand, I toss them on the bed before kneeling on the mattress, situating myself between his thighs.

"How do you want me?" he asks, already taking over stroking himself.

"Just. Like. That."

Covering his body with my own, I bracket my arms on either side of his head to kiss him again. There's equal parts leisure and aggression now, like there's still so much anger left to be released but we still want to take our time to enjoy this.

Because, deep down, we both know this can't happen again.

In the back of my mind, I'm perfectly aware it shouldn't even be happening now. I'm just too helpless—too caught up in him and us and the memories—to stop it.

Breaking away, my mouth carves a path down his chest and abs; biting, sucking, and licking at the smooth lines of skin and muscle.

"Fuck, I've missed your mouth," he rasps.

I smile against his skin and glance up, meeting his gaze. Those blue eyes are blazing as his fingers dive through the short strands of hair at the top of my head.

"Just my mouth? Or did you miss my cock too, baby?"

"All of it. All of you."

Another winning grin paints my lips before they wrap around his length. I lavish his dick with attention, licking and sucking him like it's the last thing I'll ever do.

It doesn't take long before I'm taking him deep to the back of my throat, swallowing around his shaft, only for his fingers to tighten to the point of pain in my hair.

"Oh my God, I'm already so close." He makes an effort to pull me off his cock, panting out, "Inside me, Will. Please."

My own dick leaks pre-cum from the tip, and I reach for the condom, only for Pierce's hand on my wrist to stop me.

Aiming a questioning look at him, he just shakes his head and utters a single word.

"Bare."

Fuck.

If this is the only time we'll allow this to happen, then I don't care how stupid it might be. I wanna be able to feel *all* of him. At least once.

Knocking the condom out of the way, I grab the bottle of lube, dousing my cock with the liquid. My fingers move to his crease, spreading the remnants around his hole. It clenches at first touch, and I smirk, knowing that if nothing else, I still have this effect on him. Still have the ability to make him squirm beneath my gaze and touch.

Kneeling between his parted legs, I line myself up with the tight bud. We lock eyes, and I arch my brow, a subtle final chance for him to tap out before things go past the point of no return.

"Fuck me, Will."

Not being one to be told twice, I press past his tight rim until I'm buried to the hilt. The pressure around my dick is something between torture and bliss without a barrier, his clenching and squeezing me mercilessly as his body adjusts.

"Jesus Christ," I mutter, flexing my ass to keep from coming completely undone before we even begin. "You feel better than I remember."

If I'm being honest, I've dreamt about his body more times than I can count in the past months. Remembering the way it felt beneath my touch. The way he'd tremble and quake before his orgasm would slam into him and he'd clench around me tighter than a vise.

It's something I never imagined I'd experience again after seeing him in that church, yet somehow, here we are.

Right back where we began.

My arms slip beneath his thighs and I pull him toward me, thrusting deeper inside him. A strangled sound leaves his lips, something between a gasp and a moan, and the sound goes straight to my balls.

"Love those sounds you make," I pant, pistoning my hips forward again. "Love hearing what my cock does to you."

My thrusts are hard and measured as I drive into him, putting all my aggression, anger, and hurt into each one until I'm slamming against his ass relentlessly. Punishingly. And he takes it—all the pain and hurt he's caused—while pressing and arching into me for more.

Pierce's hand moves rapidly over his length, attempting—and failing miserably—to keep time with my movements that are anything but gentle. How can I be? I'm absolutely feral for him, more animal than man when he's at my mercy like this.

Using his body to bring myself pleasure as much as to release my pain.

His ass squeezes around my length, pulsing as I drive into him, and it pushes me closer to the edge of impending ecstasy.

"God, you're so fucking tight around my cock, baby. Tell me, am I the last one who fucked you like this?"

Pierce's ocean eyes are shining with more emotions than they ought to be when he meets my gaze and gives me the faintest nod. Pride and ownership surge through me, his confirmation all I need to change my pace from relentless to downright brutal.

"Good," I snarl, impaling him as much as he thrusts onto me. "I told you I'd ruin you for anyone to come after me, and I meant it."

But even as I say the words, I know the opposite is true. *He's* the one who ruined *me*. Decimating everything I thought I knew, unraveling me at the seams. Twisting me inside out, coiling and knotting me up until I'm unrecognizable to even myself.

Or maybe it's that doing this—being like this with him—is what's turning me into someone else entirely.

"That's it, baby. Just like that," I murmur, the head of my cock swiping over his prostate as he meets my thrusts.

A soft curse leaves him and his free hand clamps around my wrist, clutching me like he's holding on for dear life. And I love it. Reducing him to pants and moans. Pulling pleasure from his body and replacing it with my own.

There's nothing I wouldn't do to make this last forever, to make him walk away from everyone and everything outside of this. To have him see the mistake he's made by promising the rest of his life to anyone else but me.

I wanna fuck his love for my sister clear out of his system.

Until I'm all that's left.

And if that isn't the most messed-up thing in the world…I don't know what is.

I'm past the point of pretending I can turn off what I feel for him. That the emotions welling inside me—the hurt, the anger, the frustration and hatred—stem from something more powerful and potent than I ever imagined.

Love.

And, God, I wanna say it. More than I want to breathe, I wanna tell him just how far he's burrowed himself beneath my ribs and nestled in beside my heart. But I can't bring myself to give him that part of me.

So instead, I say things I can.

Oh, fuck, Pierce.

Just like that.

You're so perfect.

That's it, baby.

All three words…just not the ones I wanna say.

Our bodies continue moving together in a furious rhythm more animalistic than sensual; a dire need for release driving us. Pierce's hand moves faster over his length, the strokes becoming more rapid and frantic as he chases his climax. His teeth sink into the plush, pink surface of his lower lip, and I realize I want it between *my* teeth.

And if this is the only chance I'll get to have that again, I'm not gonna hold back.

So I lean forward, and I take it.

"Fucking Christ," he groans against my lips. His free hand lands on my lower back in our new position, and every brush of his wedding band against my skin sets me on fire, and not in a good way.

It's a reminder burning against my flesh.

Of what he is. Of what I'm *not*.

Reaching behind me, I grab it and haul it over his head, and though my heart is already pounding like a stampede within my chest, when he locks his fingers with mine, I think it might explode.

My hips slam forward at a relentless pace, driving into him while dragging us both toward the cliff's edge. His hand moves quicker over his length as he attempts to match my thrusts, but from the haphazard nature of his strokes, he won't last much longer.

"Fuck," he rasps, head slamming back against the pillow and arching into me. "I'm close, Will."

My name—the one he learned first—on his lips is nothing short of sinful, especially when he's like this. In rapture beneath me while I bury myself inside him. And I want nothing more than to watch him fall apart, consumed with the pleasure my body feeds him.

"Then come for me, baby," I murmur, dropping my head to brush my lips over his. "Give me everything you have."

He clenches around my cock, and almost on command, his orgasm spills free. Cum shoots onto his stomach, covering his skin in the white, sticky liquid. My own release slams into me like a freight train as his ass bears down on me some more, and I quickly pull from his body.

I coat his abs and chest with my cum, mixing with his own across his skin, and the sight has one word ringing loud and clear in my mind.

Mine.

But in reality, I know that isn't the case.

He's only mine when the shadows creep across the moonlit floor on the Oregon coast or on rainy, starless nights when the memories become too hard to fight. In the light of day, he belongs to someone else entirely.

Shifting from between his legs, I drop to the mattress and attempt to catch my breath after what might be the best orgasm of my entire life. Sweat drips down my temple until it hits the pillow, and I glance over at Pierce to find him already staring at me.

Only, the second our gazes collide...he looks away.

He moves to get up, the bed shifting as his weight leaves the mattress, and the immediate absence of his body heat radiating toward me is like a knife to the chest.

"Pierce."

He gives no sign of hearing me other than the rigid set of his back as he heads to the attached bathroom. The sound of the faucet running as he washes away the evidence of our sins sets my body on high alert, and I quickly rise, gathering our discarded clothing left in the wake of our desire and tossing them on the bed.

Pierce returns a few minutes later, naked and not meeting my eyes as he grabs his boxers from the pile of clothes.

I wish I could reach inside his mind while I watch him. Pluck whatever errant thoughts are running through that beautiful head of his—and they have to be going wild right about now.

"*Pierce*," I try a second time, only to be met with a cruel shake of his head.

"No, Auden." His dark hair flops into his eyes as he casts them to the ground, not daring to meet my gaze.

Trying my best to ignore the foreign sound of that name coming from his lips after being Will again, even just for a few fleeting moments, I slip into a pair of clean sweats, sans underwear. It takes everything in me to push down the panic rising inside me like a tidal wave—one ready to crash into the levee that is my composure—but I manage until I look at him again, only to find him fully dressed.

And while I was just wishing to know the thoughts racing through his mind only moments ago, I've changed my mind now. Because he doesn't so much as have to speak for me to hear them loud and clear. They're written all over his handsome, broken features.

"You lied."

His brows crash together, clear irritation flaring in his eyes. "What the hell are you talking about?"

"You regret it," I state simply. "You said you wouldn't, but it's clear as fucking day the way you won't look at me."

A sharp scoff echoes through the otherwise empty room, and Pierce aims a glare at me I can only describe as disgusted. "The real question is how you don't. I cheated on my *wife*. With her *brother* of all people."

My teeth sink into my fleshy inner cheek as I shake my head. "So that's all I am now, right? The brother-in-law you slept with a time or two? That's all this is?"

"I don't *know* what this is, Auden!" he shouts, tossing his hands up in the air. "All I know is that I'm confused as hell. I'm fucking suffocating under the weight of whatever this is, and I can't even put a name on it."

"Can't put a name on it?" I seethe, stepping into his space. "Well, I've got one for it. Love."

The moment the word leaves my lips, Pierce's face goes white as a sheet. He shakes his head, denying what is and should be obvious but clearly needs to be spelled out.

"This is love, Pierce. The fight-with-you-every-day-because-I-can't-live-without-you kind. The kind where you get married and grow old together. The kind that's meant to be forever. How can't you see that?"

A tormented sound escapes him as he shakes his head some more, and I take another slow, tentative step toward him, my military training kicking in instinctively.

"You're scared, and I get that. I am too, because this isn't who I am," I utter, my tone low and husky. "I chose you over everything, even while knowing you weren't mine to choose. Even when it meant destroying people I love the most—ones I'd die to protect." The words catch in my throat as his eyes sink closed. "Tell me it wasn't the wrong fucking choice."

The agony in his gaze when his eyes reopen begs me to stop. To give him some sort of reprieve from the guilt and regret already consuming his consciousness until there's nothing left.

I'm watching him shut down before my very eyes.

Turn into a shell of the man I know—a fragment of the person I fell in love with.

"Don't go," I whisper, my voice laced with gravel. "Not yet."

I'm powerless to stop him, but I still find myself wrapping my palm around his wrist anyway. Like it's enough to keep him here. Claim him. Make him mine and mine alone.

The soft thud of his pulse beneath my fingertips creates an insurmountable ache in my chest, growing with each passing second as I wait for an answer. Hope for surrender.

Pray for a miracle.

But when I find his gaze again, I realize my prayers will go unanswered. Even still standing in front of me, I can see it.

He's already gone.

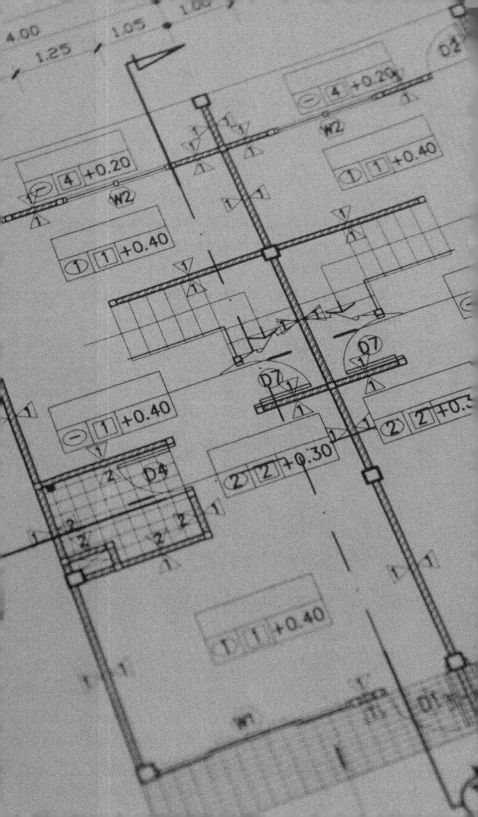

TWENTY-THREE

Pierce

There's a mallet inside my head, pounding against the inside of my skull, reminding me that alcohol is always a bad fucking idea. Except when you show up at your estranged lover's doorstep, then alcohol is the life of the party. Especially when that lover happens to be your wife's brother.

Fingers skate softly up and down my spine as a set of lips press against the back of my shoulder in soft, feather-light kisses, and my hazy mind attempts to play catch up.

Fixates on the last person who touched my bare skin.

"Mmm, Will," I mutter, tossing my arm across my eyes while a smile forms on my lips.

"Will what, baby?"

The blood in my veins turns to ice when I register the voice is soft and feminine. That the fingers tracing over my bare skin are delicate and gentle, not the rough and calloused ones that lit me on fire last night.

Emily.

"Will what, Pierce?" she asks again, and when I pull my arm off my face and blink my eyes open, I find her gazing down at me with concern. My stomach churns and rolls as I take in the surroundings of *our* room.

Clearing my throat, I attempt to talk past the boulder practically blocking my airway. "Will you please get me something for my head?"

The sweet lilt of her laughter might as well be gunshots against my eardrums, and the kiss she presses to my shoulder, a blade of guilt slicing through my skin like butter.

"Of course," she whispers before rising off the bed.

There's a black hole in my memory, the time between sleeping with Auden and me coming home, unaccounted for.

I remember the immediate regret that consumed me, and the way hurting him hurt me in return, like someone was carving out chunks of my heart with a spoon. Every touch and taste and sigh we shared as we let our bodies do the talking. The fight after, and the way Auden's face fell as I shut down on him. Everything about last night is seared into my brain, just not how I made it back home.

"You had a little too much fun last night, did you?" Emily's voice calls from the bathroom.

I can't look at her as she returns to the bedside. Can't bring myself to meet her eyes as I sit up and she hands me the pills and a glass of water to down them.

"Do I need to have a talk with my brother and the other guys about hazing?"

"No, no." I shake my head and wince in pain. "It's nothing like that."

Emily sits back down on the bed beside me, curling up against the headboard as I down the meds and water. "I'm glad you and Auden seem to be getting along."

Despite my discomfort, the mention of her brother has me shamefully meeting her gaze.

"How come?" I ask.

She cants her head to the side. "He's my brother. Why wouldn't I want my husband and brother to like each other?"

"I wasn't sure if there was some other reason."

Emily shrugs, all nonchalant and easy. "I don't know. I'm hopeful that maybe if he sees how much of a community he still has here, he'll finally decide to get out of the Army and stick around for good."

The thought of Auden staying here…fuck, I don't know how I feel about it. Not after what happened in the elevator, and certainly not after last night.

If you'd asked the man who penned letter after letter to him for all those months, this would've been the answer to all my prayers. Now it feels too late—the damage already done, and him staying here will only cause more. Yet to wish him gone feels so fucking wrong.

But if last night is any indication, the survival of my marriage, my sanity, and my conscience depends on it.

Scrubbing a hand over my face in frustration, I look over at my wife, who's smirking at me, her green eyes filled with humor and affection.

My hangover is entertaining to her, and rightfully so. To her I'm a man who went out with his friends and had too good of a time, when in reality, I went out last night and broke our wedding vows. And not for the first time; she just doesn't know it yet.

"I'm going to shower," I tell her, guilt consuming me the more I allow my mind to wallow in the sins of last night. "Maybe when I get out and feel more human, I could take you out to brunch."

Her face beams at the idea, and it's a dagger to the chest.

Leaning over, I kiss her cheek. "I'll be out soon."

In the shower, I let my forehead rest on the cool tiles as the hot water scorches my skin. Inside these four walls, I can be alone with my indiscretions. Alone with the shame and regret my actions have caused.

My heart breaks, cracking and splintering, pieces for her and pieces for him. I feel hollow and empty, and it's all my own doing. There's no one else to blame for thinking I could live a life without William Auden Thompson.

I thought I'd have occasional drunken nights re-reading his letters, secretly reminiscing and pining for the man who changed the blueprint of my heart. Then I'd put him back in a box with a lock and key so I could live the rest of my life with the woman who taught me I still had love to give.

It was never supposed to be *this*.

It was never supposed to be this convoluted family affair. Lies and broken promises that not only tarnished the love I have for Emily, but it's tainted everything about Auden and me. Our history, our love…

Because that's what it was, wasn't it?

The fight-with-you-every-day-because-I-can't-live-without-you kind. Isn't that what Auden had said?

But in reality, the love we share has now turned into the hidden, scandalous, and remorseful kind. And a man like him deserves so much more than being my dirty little secret. He deserves to be loved and worshipped in the daylight. He deserves to hear those words and know I mean them *only* for him.

Because right now, there's a woman on the other side of the bathroom door who thinks I only feel those things for *her*. Reserves those words for her, and her alone.

And while he deserves a man who lives his truth, she deserves a husband who doesn't live a lie.

———————————————

After the longest shower in history, I emerge feeling somewhat better. My hope is that the water rinsed away the cheating and lying husband and replaced him with a man determined to do better by Emily—to be the man she deserves—which includes showering her with the attention a newlywed deserves.

Which is why we're nestled together in the back of our favorite café, in the heart of Seattle, eating our weight in some of the best food the city has to offer, me purposefully steering away from some of my favorites because they remind me of Auden and Cannon Beach.

"I've missed this one-on-one time with you since going back to work," she murmurs before leaning over and pressing her lips to my cheek. "I love the kids, but after having the summer off to spend with you, it's hard going back to the old routine."

"Me too," I tell her with a genuine smile, and I find myself meaning the words just as much as the ones that leave next. "I love you, sweetheart."

She simultaneously breaks and heals my aching heart as she murmurs, "I love you too."

Emily fills me in on all the latest that's been happening for her since the new school year started, telling me all about her class of rebellious teens and the new teachers who've joined the staff. It feels nice to settle back into the normalcy of what we had previously. Before the wedding, when everything became more complicated than I could ever imagine.

"So, you know how Marie is going on maternity leave in a few months?"

I nod, recalling that, besides Julian, Marie is one of the only other teachers at the high school Emily is friends with outside of work.

"Well, she just announced she's taking a whole year off, and they want me to step in and head the school's English department in the interim."

"Em," I utter in awe. "That's amazing."

She waves me off, despite the smile stretched across her face. "It's only for a year."

"Don't do that." I slide my hand across the table and grab hers, squeezing it gently. "Don't talk yourself out of being happy for the things you accomplish. It's a step in the right direction. And a year is a long time; anything can happen between now and then."

There's barely a thought in the response I offer, but as soon as I hear it out loud, I'm immediately thinking of just how much has changed between Auden and me. Subtly, I shake my head, trying to stay in this moment and this conversation with Emily.

"I know," she agrees, albeit grudgingly. "But I don't want to get my hopes up. It's not like they're going to give me Marie's job permanently."

I offer her a shrug before going back to my food, slicing through my eggs benedict. "Maybe not, but Marie might not want to come back after giving birth. You'd be a shoo-in for the spot if that were the case."

Emily and I go back and forth talking about work, comparing the stress I was under before my big promotion to the increase in her workload once she receives hers. The conversation shifts and changes effortlessly, from topic to topic, laughing and joking, reminding me of all the reasons I'm committed to this marriage and fell in love with her in the first place.

She's infectious. Her smile, her charm, her sense of humor. She's dedicated to the things she's passionate about. Everything about her is what I'd always wanted to have in a best friend, a partner, and after the heartache and pain that was Will Thompson, I never thought I'd find it again.

But I did. With her.

After we finish with brunch, the rain forces us to go home early. We stop by her favorite dessert place on the way, picking up a selection of comfort sweets and arguing about which movies to watch on our afternoon indoors.

Emily loves movies that make her cry, and if it means detouring from another rewatch of *Grey's Anatomy*, I'm here for it. Thankfully, she isn't one for scary movies, because I can't do with another reminder of Auden today.

"Okay, so are we hysterically crying this afternoon or just a few stray tears?" I ask her jokingly.

Laughing, she throws one of the plush cushions at my head. "I'm not that bad."

"And the worst is when you rewind it back to watch a second time and cry like you don't already know what happens."

"Listen here," she says through a smile. "Not all of us think being scared to death is entertainment." She drops her body beside mine on our couch. "The only reason I ever agree to scary movies is because I get to snuggle up right next to you anyway."

And there it is. The reminder I neither wanted or needed.

Today is supposed to be about her. And yet with every passing second, comparison does what it does best, and robs every moment of joy between us. What's unfathomable is the fact that it's becoming more and more obvious there is no comparison.

There is no denying I love Emily, to the ends of the Earth. I know that like I know my own name.

But the real issue is…that I still love him too.

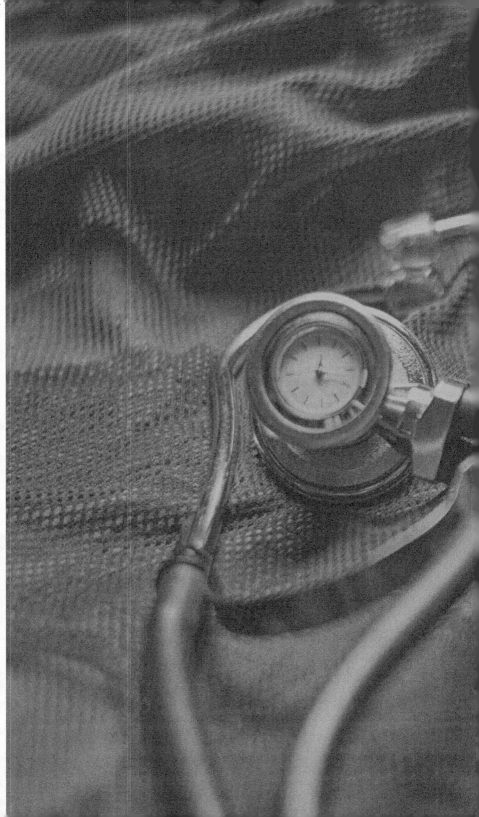

TWENTY-FOUR

Auden

I t takes me far longer than it should to find my way to Emmy's new classroom at her school, and I realize it's because I've been looking for the room labeled *Ms. Thompson* rather than one that says *Mrs. Evans*.

And while seeing his name attached to her door makes me feel sick to my stomach, it makes me feel something else exponentially more.

Guilty, guilty, guilty.

Emily's at her desk when I peek my head through the open door before rapping on the wood. "Excuse me, ma'am? I heard you were looking for a lunch delivery."

Her head tilts up immediately, and she gives me a beaming smile as I step into her room.

"There you are! I thought I was gonna have to send out a search party to find you," she says in greeting, rising to give me a hug.

Her perfume wafts over me as her arms wrap around my shoulders, and the plethora of guilt already residing within me grows.

"This place is a maze after the addition," I murmur before releasing her, the lie coming off my tongue far easier than I'd like. Fuck, it feels like all I'm doing lately is lying to her, to myself, to everyone.

And being here means I will no doubt have to come up with even more.

I set our takeout on the desk, pulling the containers of rice, tikka masala, and chicken curry from the bag while Emmy grabs another chair and wheels it over to an empty spot near the end.

She quickly scoops up the rice and curry—her usual favorite—grinning when she drops back into her chair. "You're a literal godsend. How did you know I've been craving Indian food?"

Arching a brow, I take a seat beside her to down my own lunch. "The better question is, when are you *not* craving Indian food?"

"Fair point. It's like you know me or something." She gives me a soft smile as she moves her food around. "I'm really glad you could make it. It's been really nice to know I can call you for lunch like this again."

"Of course." I shift my gaze back to my food, hedging on the question. "Is there a specific reason *why* you wanted me to come for lunch?"

"I need to have a reason now? I can't just want to see my only brother?"

I let out an awkward laugh, shaking my head. "You know that's not what I meant."

"Well, as it happens, I do have something I wanted to discuss with you." She pauses, and it's enough for me to connect the dots. "It's about Pierce."

My stomach rolls, and it takes everything inside me not to lose the little lunch I've eaten. Lifting my gaze, I feel my lips curl up in the weakest smile I can manage.

"Don't leave me in suspense."

Emmy straightens in her seat, shifting into her prim-and-proper self like she's about to give some sort of presentation or start a lesson. And fuck if it doesn't make my blood slow to a snail's pace in my veins and cause the hair on the back of my neck to stand on end.

"His thirtieth is coming up next month, and I want to do something special for it."

Relief rushes through me, as does the realization that Pierce must not have told her about what happened between us last week. If she was aware of it, there's no way she'd be able to go this long without saying something.

I know my sister well enough after twenty-six years. She wears her thoughts and emotions right on her face—one of the few traits we *don't* share.

But she is just as good at reading others as I am, which is why I'm not surprised when she frowns at my less than enthusiastic reaction.

"What's the face for? Do you know something I don't, or do you not think it's a good idea?"

"I don't have any opinion on it," I reply, trying to keep the bite from my tone. "Plus, he's your husband, Emmy. You know him better than I do."

"But you're in the process of becoming friends, right? Hanging out together with Deacon and Julian and the rest of the guys?" The inflection in her voice is so hopeful it makes me want to cry.

"Yeah, I guess," I hedge, my attention dropping back to my food. "But you still know him better than I do."

The words are acidic as they leave my lips, and there's a good portion of me that wonders if my statement is true or not. I just know all of me doesn't want to find out the answer.

"He told me I didn't need to do anything crazy, but it's the first time we're spending his birthday together. Not to mention thirty is a pretty big deal, so I feel like we need to do something, you know?"

"Why do I get the feeling you've already got something planned and you're just looking for some muscle and leg work to carry it out?"

She gives me her most award-winning grin. "Glad to see that twin telepathy is still working after all this time."

It's a bullet to the chest, those words, because if twin telepathy were truly a thing, she'd know exactly why I made that face when she mentioned Pierce. She'd know fucking everything about us, actually. But as it stands, it seems she remains completely in the dark.

"He'd mentioned absolutely loving Cannon Beach when he visited before moving up to Seattle, and I know how much you love it there too."

"Yeah," I manage to croak out, schooling my features in hopes it hides the complete carnage the words 'Cannon Beach' cause inside my chest. "I do."

"That's why I was thinking we should go down there for it. Surprise him with a long weekend on the coast," she explains enthusiastically. "I could invite Deacon and Julian, if they're available. Parker, Cohen. Possibly some of his other work friends. Maybe get his parents to fly out from Colorado for it and even convince Mom to leave the Florida sunshine for it."

"I think that sounds like a great plan, Emmy," I say, the words bitter on my tongue.

"I thought so too." She rubs her hands together excitedly. "I already booked a house on the beach big enough for eight, so that's plenty of room to start." She pulls out her phone, quickly tapping away at the screen to pull up the rental listing. Once she finds it, she turns her phone to face me with the main photo pulled up.

And my heart. Fucking. Stops.

It only shows the front of the house, which is quaint and cozy-looking from the outside. It has a turquoise door.

I don't even need to swipe through the images in order to see what the rest of the place looks like. I already know it's nestled up on the bluff with an amazing view of Haystack Rock, complete with a hot tub on the back deck. Just like I know it has a whisky-colored leather couch in the living room, and that the en suite off the primary bedroom has one of the most amazing showers I've ever seen.

I know all this…because it's the same fucking house I stayed at last time I was in Cannon Beach.

With Pierce.

Bile congeals in my throat, and I'm forced to swallow it down as I take the phone from her. I swipe mindlessly through the photos, more and more anxiety building inside me as my theory is confirmed.

Another forced smile paints my lips when I reach the final image and hand the phone back to her. "The house is breathtaking, Emmy."

She frowns. "Why do I hear your lingering *but*, then?"

My tongue wets my lower lip as I look for some fucking reason or excuse that doesn't include *but I've fucked your husband on every horizontal surface in that place.* Literally *anything* but that.

"But I don't understand why you wouldn't just make it into a romantic weekend away for the two of you." Her frown deepens, and I quickly tack on, "I mean, as fun as it would be to get everyone together for a long weekend on the coast, wouldn't you rather have the privacy as newlyweds?"

As much as it kills me to say it, I don't think I can spend time in a place that was *ours* with him…knowing he isn't mine.

"I figured that's what the honeymoon was for."

Very true.

"Look, if you think it's something he'll like, I say go for it. He's clearly crazy about you, so I doubt you could really go in the wrong direction." My pulse quickens in anticipation as I brace myself for the answer to my next question. "So what is it you need from me?"

"Would you be willing to drive him down?" she asks. "I want to get everyone down there and settled before he arrives. Plus, it'll keep him guessing as to what's going on."

My skin tingles with discomfort, my brain flipping through a list of excuses I could use to get out of this.

"I'll have to check my schedule for that weekend—"

"Okay, but if you're available." She cuts in before tacking on, "Please, Auden?"

Because I can never say no to my sister, I concede to her impossible request. "I'll double check and let you know, okay? But if I can, I will."

Even if it kills me in the process.

The smile stretches wide across her face. "I knew I could count on you."

It's all I can do to force the food down my throat as we continue our lunch, idly chatting about her class, my work, and other nonsensical things. I'm thankful the conversation steers away from Pierce for the most part, him only coming up in brief passing.

But I don't miss the way she smiles as she says his name, or the way she'll glance down at the diamond on her hand.

Her lunch hour ends rather quickly, one of the bells signaling the end of the student's lunch break, and I take that as my cue to head out.

"We should get back to doing this more often," Emmy says as I gather our trash to toss in the garbage near the door.

In truth, I'd love nothing more than to spend time like this with Emmy again. After all, it was a regular thing for us prior to my deployment, and it's nice to sink back into a familiar routine after returning. But I'd be a liar if I said any part of me wants to be around her while she's in this newlywed bliss.

It's too fucking painful. Especially after what Pierce and I did.

"Auden? Hey," she says, catching my arm to halt me. When I lift my gaze to meet hers, she gives me a warm, sincere smile. "I hope you know how much I appreciate you spending time with him and getting to know him. It really means a lot to me."

"Of course, Emmy." I give her a tight smile in return, doing my best to ignore the stabbing pain in my chest or the returning acidic taste on my tongue as I mutter, "He's family now, right?"

"Exactly."

I'm almost to the door when she calls out behind me again. I'm not prepared for the question that leaves her lips. "Do you think Dad would've liked him?" When I offer her nothing but wide eyes, she continues. "I like to think so, but you know how he was. Sometimes, I swear he thought no one would be good enough for either one of us."

I never imagined this would be how this lunch would go, and honestly, I didn't anticipate the direction of our conversation, but history should've prepared me for it.

When you lose a parent at such a young age, there are a million life-changing milestones that happen without them. Birthdays, prom, graduation. Enlistments…weddings. The list is endless. And every time you think you can't possibly miss them any more, the thought of them not being here for the next big moment makes the loss feel even greater.

Pushing my guilt aside, I hold my arms out and Emily steps into them. Hugging one another tightly, we reminisce in silence about the father and soldier we both loved and lost, finding solace with the only person who will understand what it's like to exist in the bittersweet.

"Dad would've approved," I say softly, kissing the top of her head. "There's a lot to like about him."

With the unexpected emotional ending to our lunch, Emily and I finally manage a second round of goodbyes, and I head back to the office to let the receptionist know I'm leaving. Opening the door to exit, I find myself almost running smack into Julian.

"Sh—oot. Hey, Auden." He glances around, making sure no kids heard his almost-slip. "What're you doing here?" he asks. "Are you looking for your sister?"

"Just came from there, actually. Brought in some lunch to have with her."

He chuckles softly. "Back in the routine of it, huh?"

I give him a wry smile. "You know it."

"You and Pierce will have to work out a rotation so you don't surprise her on the same days."

The smile on his face, and his flippant revelation, cause my forehead to crease with a frown. "A rotation with Pierce?"

Julian nods, his eyes narrowing on me. "Yeah, Pierce will do that with her sometimes too. Glad she can have both her favorite guys come in for lunch dates now."

I swear, I feel my eye twitch at the mention of Pierce taking my place, and the high octave of Julian's voice giving away that he knows far, *far* more than he's previously let on.

"Yeah, I'm glad he's stepped in while I've been away." I run a hand over the back of my neck. "Anyway, I've got to go. I'll see you around, yeah?"

If he notices my discomfort, he doesn't comment on it, just offering me a nod and smile before we part ways.

My steps are full of purpose as I walk to my car, the thoughts in my mind volleying from anger to frustration to hurt and right back around again.

I slam the door closed behind me, letting out a soft curse while pulling my phone from my pocket. Fully aware of what a bad idea this probably is,

I pull up his contact anyway and type out the four-word message.

Me: We need to talk.

The message is instantly marked as read, like he was sitting there waiting for me to text him. The three little dots showing him typing appear immediately.

Pierce: When and where?

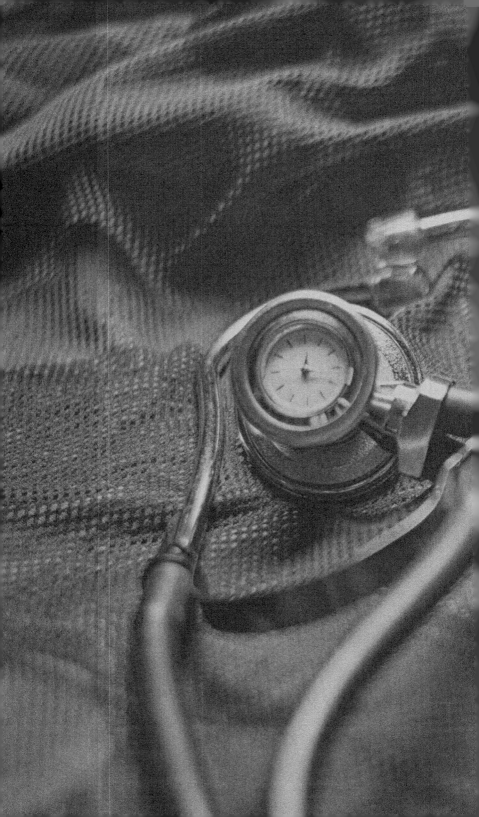

TWENTY-FIVE

Auden

Pierce is already at the coffee shop and seated at one of the tables near the corner when I arrive the following morning. He's as delicious as ever, wearing a dark gray suit, white dress shirt, slacks that are perfectly tailored for his long legs, and a royal blue tie that enhances his eyes more than I should notice.

I fucking hate that I notice.

Heart crawling into my throat, I pull the chair out across from him and slide into place.

"Thanks for meeting me," I tell him, glancing around the shop anxiously.

He gives me a weary smile, if it can even be called that. "I think I owed you a conversation, at the very least."

My mind detours back to the way he left the other night, the anguish on his face, the blade through my heart. It's true, a conversation is a measly peace offering.

I discreetly peruse the man in front of me now that I'm seated across from him. He's a far cry from the man I'd come to know during our week on the coast, and sometimes I wonder which version of him is the real one.

Did he lie to me? Or is he lying to her?

There's an edge of worry in his eyes as he leans forward, cupping his coffee between his palms.

"I'm assuming you wanted to talk about something—"

"Yeah, I'll cut to the chase," I say, interrupting before he can finish the thought. "It's more of a heads-up than anything, but my sister is planning a surprise for your thirtieth."

Pierce's eyes widen, and he looks at me like I've just lost my mind before he bursts out laughing. It takes me off guard, because nothing about my statement has any humor to it, yet here he is, laughing like a maniac.

He shakes his head as he calms himself down enough to speak. "I'm sorry, I know it's not funny. I just…" There's another awkward laugh, before he sighs. "After everything that's been going on, that's not what I thought you'd say."

I cast my gaze down to the table and let my finger trace over the grains in the wood. His line of thinking is obvious, though if I'm being honest, that's the very last thing I want to discuss.

"Right, okay," he says, clearing his throat. "Well, I already told her she doesn't need to plan anything for it. It's just another day, and I'm more than happy to treat it as such."

"Yeeeaaaah." I drag the word out. "That's not going to work. It appears us Thompsons are a stubborn bunch."

He grazes his teeth over his bottom lip. "Apparently so."

Our gazes collide, and there's a hint of acknowledgment in his. Like he's perfectly aware of all the things my sister and I share. The traits that both of us are either blessed—or cursed—with.

"Okay," Pierce says, his eyes darting between mine. "While I'm happy to see you, what's with the urgency? Why are you ruining the surprise?"

I want to laugh at the notion that I'm the one ruining it and not that it was already doomed from inception.

"Because she wants to do this with everyone," I explain slowly. "Your parents, our mom, Julian, Deacon, some of your work friends…me." Holding his bright blue gaze, I pause, hating everything about this. "And she wants to do it down in Cannon Beach."

All the color drains from Pierce's face, and he slumps back against the chair. "You're kidding."

I shake my head, wishing this was a goddamn joke instead of the nightmare I've been forced to live. "She even showed me the house she booked."

If possible, Pierce gets even paler, and he swallows. "Please don't tell me…" He trails off, his eyes fixed on my expression, doing his best to get a read. And when my lips harden into a tight line, I know his thoughts are exactly where mine are. "Fuck."

I don't know if I say it for him or my own self-preservation, but the words come out regardless. "I can see if I can get out of it, to make it a little less awkward, but if I know my sister, she—"

"There's no way she will let you miss it unless you're dead or dying or halfway around the world."

"Yep," I murmur, only to fill him in on the worst part of it all. "And she wants me to be the one to bring you down for the surprise. To 'keep you guessing'; her words."

Slumping forward, he rests his elbows on the table and buries his head in his hands. Every part of me feels like I'm a square peg trying to fit myself into a round hole, trying to be the best brother and brother-in-law, when all I want to be is his.

I wring my hands together to stop the burning need I have to comfort him.

Is it always going to be like this? Will we always hurt this much?

Eventually, Pierce raises his head, his sapphire gaze meeting mine, and there's so many emotions swimming in it, I can't even begin to unpack them, nor do I want to hear him try to.

"Look, what happened the other night—"

"Can't happen again, I know," I say all too quickly, my focus dropping to the table again, not wanting to look him in the eyes. "It shouldn't have happened in the first place. You were drunk—"

"I wasn't that drunk," he counters.

"And I should've called you another cab and made you leave, so that's on me."

A sharp scoff leaves him, and I glance up in time to catch him shaking his head. His jaw tics with effort before he utters, "I'm not blameless in this, Auden. Not even fucking close. This conversation isn't going to be over any quicker if you try letting me off the hook." His chest heaves as he tries to lower his voice and frustration. "I was perfectly aware of the choices I made, just like I'm more than capable of owning up to their repercussions."

What repercussions?

It feels like I'm the only one paying the price each and every fucking time.

"And what would those be?" I finally ask.

"To start?" His throat bobs before answering. "The guilt."

I want to ask whether his guilt is for Emily or me, but I settle for something else, hating this version of myself that *needs* his attention, his validation. Hating myself for seeking constant reassurance that I'm not alone in this hellhole of deceit and betrayal.

Which is why I find myself uttering a single word.

"Question."

He stares at me for a moment like I'm insane. "God, you still have some of those left, don't you?"

"What can I say?" I murmur with a little smirk. "I knew I'd need them later."

The intimacy of this moment is dangerous. Falling back into a world where we have our own secrets and inside jokes is more like jumping off a cliff rather than a gradual, slippery slope.

From the apprehension written in the lines on his face, he knows it too.

But like me, he's still helpless to stop himself from throwing himself off the edge, no matter the destruction waiting at the bottom, and that's the guilt-inducing reassurance I need.

"Okay, I'll bite."

Rolling my teeth over my bottom lip, I utter a question that I don't even know how to answer for myself. One I have a hard time thinking about since it has the power to shred my heart into a thousand tiny pieces.

"Do you regret it?"

Pierce's expression is unreadable as his gaze lifts to mine, and a somber smile curls one edge of his mouth. "Only when I think about it."

The words cut, though I'm not sure they're meant to. After all, I understand it. But jealousy has me wanting to be in his every waking thought, the way he is in mine.

No part of me regrets him or what we were to each other, but fuck, life would be so much easier if that wasn't the case.

"Sometimes I wish I'd never met you, you know? Or that I'd just left with the goddamn bartender that night, because that decision sure as hell would've saved us a ton of confusion and heartache," he says sheepishly, and I'm reminded of the insane amount of jealousy I felt toward the stranger. "But I also know that I wouldn't trade the time I've spent with you for the world. Not back on the coast, and not here either. Not a single fucking second of it."

His confession mirrors my thoughts, and it hurts as much as it fills me with relief. We were undoubtedly stuck between a rock and a hard place, living in limbo and denial, believing there was any way this could end other than badly.

"I'm stuck constantly comparing the two of you," he admits, and it makes me feel uneasy. "Not just who you are, but how you make me feel. And sometimes it's hard to tell where one of you stops and the other begins." He holds my stare. "If maybe I jumped into things with her because, subconsciously, she reminds me of you?"

Feeling uneasy, I leave his question unanswered.

Do I want to know all the reasons why he fell in love with my sister?

I shift my focus solely to the one person we should've been thinking about this whole time, and acknowledge that the only reason we feel any amount of guilt and regret is because of Emily. If I understand anything he feels, it's that. And that should be enough.

Goddamnit, I'm determined to make it be enough.

"She's important to both of us," I say firmly. "We both love her, care about her, want to see her happy. And this would destroy her." My stomach heaves in disgust at how much I've already unknowingly hurt her. "I can't fucking do that to my sister. Not anymore, no matter how strained our relationship has been. She's still my number one. She's still someone

I'd do anything to protect." I swallow past the thick wedge of emotion in the back of my throat. "I'm a soldier through and through, Pierce. And outside of the military, my duty and honor is to her."

His expression turns somber, the sadness in his eyes unmissable, but he nods, and says exactly what I need him to say.

"I know. We have to find a way to make this work, to exist together without..." He stops, leaving the sentence hanging over us.

Without ripping each other's clothes off and fucking each other into submission.

Without turning into the worst kind of people on this planet.

Without hurting the woman both of us love to pieces.

An idea forms, and though it just about kills me to speak it, I do anyway.

"My reenlistment window is next month," I murmur, tracing my thumb over the condensation on the glass in front of me. "I can talk with my retention officer about what's open and be sent anywhere else in the world."

"Auden, no." The firmness in his tone has my gaze lifting to meet his, and I'm not prepared for the sorrow I see brimming in his. "You have to know that's the last thing she wants."

In truth, it's the last thing I want too. Seattle became my home after Dad died, and getting stationed here has been one of the biggest blessings I've received since joining the Army. Even though I know moving around is part of the military lifestyle, getting reassigned to anywhere not here still feels all sorts of wrong.

But if I have to, I will. After all, I have before.

I've spent my entire life sacrificing my wants and needs for the good of everyone else. At this point, what's one more time?

"It's the best option, and we both know it." I tap my finger on the table. "Once I'm gone, I'll only be around once or twice a year. Maybe less if I get put on another deployment. I'll do my best to put as much distance between us as possible without it looking too suspicious."

Pierce's jaw clenches, and he leans back in his chair before glancing out the window.

I'd do anything to know what he's thinking. To crack open that skull of gorgeous hair and revel in every thought coursing through his brain.

To the point where I can't stop myself from asking for them.

"Tell me what you're thinking."

"Something selfish." His lips lift into a sad smile while his attention stays fixed out at the street. "When it comes to you, it usually is."

Fuck.

"Pierce—"

Bringing his attention back to me, he shakes his head. "No, just let me get this out. And I know you're sick of hearing these words from me, but I'm sorry, Auden." The sincerity and regret in his eyes steals my breath as he continues. "I was able to lock away the part of me that was screaming how selfish and fucking stupid I was being by showing up at your apartment, because all I wanted was more of you. More time and moments and pieces of you that always seem to fit so well with who I am. But I swear, I'm doing my best to let you go."

For what might be the first time in a long time, I can read every thought written in the lines and planes of his handsome face. They're clear as day.

You aren't the only one making sacrifices.

"Thank you."

He nods, and a moment of silence settles between us as he takes a drink from his cup, his expression pensive, his eyes full of questions.

"How long would it be until you're gone again?" he asks, voice low and gentle.

"I'll know more after I reenlist and have orders." I glance at my watch for the date, working through a possible timeline in my head. "Hopefully, we can get things moving as quickly as possible, though, and I'll be gone within the next six months, should everything fall into place."

When my gaze returns to his face, I find his mask has been completely removed, the stoic expression he's attempted to hold around me crumbling to nothing. Now, all I see is pain. Regret. Loss. Worry.

And while it might be foolish to think, it seems the last one isn't just for the state of his marriage.

Sinking his teeth into his lower lip, Pierce glances back out the window at the street. The set of his jaw and drum of his fingers on the tabletop are physical manifestations of his rampant thoughts. He's holding himself back from speaking them, but it's like the pressure on a dam building far past the point it can hold. And because I know him, it's only a matter of time before the dam breaks, and it all gushes out.

I can't be here when it happens.

We're past the point where I can enable his emotions, allowing them to overwhelm my own. God knows I've made enough mistakes to last a lifetime already because of that.

"Look—"

"I better get going," I say while rising from my spot across from him, ready to bolt like the coward I've become. But he's quicker than I expect, and his hand snags my wrist, preventing me from walking away.

"Will."

My eyes sink closed, that name on his lips now more torturous than ever, before steeling myself to turn back to him. If I thought his features were cracked open before—emotions on full display—it's got nothing on the anguish he's wearing now.

I've seen warzones less desolate.

"I never wanted it to be like this," he whispers, agonized blue eyes staring up at me as he releases my wrist.

My heart feels heavy in my chest, aching with every beat it takes.

"That makes two of us."

TWENTY-SIX

Novemeber

Auden

The brewery we're holding Pierce's birthday dinner at is packed, despite it being early November on the coast. I'll attribute it to the rather warm weather for this time of year, though I'm starting to realize there's no bad season to visit Cannon Beach.

Our evening has been mildly uneventful, but after being drilled for an hour by my mother about whether I plan to reenlist, followed by everyone fawning over how cute my sister and Pierce are together, I'm about ready to toss myself into the ocean and pray for a shark attack. And that's not even touching on the painfully awkward three-hour car ride Pierce and I shared down here, where neither of us spoke more than five words to each other.

Probably because we both knew we were heading back to a place we'd made into our sanctuary, only for it to now be tainted by a cruel, harsh reality.

"Back for another surf lesson?" a voice says from my left, conveniently pulling me from my thoughts.

I glance over, only to find the familiar gray eyes of Easton. A small grin curves my lips, and I motion toward the barstool beside me. "Hey, man. How're you doing?"

"Oh, you know. Still keeping busy, despite us being well into fall," he says, taking a seat with a wry smirk. "What brings you back to good ol' Cannon Beach, though? This isn't your usual time of year to swing through town."

"Sounds an awful lot like you've kept up with my comings and goings all these years," I muse, doing my best to ignore the pit in my stomach at the mention of our current location.

If I had any choice in the matter, I wouldn't be back here at all.

Not in Cannon Beach, and certainly not in the same goddamn house Pierce and I fucked on every available surface of for a whole week. But fate is as cruel as she is a bitch, thrusting me into what might be the most hellish form of torture imaginable. No doubt because of the filthy, vile piece of trash I've become by fucking him when I swore I'd do my best to keep my distance so he and Emily could live on in their happily ever after.

But it's distance I've managed to maintain the past three weeks, ensuring, at the very least, that it doesn't happen again.

Easton snaps his fingers in front of my face, trying to snag my attention. "You hear anything I just said, or did seeing my pretty face cause you to have some kind of stroke?"

I scoff and shake my head. Easton's always been one to keep me on my toes the times we've chatted over the years, and I'm not at all surprised this time would be any different.

"Anyone ever tell you you're a bit full of yourself, East?"

"Cannon does every fucking day, not that it helps."

"I guess not." My gaze shoots over to where Easton entered the brewery, waiting for his husband to make an appearance. And when he doesn't after a minute or two, I give him a questioning look and ask, "Are you here by yourself?"

Easton raises his brow, a hint of amusement in his gaze. "You might wanna reword that question unless you're trying to proposition a married man."

I let out an awkward laugh. "I meant here eating alone."

"I'm just giving you shit," he says, slapping my shoulder. "I'm grabbing takeout for the hubs and me before heading home. But one of my buddies owns the place, so I usually try catching up with him while I wait."

Realization hits me, and I immediately stutter out an apology. "Shit, sorry, then I'll—"

"Relax. Apparently, he's not in tonight." Easton shifts, his eyes trailing up and down my body in an assessing, yet nonsexual way before shrugging. "I guess you'll have to do as a replacement until my food's ready."

I roll my eyes. "Glad I can be up to your standards."

Easton orders himself a beer to go with his takeout order, and once the bartender sets it in front of him, he eyes me from over the rim as he takes a sip.

"I was half expecting you to buy me a drink too, seeing as you were so quick to get me alone."

Another bark of laughter leaves me. "Oh my God. Please tell me you didn't actually think I was about to hit on you."

He chuckles, shaking his head. "Absolutely not. I know you better than that. Plus, I saw your guy over at one of the tables with your sister when I came in."

My stomach heats with a bout of irritation at the mention of Pierce, and when I catch Easton's attention sliding over to the table where everyone is gathered, I feel my blood pressure rise. I don't bother looking, instead pressing my tongue to my cheek and muttering a clipped, "He's not my guy."

There's a brief moment of silence as Easton's attention shifts back to where they are, watching Pierce and Emily. I don't have it in me to look—no doubt I'd be greeted with the sight of them laughing and smiling together with their friends.

My companion remains quiet for a few minutes as he analyzes them before his focus returns to me. "I swear I felt vibes between the two of you last fall, but I must've read the situation wrong. My bad."

Biting the inside of my cheek, I debate how much to reveal before settling on giving him a watered down version. "You weren't entirely off base."

"I'm usually not."

Again, so sure of himself.

"It's complicated," I offer, still not positive I even *want* to elaborate on this mess I've found myself in, regardless of how much it kills me to keep it all in.

"Clearly." Easton's gaze flicks from where the two of them are chatting with Mom and Parker at our table from dinner. "Because from where I'm sitting, he looks pretty married too."

"Like I said, it's complicated. And messy."

"It usually is. But the messiest ones are usually the ones who end up being worth it, right?"

Shaking my head, I mutter, "I don't think that's gonna be the case here."

His eyes shift back to me. "Stranger things have happened, my friend. I know that better than anyone."

He has a point, but he's also missing the bulk of the story, and while my desire to rehash it is non-existent at best, I find the words slipping from my lips regardless. Each and every gritty, sordid moment of this tragedy Pierce and I have found ourselves in.

Easton listens, absorbing the information until I finish talking. He remains silent for a moment, eyes locked with mine, before letting out a low whistle. "No fucking shit."

"Yep," I mutter, popping the *p* and taking another swig from my beer. "Complicated and messy, which is why I'm signing a new contract and getting as fucking far away from it as I can."

"Even if it means losing your sister *and* the love of your life?"

My blood runs ice cold, freezing in my veins. "Who said anything about him being the love of my life?"

Easton arches a brow. "You didn't have to say it, man. It was written all over your face when you looked at him as you were talking about it." He lifts his beer and takes a drink, allowing me to process the information before tacking on, "Most people wouldn't see it, but it's a look I know well. I wore it myself for years."

Scraping my teeth over my lower lip, I let out a long, disheartened sigh. There's no part of me that'd wish the heartache and pain I've been living through on anyone, but knowing I'm not alone in the misery takes a bit of the sting away. And maybe a little hope that something—or someone— better waits for me on the other side.

"Then you understand why I have to go." I glance at him, a somber smile curling the corner of my mouth. "Time and distance will make things better. Easier. Outta sight, outta mind, right?"

Who knows, maybe I can come back eventually and seeing the two of them won't be like a dagger to the gut anymore. The space will give me the chance to truly move on, possibly even find someone else.

One can hope, at least.

"Running away from him is easy, but you're gonna have a helluva time running from the feelings," Easton points out, his tone softer than it's been most of the night.

My fingers tap along the bar top, fidgeting with indecision despite already having made a choice. "I'd rather try that than become some kind of an interloper on their perfect little life. I do hope they're happy, because they both deserve it, but I refuse to sit here and watch."

"I get it. Believe me, I do. But look at it this way," he says slowly. "You spent months on the other side of the world from the guy. Then you came back, and despite every circumstance in both your lives changing, the two of you fell back together like everything was exactly the same as before you left. Do you really think any amount of time and distance is gonna change that?"

"It has to," I whisper, more of a plea than a statement.

Easton's expression is somber, and he nods solemnly. "I know we don't know each other all that well, but I can tell you, fighting for what you want will always be the best option, not walking away. Take it from someone who almost pushed the love of his life into the arms of someone else."

Gnawing on my lower lip some more, I process his words, my brain catching on a single one.

"Almost?"

"It wasn't all that different from where you're at," he murmurs in confirmation. "He wasn't quite locked into a marriage…yet. But when I say I know messy, complicated, and painful, well, I mean it. And sure, it wasn't easy, but I'd do it all over again if it meant coming out the other side with him."

He makes it sound so simple, and while I know it was probably anything but, I can't help the spark of hope he's ignited in my chest. That is, until I'm immediately sobered by the level of destruction I'd cause, and more importantly, *who* I'd be destroying in the process.

"She's my sister. I don't think I could live with myself if I took this from her," I mutter, scrubbing a hand over my jaw. "I might want him, but I wouldn't be able to look at myself in the mirror if I was the reason her world fell apart."

"Again, I get that. But at what cost to you?" His brows crash together, a frown on his lips. "How much more of yourself can you sacrifice before there's nothing left for you?"

I hate the amount of validity in his question. I hate this entire situation. I hate the Army for taking me away from everything I could've asked for. I hate myself for realizing it far too late.

And part of me even hates the man across the room from me, who I love more than anything else in this world.

"I don't know what else to do," I whisper, tears pricking my eyes.

Blinking them away, I lift my gaze, only to find Pierce's eyes on me from his seat next to my sister. They're hard and penetrating as they bore into mine, and I catch his lips shift into a slight frown before his attention flicks to Easton. We wouldn't have needed to spend an entire week together for me to read his mind; the jealousy flaming in his stare does the job on its own.

"Yeah, fuck this," I mutter before downing the rest of my beer.

The bartender chooses that moment to appear with a plastic bag full of take-out containers and sets it on the bar in front of us.

"Hey, East. Here's your order."

"Thanks, Jake," he says as he hands some cash over to settle his bill. "Keep the change."

Jake smiles, nodding. "Appreciate it. And tell Cannon he's allowed to show his face in public every once in a while. We miss him around here."

Easton lets out a wry laugh and grabs the bag from the bartop. "I'll get right on that." He glances at me and explains, "Cannon helped get the zoning taken care of for this place a couple years ago, so they're always asking about him."

I can only nod, not knowing what the hell that really means.

Another chuckle comes from Easton as he slides off his stool, and he nods toward the rest of my party still conversing and enjoying their evening on the other side of the establishment. "You look like you wanna go back over there as much as a horny boy wants to wear a condom."

I choke out a laugh, because he hit the nail on the head. "I'd rather be six feet under, if we're being honest."

"I don't normally take in strays, but I doubt Cannon would mind if you chilled with us for the weekend. At the very least, it would save you the awkwardness around the house."

"You're serious?"

"Of course," he assures me. "Besides, the waves are supposed to be great tomorrow, and I'd love to drag your ass back out on them."

"Yeah, I might take you up on that." My attention flashes to the rest of the group, and it only takes seeing my sister giggling and pressing a kiss to Pierce's cheek before I make my decision. "Just give me a minute."

Heading back toward the table, I keep my eyes locked on my sister. Pierce's gaze is a white-hot brand on the side of my face as I approach, searing me with every step, and it takes every ounce of my willpower to act unaffected by it.

"Hey, Aud, what's up?" Emmy asks, a big grin on her face when I rest my hand on the back of her chair.

"What's the code for the house?"

"Last four of my phone number and then the enter button," she says, her face twisting into confusion as she speaks. "You're heading back already? It's still early."

Debating for the briefest moment on how much to tell her, I decide to go with, "I'm actually grabbing my stuff and gonna stay with a friend. It'll be more comfortable than the sofa."

She frowns. "Aw, are you sure?"

"Yeah, it's fine. He doesn't live far from here."

Emmy's eyes dart over my shoulder to where Easton must've disappeared outside, and it's then I take the opportunity to shift my gaze to Pierce before immediately wishing I hadn't.

I've never seen those blue eyes quite so cold, yet so full of searing rage at the same time.

"I'll say this…" Her attention flicks from the door back to me. "He's a pretty cute friend."

I don't answer her, instead giving her a smile and bending to kiss her cheek. "I'll be back over tomorrow in time for breakfast. Just text me when."

"Absolutely."

Rising to my full height, I give the rest of the table a quick farewell, all the while keeping my gaze attached to anybody that isn't Pierce. There's no way in hell I'm giving him the satisfaction, especially knowing he just heard every word of my conversation with Emmy.

It's only once I've said my goodbyes to everyone else that I finally allow myself to meet his furious gaze; a complete contradiction to his stoic, cold expression.

"Happy birthday, man," is all I tell him, doing my best to erase any hint of emotion from my face.

And then I head out to join Easton without a backward glance.

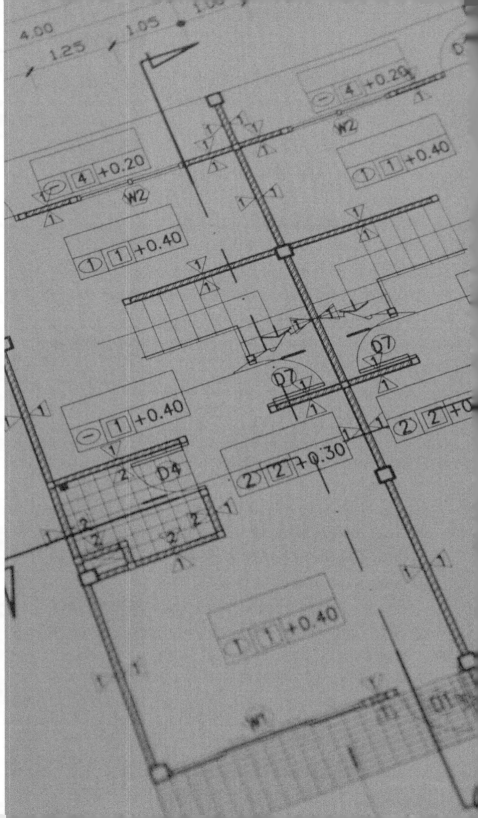

TWENTY-SEVEN

Pierce

My eyes are glued to Auden as he disappears out the front door of the brewery, white-hot rage blinding me until all I see is red. Or maybe it's green, because despite the irrationality behind it, I'm more than aware of the feeling that's the root cause of my anger.

Jealousy.

An insane surge of jealousy, to be exact, flowing through me like a river of molten lava, scorching any rational thought in its path.

Apparently, all brain function has left the window at the sight of Auden going home with someone—the mere thought of anyone else touching him being too much to bear—because I find myself leaning over to Emily and pressing a kiss to her temple. "Sweetheart, I'll be right back."

"Okay," is all she says, though I hear her pitch rise at the end, making the word come out as more of a question, as I rise to my feet.

I can feel the questioning stare of Deacon and Julian as I grab my jacket, but I ignore them in favor of rushing out after Auden and Easton. They'll have questions later, I'm sure, but I've got no answers for them right now. Nothing that'll make sense.

Bursting through the door, I frantically search the lamplit streets, finding the two of them about twenty yards down the sidewalk to my left.

"Auden! Where are you going?" I shout, unable to help myself.

Auden's back stiffens, and he halts first, with Easton only making it a step or two in front of him before pausing too. They share a brief look before Easton's eyes land on me in a cryptic, assessing way.

"Looks like you have some stuff to get sorted out after all," Easton concludes, attention still fixed on me. "But the offer still stands if you need a place to crash for the weekend."

Auden only nods and gives him a clipped, "Thanks, man."

Easton disappears down the sidewalk, hopping into the Bronco parked on the curb before Auden finally turns to me. His glare is full of fury as he stalks toward me like a predator about to go in for the kill, his teeth bared in a snarl.

"Seriously? You've got a lot of fucking nerve, Pierce."

Me? He must be joking, considering the last time we were here, he told me he held little interest for the guy, yet here he was about to go home with him for the whole damn weekend.

And just like that first night we met, words tumble from my lips without my permission.

"Yeah, seriously," I snap right back, not bothering to hide my irritation. "I guess I shouldn't be surprised you'd go home with him. After all, picking up strangers at a bar in this town is kinda your thing, isn't it?" My lip curls back in a distorted sort of grin. "Though I could've sworn you told me Easton wasn't single or your type."

"Not that it should fucking matter to you, but there's nothing happening with Easton and me. He's just a friend, not to mention *married*. Or did you fail to notice the wedding band on his hand when you were glaring at us from across the room?"

I bite out through clenched teeth, "Married doesn't mean anything."

Auden arches a brow, a sardonic laugh slipping from his lips as he mutters out a soft, "To you, clearly not."

Oh, screw you.

"So we're taking cheap shots now, are we?"

"Might as well, because you're out here acting like some kind of jealous boyfriend when *you're* the one who is standing here with a goddamn ring on your finger," he growls, grabbing my left wrist and yanking my hand up in front of my face, forcing me to look at the piece of jewelry.

I shake free from his grip, hating the zap of electricity from his skin on mine, but hating the accuracy behind his words even more. Whether it be Easton or anyone else, I have no right to stop him from winding up in their bed. At the end of the day, he isn't mine. He never really was to begin with, but certainly not now.

I'm unable to get a word in before Auden continues spewing anger, venom dripping off his lips with every word.

"And even if Easton *was* single and I had the intention to take him home, that's not any of your concern." A grimace mars his features, and he shakes his head. "God, Pierce, what did you think would happen? That I'd sit here and pine for you for the rest of my life? Be the dirty mistress that'll fuck you when you're drunk and lonely and stuck in the past? Because that sounds like the worst form of torture, and I deserve a fuck of a lot more than that."

His heated words and harsh tone are like a slap in the face, one I hadn't realized I was in desperate need of. But they bring me back to reality—to the cold, hard truth that no matter what happened between us in the past, he doesn't owe me a damn thing.

The thought alone is sobering, and my fingers weave through my hair as frustration, exhaustion, regret, and fear battle within me. I turn away, unable to look at him while I fight a losing battle inside my mind. The one that would have me dropping anything and everything to be with him. To sink back into the familiarity and safety we found within each other in this very town.

But I just…can't.

Yet, as hard as I've been trying, I can't seem to let him go either.

I hear Auden's footsteps behind me, and when I turn back to face him, he's closer—only a couple feet away. In the glow of the street lights, I can see the anger in his eyes, the same resentment and frustration I'm sure is present in my own.

But I see the sadness in them too, and it's all the more gutting.

"I fought. I fought like hell, sending letter after letter with no response. I fought for far longer than I should have. I fought for the thing you gave up on. But I'm done fighting. " His words come out in a gruff whisper, dragged over shards of glass. "Now, I just wanna move on with my life. And I'm trying, Pierce, but you won't fucking let me."

A sharp laugh comes from me, and I practically rip the hair right out of my head when I throw my arms out beside me. "Do you think this is fun for me? To want you still? Because I didn't ask for this."

"I didn't either!" he shouts, stepping up into my space, no more than a foot separating us. "You think it doesn't eat me alive to see how happy my sister is with you, yet knowing that I had you first? You think it isn't a bullet to the chest every fucking time I have to bite my tongue and hide everything that happened between us?"

"I offered to come clean," I point out. "You're the one who disagreed; who was more than happy to pretend we were nothing more than fucking strangers since the moment you saw me at the wedding."

His lip curls back, the words coming out with a sharp bite as they leave his mouth. "You know damn well I was anything but happy at that wedding, Pierce. Don't try pretending any differently."

The statement slices through me, but not nearly as much as the hint of hurt behind his rage as yet another careless statement finds its way past my lips.

"Well, that makes two of us."

There's nothing but venom and disdain in his words as he hisses, "What the fuck is that supposed to mean?"

I shake my head and remain silent, but Auden isn't having it. No, I've lit a fuse, and there's no way this charge between us is gonna do anything except detonate.

"You don't get to toss shit out like that and not put your weight behind it," he snaps, heat and rage radiating off him in waves. "So spit out what the hell you actually mean. For once, just tell the goddamn—"

"It means you weren't the only one who felt like your heart was being ripped from your chest and thrown on the fucking floor that day, Auden!"

His nostrils flare with what must be equal parts fury and…dare I say, hope. But it's still the anger that wins out in the end, because he shoves me until I stumble back against the building's exterior.

"What the hell?" I hiss when my back hits the wall.

"I should be asking you that," he growls, annoyance and disbelief tainting his voice. "Where do you get off, Pierce? You expect me to believe it hurt you nearly as much as it did me by actually going through with it? I had to sit there and watch you marry my sister, all the while acting like I meant fucking nothing to you."

My jaw tics as I press my palms to his chest and give him a little shove backward. The close proximity of his body to mine makes it hard to think sober, let alone with even the slightest hint of alcohol running through my veins.

"Yeah, Auden. I do," I mutter in barely more than a low whisper. "Because standing up there, promising Emily the world while it felt like my entire existence was being drawn to you—to take your hand and run away—was the hardest thing I've done in my entire life."

His lip curls up in a sneer, but there's something else lingering in his eyes glimmering in the street lamps and moonlight. And again, I swear it looks like hope.

"You've got a funny way of showing it."

"Maybe," I mutter, my hand trembling with effort not to touch him. "Or maybe I'm just finally done pretending I love her more than I love you."

Yet more careless words tumble free, ones I didn't mean to say—to bring life to despite having thought and felt them for months now. But now that it's out, I don't regret it. For once in my fucking life, I don't regret this. Him.

Us.

Yet from the way Auden's face falls, quickly switching from anger to agony, it's clear he wishes I would've kept this little revelation to myself. Would've preferred me to say anything else.

"Pierce, you don't—"

"No. Don't you dare. Don't give me that," I snap, my own temper flaring now. "You were right that night I showed up at your apartment, okay? I'm scared. Fucking terrified, actually. But I'm done hiding behind this fucking ring. I broke my vows before I ever made them by telling her I'd only love her for the rest of my life." One hand slips into his hair impulsively, the other cups the side of his face like I'm handling a live grenade. "I ripped those promises to shreds by falling into bed with you, and here I am, running them through the dirt yet again by telling you words that are supposed to be meant for her."

I lean my forehead to rest against his, inhaling his scent. A warm, oaky musk that sinks through my skin and grounds me. Soothes the ache in my chest with every breath I take. Consumes me in familiarity and a sense of belonging.

Of a place that feels like *home*.

My forehead rolls back and forth against his as I shake my head. "It's selfish as hell to tell you this way, I know that. But I'm in love with you, Auden. I *have* been. And I know that makes this messy and more complicated than either of us asked for, but I can't change how I feel. Attempting and failing to fight it is exhausting, and I can't do it anymore. I won't."

He's silent and unyielding for a few moments, and though it terrifies me, I don't regret telling him. He's owned my heart for a while now—even with his sister in the picture. Hell, I'm starting to realize the love I have for Emily is partly due to Auden. To the similarities they share when it comes to who they are.

A full minute passes without him making a sound, and panic starts setting in. Like maybe he hasn't just *tried* to move on.

Maybe he actually has.

Pulling away, my eyes trace over his features. "Say something," I plead, my thumb brushing over the ridge of his cheekbone.

His gaze flicks back and forth between my eyes before bringing his forehead to rest against mine again. "I don't know what to say. I don't know what to do."

I can't help myself from being selfish when it comes to him, which is why I say exactly what I want—what I *need*—from him in a moment like this. "Tell me you love me too. And then kiss me."

A soft sound—some mixture of a groan and a whimper—slips from him, and I can feel his body vibrating with indecision. Torn between right and wrong, just like he was that night in his apartment. And just like that night, I can tell he's so close to giving in to what I want. What we *both* so clearly want.

Each other.

But rather than acting on it as he did last time, he pushes away from me. His head shakes back and forth, over and over again, like the action is enough to make me take back the words—the plea for him to return them. To remove that one four-letter word from our vocabulary, because at this moment, it's just too painful to bear.

"Auden," I plead, stepping toward him, only for him to take another step away. And he continues backing away, each movement acting as another dagger in my already bleeding heart.

But it's still not enough for me to give up. Not again.

I'll fight—even if it's too late.

"Will," I whisper, using the name he'd first given me instead.

Another grimace crosses his features, distorting them in agony, and a mangled, choked whisper comes from his throat.

"We can't."

He doesn't wait for a response before putting some much-needed distance between us. Glancing around, he crosses the street before heading off down the path leading to the beach, only the brightness of the full moon illuminating his way.

Though I know I should go back inside to where my friends, family, and wife wait for me, I can't bring myself to let him go, which is why my feet start moving after him. I don't let him get more than thirty yards away, tracking him through the sand toward the north end of the beach.

I realize where he's headed almost immediately, and my heart crawls into my throat as he walks straight into the icy water near the cliff's edge. *Crescent Beach.*

He doesn't pause when he reaches where the waves lap against the shore, wading through the knee-high water until he reaches the patch of sand on the other side.

Not pausing, I follow him—the way I always will.

The water is frigid as it hits my skin, and my jeans are soaked once I make it the twenty feet to the other side, but I don't care. Nothing short of a fucking hurricane is gonna keep me from getting to him so we can talk about this.

"Will, come back," I call out as I step out of the cool water and trudge across the sand after him.

He doesn't answer me, though I know he's close enough now to hear me. So instead, I pick up into a sprint across the wet sand until I'm no more than three paces behind.

"Will," I say, grabbing his arm. He's quick to shake me off, though, and continues storming down the beach like the soldier he is. A man on a mission.

Objective: Get as far away from me as humanly possible.

"Go back to your wife, Pierce."

"Not until you talk to me."

"Talk to you?" He scoffs, shaking his head as he rapidly approaches the mouth of the cave. "Pierce, what's the point?"

"I literally just told you I love you, and just like you did at the wedding, you fucking ran away."

He stops dead in his tracks and whirls on me, and I don't think I've ever seen him more disarmed than he is right now. The hopeless look on his face, lit by the moon and half-cast in shadows…it's haunted.

As if I reached into his chest and yanked out his heart myself.

"I ran because I can't *do this*. Don't you get it, baby? I can't fucking want you this way anymore. I can't love you, because…because you're with *her*, okay?" Anguish and hurt shred his voice, causing it to crack and crumble as he speaks. "You aren't mine to want, you aren't mine to love, and knowing that is tearing me apart. It's destroying every single piece of honor I have left."

My hand wraps around his wrist, and I pull him toward me. "Except I *am* yours. You know as well as I do, I always have been."

"Not in the way that counts." He shakes his head, the moon and starlight glittering in his eyes as he looks up at me. "Pierce, I'm not strong enough for this. I can't—"

"This isn't war! You don't have to be strong and resilient and silent in a relationship. You can love me out loud." I lift the wrist I'm holding and press his hand to my chest, placing it directly over my heart. His eyes widen as I cover it with mine, pushing hard enough that he can feel the organ pounding behind my ribs. "You feel this? The way it stumbles and stutters when you're near? It's because it beats for you, Will. For you and for fucking *only* you. And believe me, sometimes I wish it didn't. There are times I think I'd do just about anything for it to not be the case, especially over the past couple months. Just like I wish it were as simple as pushing you out of my mind and shoving the feelings to the side. But we don't always get a choice."

A strangled groan rips from his throat, and he tries to pull away, but I don't let him. My hold on him remains vise-like, locking him in place. If I have it my way, he's not going anywhere without me ever again.

"We don't get a choice," I whisper again.

His gaze collides with mine, and the unshed tears pooling on his lashline are a knife to the gut.

"No, we don't." He visibly swallows, Adam's apple bobbing with effort. "But we *can* choose to walk away from one another. It's the right thing to do."

Bringing our foreheads together again, I brush the tip of my nose along his, reveling in the heat of his breath on my lips only centimeters away. And God, I fucking ache for them.

No part of his plan feels like an option. I don't care about the conversation we had last month at the coffee shop or if it's the thing that will keep our lives from falling apart.

The only thing I care about right now is him.

Getting him back…and fucking keeping him.

"But that's just it. We both know the right thing is you and me."

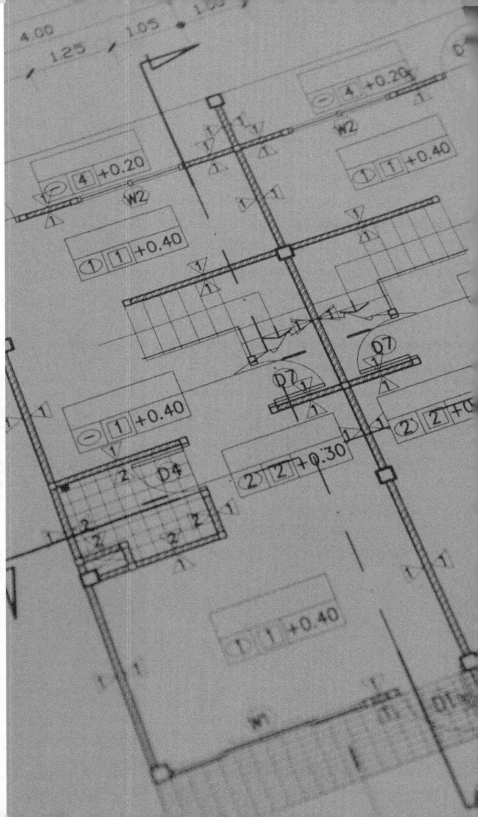

TWENTY-EIGHT

Pierce

A uden's fingers dig into my hips at my declaration, kneading and squeezing there like the hold he has on me is the only thing keeping him tied to Earth. Like if he isn't hanging on as tight as he can, he might float off into space.

Or be swept away in lust and longing.

"We shouldn't," he murmurs, his mouth so close to mine, I can practically taste him.

"You're right."

His hands grip me tighter. "This is the definition of insanity."

"Maybe."

"Not to mention it makes us terrible fucking people."

I nod, my nose brushing his. "I know."

His forehead presses harder into mine, the heat of his skin keeping me warm against the cool autumn breeze. I can feel the way he's warring with himself at every point our bodies touch. Can feel the anxiety and guilt flowing off him and into me.

"It's a burden we can share together, Will," I whisper, my fingers snaking around the back of his neck.

His resistance crumbles at the sound of his name, and our mouths collide with a brutal force. A tidal wave of desire and need crashes over us, pulling us under and dragging us out to sea.

I grip the back of his shirt, clawing at the fabric and pulling it over his head. He does the same, yanking mine off before setting to work on my belt buckle.

"Are you gonna regret this?" he asks, a gritty rasp in his voice as his fingers swiftly slip the buttons open. "Because I don't think I can look at you and see it etched in your face again. I can't have you looking the other way or acting like I don't exist because you're being eaten by guilt all over again. I'm not that fucking strong."

My hands cup either side of his face, drawing his gaze up to meet mine. It's frantic and heady in the moonlight, filled with equal parts want and worry.

And while I have no desire to quench his lust, I can ease his doubts.

"I don't regret you," I utter, my words a whisper against his lips. "No matter what happens, no matter where this world takes us…I will never, *ever* regret you."

He doesn't answer, only pulls my mouth back to his in another feral kiss. It doesn't take more than thirty seconds for the both of us to be stripped down to nothing, our bodies falling to the sand.

The mouth of the cave allows the light from the full moon to filter in, illuminating Auden's face as he rips open a little foil packet with his teeth. His eyes lift to mine when I let out a little snort, brow arching in question.

"You and those fucking to-go lubes."

A small grin appears on his lips. "It's like hot sauce. You never know when you're gonna need it." He coats himself, spreading the lubricant down his shaft before leaning back in the sand. "And are you really planning to complain about that right now?"

At the sight of him splayed out in the moonlight?

"Not at all."

My knees sink into the sand as I straddle him, lining myself up with his length. There's a gleam in his eyes, and I swear, he's never been more fucking perfect than he is in this moment.

It's enough to have me whispering those three words I have no right to speak.

"I love you, Auden."

There's something in his gaze that tells me he wants to say it—a glimmer in those gorgeous greens that speaks the words, though his mouth might not. And while I might want to hear them, I also know I have no right to demand them.

Because there's a very real possibility that there's no future for us past this moment, no matter how much I might want one.

I sink down on his length, loving the glorious stretch of him filling me to the brim. He bottoms out inside me on the first drop, a low hiss escaping him as his hands shoot to my hips.

For the briefest moment, neither of us moves, thinks, or breathes—instead choosing to exist in a tiny blip of time where there's nothing keeping us apart. Nothing saying this is wrong or immoral, because we're one.

I start moving over him, rising up off his dick and then sinking back down again. Every drop of my hips draws out harsh pants from his lips, soon forming into full groans as I fuck myself on his cock.

"Mmm, fuck, I love it when you do that."

Words of praise I love start leaving his mouth, coming out in that gritty rasp I'll never get enough of. The more he says, the more I wanna hear.

His head sinks back into the sand as I ride him, a sinful grin curling his mouth. Auden's hands never leave my waist, using his hold there to guide me up and down his length. It's sexy and commanding, like he's still somehow the one in charge.

"I love the way you feel around me, baby. You're clamping me like a vise," he rasps when I start picking up speed. "Your ass was fucking made for me."

A smile that can't be helped hints at the edge of my lips, and I lean forward to press my mouth to his in a toe-curling kiss.

It's not just my ass that was made for him. It's all of me.

Every part of who I am is meant for each piece of him.

Breaking the kiss and straightening, I lift up before dropping my hips again at an agonizingly slow pace. His hands on me give the illusion of him in control, even from the bottom, and it's somehow sensual and carnal at the same time.

Raw fucking while also making love.

"That's it, baby. Use me. Ride me." His teeth sink into his lower lip as I move. "I love watching you bounce on my cock."

A soft moan sneaks free as I pick up speed, loving the way the crown of his cock swipes over my prostate with every drop of my hips. I sink down on his length over and over again, and I don't think there's ever been a more beautiful sight than this man beneath me while I ride him.

One of his hands wraps around my dick, stroking my aching length in time with my movements, and I know there's no better feeling in the world than this. If I could, I'd seal off the entrance to this cave, keeping us trapped here forever. If only so this moment would never pass, becoming only another fleeting memory.

Pre-cum seeps from my cock, and Auden smears it down my length as he jacks me. His thumb swipes over the tip to collect more of it, bringing the bead to his mouth and sucking it clean.

"Mmm, I love the way you taste."

Even in the dim moonlight, I can see the desire and want in his gaze. I can feel it as he wraps his palm around me again, stroking in time with my movements.

"God, you feel so good," I tell him, my breaths coming out in harsh pants as I cant my hips into his touch.

Auden's grip tightens on my hip, and he uses his hold to drag me down on his length even harder. I can tell he's getting closer, his breathing picking up and his movements becoming sharper and more defined.

A groan slips free when he pegs my prostate again, lighting me up like a match and setting me ablaze.

"I love those sexy little sounds you make," he rasps, his hand at my hip moving to coast up and down the top of my thigh. "I love that they're just for me."

It's not lost on me how he continues using that word while he praises me, giving me what I so desperately want to hear while not losing himself in the process. And it makes my heart swell just as much as it shreds it to pieces.

Because, as much as I love hearing it, I'd give just about anything to hear a single, three-letter word after "I love."

If this is all I get, though, it'll be enough. It has to be.

"Take over for me, baby. Fuck your fist and come on my chest."

I do as he asks, wrapping my palm around my leaking dick, and Auden's hands fly to my waist, fingers digging into my skin as his hips snap up. He wastes no time, impaling me on his length, fucking into me with reckless abandon; all finesse and rhythm gone. Now, it's only about release. Finding it together.

His back arches off the sand, and he lets out a tortured groan.

"Let me feel you clench around my cock while I fuck you until you can't think straight."

My ass squeezes around him involuntarily, the filth falling from his lips never failing to turn me into a melting puddle of goo. My tip leaks in my palm, pre-cum seeping through my fingers, and I shuttle my hand as fast as I can.

We chase our climax together, the place we're joined drawing pleasure from both our bodies.

"Come for me, Pierce," he commands. "One more time, baby."

Barely a second after the endearment leaves his lips, his thrusts stutter and he explodes inside me. My own release spills from my throbbing cock, coating his stomach and abs in ropes of cum. He continues dragging me up and down, my ass clenching around his length, milking his orgasm.

I collapse onto his chest, my cum sticky and wet between our chests, our breathing ragged and loud, mingling with the sound of the waves in the distance. We lie like that, melded together as one, for I don't know how long.

Fingers trail up and down the knobs of my spine lazily, the action a loving caress that has me sinking deeper into his warmth.

"What're you thinking about?" he murmurs some time later. Long after the cum between our bodies has gone cold, and his softening dick has slipped free from my body.

A small huff slips out of my mouth, his words reminding me of our week of mornings together. "I can't keep doing this, Auden." I feel his body tense beneath me, but I continue talking. "I can't keep living like this. Being ripped in two by the both of you has been a nightmare since the beginning."

I raise my eyes to meet his, hoping he sees and hears my sincerity. "But if I'm sure of anything, it's that I should've chosen you. Fought for you. *Waited* for you."

Auden goes stark white in the moonlight. "Pierce—"

I shake my head, cutting him off before he can object. "No, Auden. I'm serious. I'm gonna come clean to Emily. I'm gonna tell her the truth." I shift and lean over him, my fingers tracing the skin on his shoulder. "Fuck. I meant everything I said earlier. I can't keep pretending I don't feel the way I do, and we sure as hell can't keep doing this. The guilt is gonna eat us alive."

"Yeah, but, Pierce—"

Again with his objections and excuses. "Look, I know it's not ideal. And I know it's gonna be messy as hell—"

"Pierce, *no.*"

I frown, leaning back like he just punched me across the jaw. "What do you mean *no?*"

"Don't tell her."

There are so many emotions written in his expression, it'd be nearly impossible to list them all. Yet if I know anything for certain, it's that he's as torn apart as I am right now. He's struggling just as much. Maybe even more.

But it still isn't enough to have me backing down.

"Give me one good reason not to," I murmur, barely loud enough to hear over the waves crashing against the rocks.

His eyes bore into mine, searching silently for what feels like an eternity. "Because I'm signing a new contract in two days, Pierce. On Monday when we get back."

"You're leaving again." My words are a pained whisper, but the ache in my chest is familiar, his absence forever hurting, then and now.

"That was always the plan, baby," he says a little too easily. "One we both agreed would be best for everyone."

"Yeah, but that was before." I shake my head vehemently. "Now—"

"Now..." He places his hand over my chest, the bravado gone. "Now is even more of a reason for me to go." His eyes turn soft and glassy. "It's exactly why we agreed to it in the first place."

When I do nothing but stare at him, he continues talking, continues trying to talk me out of my decision—out of choosing him.

"You still love her, right? Had I never shown up here and fucked it all up, you'd still be happily married to her? Then be with her, Pierce. Love her the way I know she loves you."

He can't hide the complete devastation this time, his voice cracking, his eyes filled with unshed tears. He's breaking his own heart to save everybody else.

Duty. Honor. Sacrifice.

"There's no other way around it," he finishes simply before brushing strands of hair out of my face.

"I can't say goodbye to you all over again," I whisper, unable to rein in the emotion filling my voice. "You told me you couldn't bear to see me full of regrets? Well, this is what *I* can't handle."

"And you don't have to," he says calmly. Too calmly. So painfully calm. "I'd never expect that of you. You don't owe *me* anything."

Except he's wrong.

The man I've become—the one he helped shape—owes him everything.

TWENTY-NINE

Pierce

The rest of the weekend went by in a blur, and both Auden and I did our best to keep our distance from one another without raising any suspicion. Especially in front of Julian and Deacon, who hounded me with questions once they came back to the house with the rest of the party, only to find me there already. I'd told them—and Emily too—that dinner hadn't agreed with me, and I decided to head back to the rental early. But while Emily might've bought the lie, I could tell they didn't believe a word of it.

Now we're back in Seattle, and I'm wrecked. I haven't slept a wink, my mind on a constant loop, alternating between thoughts of Cannon Beach the first time—*and* the second—and my wedding day. Each of these moments in my life just as significant and crucial as the next, and they've got me in a downward spiral by Monday morning when Emily walks into our kitchen, startling when she sees me sitting at the island.

"Shit, baby, you scared me. Aren't you supposed to be at work right now?"

I spin my coffee cup on the countertop, silently working up the nerve to say what I need to say, knowing there's no way in hell this decision will cause anything other than pain.

"I took the day off, actually."

Her lips pull down in a frown. "You not feeling well?"

"No, it's nothing like that." I take a quick sip of my hot drink, as if it will somehow make the next words out of my mouth hurt less. "But I do think we should talk."

"About what?"

Her question is so nonchalant, barely even curious, not an ounce of concern on her face. It makes me hate myself so much more, because she doesn't even see it coming.

"There's something I need to tell you." My leg starts bouncing out of anxiety, and I quickly place a hand over it, giving me away. I don't think it's gonna be an easy conversation.

Glancing down at my leg, Emily sets her mug on the counter, finally the appearance of a worried expression crossing her face. "Pierce, what's going on? You're starting to scare me."

I reach across the counter and take her hand, my thumb brushing over the diamond on her ring finger as I look for the words I need to explain this, only for nothing to sound right.

So I decide to rip off the Band-Aid entirely.

"Do you remember how I told you I was kind of healing myself from someone in the past when we met and first started dating?"

She frowns again and nods. "I do."

I steel myself, blowing out a breath before uttering words I never in my life thought I'd say. Ones I know will change absolutely everything in the blink of an eye.

"Well, the person I was healing from…was your brother."

She's silent for a moment, her brows draw together as she works through what I just said. "Wait, I don't understand." Her head cants to the side as she studies me. "*My* brother? Auden? The one you met as we were literally getting married?"

"Yeah, Em. Auden." Pasusing, I give her time to process before continuing. "But the wedding wasn't the first time I met him." I roll my tongue over my lower lip and decide the best place to start is from the beginning.

"I met him in Cannon Beach just before moving to Seattle. He'd introduced himself to me as Will when we met at a bar in town. He'd been there before setting off to deploy, and though it was only supposed to be a single night, we ended up spending an entire week together. And once the week was over…" I trail off while producing the stack of letters he'd sent me during his deployment, and set them on the counter in front of her. His whole heart and mine. "We wrote to each other. Often."

If possible, her frown deepens as she subtly shakes her head. Her hands reach for the stack of envelopes, looking down at them in a mixture of confusion and doubt, her fingers tracing over my name and apartment address. "I'm sorry." She raises her head, glassy green eyes meeting mine. "Are you sure we're talking about *my* brother?"

"One and the same." I point to the letters. "These can explain it a lot better than I can."

With a shaky hand, she pulls the stack toward her and takes a seat on the barstool beside me. She glances up at me, suspicion and a bit of curiosity in her eyes as she carefully opens the first envelope and unfolds the letter.

And she gasps, her hand covering her mouth and tears welling in her eyes the second she looks down at the letter to find her brother's handwriting addressing me by name.

It's the most painful, heartbreaking thing, watching her expression as her eyes skim over the page and absorbing the secretive, intimate words written on them, but I know it's what has to be done. It's the only way this might make even an ounce of sense.

"Pierce," she murmurs, her voice cracking on the single word as she shakes her head back and forth.

Her gaze lifts to me after finishing the first letter before flitting back to the stack of others just like it. There's no way either of us are making it through this conversation without breaking down in tears.

Emily takes her time reading through the letters, one by one, and the silence in the air between us becomes stifling. I watch as she processes the information, attempting to make sense of the situation as best she can, and I'd be lying if my heart wasn't breaking right alongside hers.

Breaking for her, for me, and for Will. For all the good intentions and all the unnecessary pain.

She hands the stack back to me, tears in her eyes, and shakes her head. "I just... I don't understand *how*." Her voice rises an octave. "Pierce, how?"

"I wish I knew," I murmur, reaching up to wipe away her tears threatening to spill over. But what might break my heart more than the sight of them in the first place is the way she pulls away from my touch to wipe them herself.

Fuck.

She clears her throat softly and shakes her head again, leaning away from me to put distance between us. "And you decided it made more sense to act like you'd never met, rather than telling me?"

Shame consumes me, the question she poses proof of just how very wrong we were. How wrong *I* was. "We both agreed that the past made sense to stay in the past. I'd fallen in love with you, after all, and was fully invested in us and our relationship."

"*Was*," she echoes, and I don't miss the tears she rapidly blinks away.

I hadn't even realized I'd spoken in the past tense, and when I replay the words in my head, I can't help but wince. "I'm so eternally sorry, Em. I never wanted to hurt you." I can only hope she hears the truth in my words. "That's the last thing in the world I ever wanted."

"But it's him."

Her composure fractures, eerily similar to the anguish I've seen on Auden's face so many times in the last few months. Both of them torn between their loyalty to family and torn between their love for me.

The love she has for her brother and the need to see him happy and settled has been part of her makeup before I ever came along. And if I know Emily well enough, it will be the single reason she forgives Auden before she ever forgives me.

I swallow past the knot lodging itself in my throat, but my words still come out choked and filled with emotion. "Yeah, it's him. I think it always will be."

Tears spill over her lashes, and she doesn't try to hide them anymore. Makes no attempt to wipe them away, and I watch as her heart cracks and shatters right before my eyes. Her shoulders shake as she's racked with sobs, and instinctively, I pull her into my arms.

She burrows her face against my chest, and I don't care that her makeup is probably staining my shirt or that I should be the last person comforting her broken heart when I'm the same person breaking it.

But the love I have for her brother doesn't make the love I feel for her any less real, and it's no one's fault it doesn't run as deep.

I hold her like that, whispering her name and countless *I'm sorrys* against her hair, knowing how worthless and hollow they probably sound. It's all I can do, though.

I'm not sure how long we stay like that: her silently shaking against my chest while I attempt to hold all her pieces together. It could be hours or only five minutes. All I do know is it feels far too soon when she finally pulls away to wipe her tear-stained cheeks.

"What do you need, sweetheart?"

She lets out a raw, watery laugh. "Well, I guess a divorce, for starters."

I offer her a sad, somber smile. "Anything besides that?" I prepare myself for questions, accusations, anger or fury. "Are there any questions you need answered or—"

She shakes her head. "No, nothing like that."

"Are you sure?"

She's silent for a second before she whispers, "I don't need to know the details of your indiscretions, Pierce. Knowing they exist is more than enough."

I don't know if I'm relieved or want her to drag me over the coals, but I insist on making sure she knows just how truly apologetic I am. "I wish 'I'm sorry' would be enough to take away how I've hurt you."

"I'm not even going to pretend I understand." Her voice hiccups. "And I don't really know what to think or feel about this." Her smile is weak when she looks up at me, those green eyes closer to emerald than their normal mossy color, thanks to her tears. "It's so messy, you know, because it isn't just that you don't love me or don't want to be with me." More tears spill out of her eyes. "But it's so tied up with Auden, I can't even…"

She pinches the bridge of her nose, and I give her the space to think out loud.

"But I do know," she says more firmly, "I don't want to be with someone who is still in love with someone else—no matter who it is. I'm not a second choice or a consolation prize."

I rise, my hands immediately cupping either side of her face, and I pull her forehead against mine. "You're not. You're the grand fucking prize, sweetheart." The last word catches in my throat, coming out over gravel. "And who knows what would've happened if I hadn't gone to the coast or the bar, or done anything else that would've changed what happened. If I'd have met you first—"

She lets out a soft squeak as her forehead rolls against mine. "Don't. There's no point in playing that game. All it's gonna do is hurt both of us more."

She's right. Auden and I had wished for those things too, but it wasn't fair to any of us. To live a life void of true feelings and truths wasn't a way for any of us to live.

Pushing herself away from me, she wordlessly walks into our bedroom, and like a dog with a bone, I follow. My guilty conscience makes it extremely difficult to watch her walk around the house, shoulders hunched, eyes constantly leaking.

I follow her into our en suite bathroom, leaning on the door jamb as she tries to wash the tears from her eyes. "Em, I will never be able to apologize enough for this. Had I known this would happen, I never would've even listened to Julian and Deacon when they insisted I meet you."

Turning, she grabs the lapels of my shirt. "You're a lot of things, Pierce, but a bad guy isn't one of them."

"Why do I feel a lingering *but* at the end of that sentence?"

She lets out a humorless laugh. "Because knowing you aren't a bad person doesn't make this any easier to swallow."

Stepping back, she grips the bathroom door. "I still have to go to work. But I'd really appreciate it if you'd give me a few days without you here."

"Of course," I say, knowing if she asked me to light myself on fire right now, guilt would have me doing it in a heartbeat. "Whatever you need from me, okay?"

She looks lost as she closes the door on me, effectively ending our conversation.

Then again, isn't that what normally happens in the midst of heartbreak? When the whole entire world shifts on its axis in a single moment, and all of a sudden, the future is completely uncertain?

Anyone would feel lost in moments like those.

Not knowing what else to do, I search the house for a suitcase, something big enough to fit everything I'll need over the next few days. I don't have plans or a place to go, but my conscience is clear, and that's more than enough for now.

When Emily steps out of the bathroom, she's wrapped in a towel, her eyes red and her wet hair dripping down her shoulders.

"Sorry," I murmur, knowing she needs her privacy. "I'll be in the kitchen."

As I drink my second cup of coffee, Emily appears, looking as put together as the circumstances will allow. She grabs her purse and keys from the counter, ready to walk out without another word.

"Are you okay to drive?" I blurt out.

"Yeah, I'm good."

"Are you sure? I can drive you," I insist.

"Pierce, please don't," she says with a heavy sigh. Her eyes hold unmatched amounts of sorrow as she meets my gaze. "If I have to fall out of love with you, the least you can do is stop treating me like you still love me."

If there's anything more confusing in this moment, it's that I do still love her. But I know those words are too selfish to say at a moment like this. They'd only be to help me, not her...and I've already been selfish enough in this marriage to last a lifetime.

"I'm sorry, you're right. I'll give you space." I rub the back of my neck. "But everything between us was real. I hope if you can believe anything, it's that."

She smiles sadly. "I know it was. You just don't love me enough."

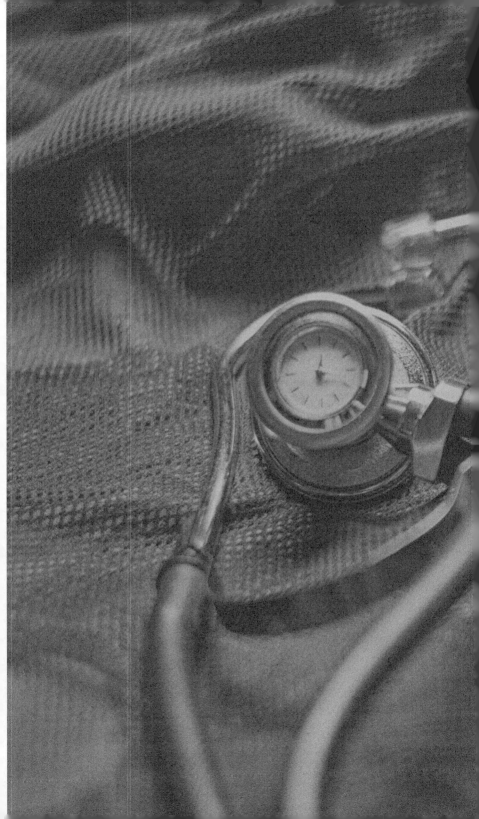

THIRTY

Auden

A lingering sense of disheartment has been coursing through my veins since leaving Cannon Beach yesterday, growing more intense as distance was put between myself and the place that stole my heart.

Or, I guess the place where my heart was stolen.

The only solace I have at this point is that it wasn't necessary for me to bring him back to the city—a three-and-a-half-hour drive I doubt I'd have survived after the revelation he shoved into the light.

I can still hear his words in my head. The three that I'd have given anything to hear spill from his lips.

Except, when they finally came, I couldn't allow myself to sink into them.

Couldn't form them or let them fall off my tongue for one simple reason.

Saying them under the circumstances we find ourselves in…taints them. As much as I love Pierce Evans, he isn't mine to love. And by telling him to stay with Emmy, I've made sure he never will be.

Part of me wonders if it would be easier if he'd kept quiet instead.

I do my best to shove that line of thinking to the side as I grab my wallet and keys from the counter. All it will do is cause me more heartache and grief than is already consuming me, and I can't allow those things any power over me. Not today, and especially not as I'm heading to post so I can sign my life away for another four years.

Which is a way of thinking I never imagined having, yet here I am.

Ignoring the newfound dread in my stomach at the thought, I yank open the front door to my apartment, only to find the last person I'd expect on the other side.

"Pierce."

His name comes off my lips in some mixture of awe and excitement, and my adrenaline spikes when his ocean-blue eyes bore into mine.

He has a death grip on the door frame as he catches his breath, and his other hand that was raised and ready to knock drops back to his side.

"Please tell me you haven't gone to base yet."

My brows crash together. "What?"

"Your contract," he clarifies, still panting slightly. "Have you signed it already?"

"I was just heading out to do it."

"Well, don't."

I swear, my heart stops the moment those two words leave his lips. It's a plea I've already heard before, though. From my mother, my sister. Even from him no more than forty-eight hours ago. But every time I've heard it in the past doesn't compare to the way the organ in my chest physically aches to listen to it now.

To just…stay.

It can't be reality, though, and we both know it. His marriage—and my heart—won't survive it.

"Pierce, I have to," I whisper, shaking my head. "It's the only thing that makes sense. It's—"

He steps forward, and my words die on my lips as he closes the distance between us to wrap his hand around the back of my neck. The door slams closed with both of us inside my apartment as his fingers dive into the short strands of hair at the base of my skull, and there's no doubt in my mind he's about to do something we'll regret.

"Pierce—"

"The only thing in this whole fucking situation that makes sense is you and me, Auden." The words come out low and gentle, like he's speaking to a skittish animal. Like if he says one wrong thing, I'll run away all over again.

He searches my face as we stand just inside my apartment, his expression full of…hope, maybe? For what, I can't begin to fathom, because there's none left when it comes to the two of us.

I'm a few signatures away from solidifying that.

Pierce's free hand reaches up, thumb brushing lightly over my lower lip as he murmurs, "You remember when we were stuck in that elevator?"

Remember?

A soft laugh leaves me. "As if I could ever forget."

"Just making sure. Lord knows there was enough whiskey involved to make some of the details blurry." His blue eyes brighten as one of his heart-stopping smiles crosses his lips. "Then you remember how adamant I was that you gave those letters back to me once you'd found them, right?"

I arch a brow. "They were my letters."

He shakes his head before producing a sealed envelope from the back pocket of his jeans and holding it up between us.

"Not all of them."

My heart might as well crawl into my throat as I eye the letter like it's a live grenade. "What is that?" I ask slowly, my voice coming out grated and raw.

"The one letter you didn't burn to ash. My real last letter," he says with an ironic smirk. "The only reason for it still being here is because I never had the balls to send it. I just put it in that box with all the ones you sent me."

All the oxygen might as well have been sucked out of the atmosphere as I process his words. Unfortunately, his proximity and sudden appearance make it a little difficult for any thoughts to form besides the one that spills from my lips in disbelief.

"You're joking."

Yet from the look on his face and the damn thing being held right in front of me, it's clear he's never been more serious.

Pierce releases me and steps back before sliding his finger beneath the envelope's flap. I'm shell-shocked, frozen in place as he pulls out the paper residing inside it and unfolds it.

His eyes scan the page briefly before they dart up to me. "I think it's about time you know what it says."

The mere thought of knowing what's on that paper creates a thrum beneath my skin, my pulse skyrocketing into hyperdrive. Yet there's part of me that doesn't want to know what he chose not to say to me. Not after having to find my own closure with the one he *did* send.

I don't have a chance to decide, though, because Pierce clears his throat and starts to read.

"March 31. Will. This letter might go down as the hardest thing I've ever written,

maybe even more so than that very first one. I don't know where to start with it or how to ease into what I have to say, so I guess the best thing to do is just say it. I've met someone." He pauses, gaze darting up to me briefly before continuing. *"Her name is Emily, and my God, she's amazing. She's downright hilarious, sweet in that not-so-innocent way, and so fucking smart, it's insane. And I've fallen head-over-heels in love with her in what might be the blink of an eye. But the reason this letter is so difficult to write isn't because of Emily. Not entirely, at least. It's because I'm planning to ask her to marry me. By the time you receive this letter, I probably already will have.*

"This information probably seems irrelevant to you, seeing as when you left for the other side of the world, you left anything we could've possibly become too. But over the course of our week together on the coast, and even more while we've written these letters, I've fallen in love with you too. Not ideal, I know, and believe me when I say I did everything I could to stop it from happening. But everything about you is intoxicating to the point where I know if we continue down this path, I'll only fall harder and deeper for someone I can never have."

My throat constricts, all air leaving my lungs as pieces of the puzzle I'd been missing start to fall into place. And in the strangest way, they're healing me as much as they're breaking me apart all over again.

Pierce's soft voice continues filling my otherwise silent apartment, speaking the thoughts he'd inked onto the page.

"It might not make sense—I can barely make sense of it myself—how I can love two people at once. How can I be so torn between a woman who is everything I could want, all I could ask for, standing right here in front of me, in comparison to a man who is the very definition of unavailable? Yet here I am, feeling like there's some monumental choice to make, when there's no choice at all.

"I have to give you up. I have to end whatever this is with you, no matter how deeply in love with you I might be. Because you aren't here, and I can't have you. I can have her, though. The funniest part is, I really think you'd like her. She reminds me a lot of

you at moments—both in good ways and bad."

I can't help the laugh that comes out as he says it, and he glances up with a solemn smile before reading more of his thoughts.

"I'm not sure how to end this. Nothing feels right, and maybe because it's not and I'm about to make a massive mistake. I honestly don't know, because cutting off whatever this is with you feels like the equivalent of cutting off one of my own limbs. But I can't wait around for you, hoping and praying that I might be enough for you to walk away from a life and career that clearly mean everything to you. So even if it feels wrong, even if I don't want to...I have to walk away. If only for my own sanity, I have to let you go."

Pierce's voice cracks on the last few words, emotion clogging his throat while also pooling in his eyes. He makes an effort to clear it again, blinking back the tears as he does, but his voice still cracks on the last few lines.

"Just know you have a piece of my heart with you over there on the other side of the world...and it will always belong to you. —Pierce."

Once he's finished, he folds the paper and tucks it back inside the envelope before holding it out to me. Gingerly, I take it, holding it in my hand as if it were his heart instead.

Maybe because, in some way, it is.

"Emily and I are over, Auden," Pierce starts, his voice soft and raspy. "That's true and needs to be said regardless of whether you want to be with me or not."

His shoulders rise and fall in a shaky breath, and it's hard not to notice his nervousness sitting beneath all the emotion. It's always been endearing to me how much of a bleeding heart this stoic man in a suit turned out to be.

"I didn't come here expecting one letter to change your mind, especially if your heart is set on another contract. But the things we've shared are etched into my skin and memories burned into my brain.

"You told me you wouldn't be you if you weren't in the military, and that your duty and honor is to your sister. *Always.* The last thing I ever want is for you to be a different version of the man who said those things to me, so please don't take this as some sort of ultimatum; me or the military. I don't want you to feel or be anything less than the man I fell in love with."

My brows narrow in confusion. "Then…why—"

"I wasn't going to let you reenlist without knowing the whole truth," he cuts in. "And the love I have for you is a big part of it. It's *always* been part of it."

Stepping toward me, Pierce offers another gentle smile and grabs hold of my hand.

"I tried to hide from it, push it down, run away, and even replace it. But your person is your person. No matter how hard you fight it, no matter how many times you say they're just a fluke or a passing phase. It's written in the stars. It's chemical. It's fucking undeniable." His fingers wrap around the back of my neck, anchoring there while his sapphire eyes bore into mine with nothing but love and certainty. "You're my person, Auden. *You're* my fucking person. Not your sister. *You.*"

His words fill me with the same kind of assurance, and for the first time since seeing him again in that church, the only thing I feel is hope. Real, true hope that this is the end of the pain and heartache. That Easton was right after all, and we've finally made it out the other side.

Actually, I've never been more positive about anything in my life.

"I don't know whether to kiss you or kill you right now."

His grin is the best thing I've seen in weeks, and my heart beats harder in my chest when I realize it's the same one he'd aimed at me countless times in that very first week.

The one I fell in love with.

"At the risk of saying it another time without hearing you say it back, I love you. And if you're dead set on staying in the Army, then I'd love to be considered as a plus one for wherever you head to next."

Still holding one another, I press my lips to his in a kiss that can only be described as a prelude to the rest of our lives. A kiss that says I love you, over and and over again.

"I love you." The three words come out on a relieved exhale, my lungs, my chest, my heart—everything about us, finally free. "I love you so fucking much."

The sound of an alarm ringing interrupts us and Pierce's gaze darts around the apartment searching for an explanation.

"It's just my cell," I tell him, pulling it out to silence. "I'd set a reminder to go to base."

He wets his lips, trying to hide his apprehension, while his eyes search mine expectantly.

"Fuck it if it means I can't have you." They're words I never thought I'd hear myself say, but that life has nothing on the life I want to build with this man. "The military, the career...fuck it all, all right? I love you, and you're the one worth leaving it all behind for, Pierce. It's always been you for me, and it always will be."

"You mean that? I mean, leaving the Army. Are you sure that's what you'd want?"

My hands cradle his face. "What I want is *you*. I wanted you then, and I want you still."

"Okay, but then what are you gonna do for work?"

"I'll figure it out. I've got plenty of time to do that between now and the end of my contract." The look on his face makes his unease with this plan more than evident; Pierce the Overthinker is back in the building, so

I kiss him again. "You're worth it, Pierce. You're so fucking worth it, it's not even funny."

His hands circle my wrists, blue eyes earnest and sincere. "I just don't want you to give everything up for me."

"Haven't you realized yet, baby?" My lips find his, brushing against them before capturing his mouth in a searing kiss. *"You. Are. Everything."*

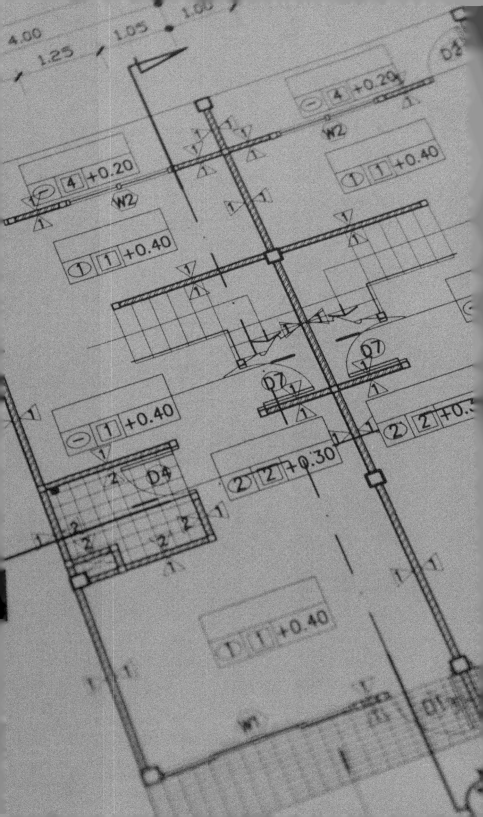

THIRTY-ONE

Pierce

O nce Auden's mouth meets mine again, there's no chance in hell of him getting away anytime soon.

Because, while keeping our hands off one another has always been a problem, being able to touch Auden guilt—and consequence—free feels like euphoria. Like heaven. Like every dream and hope and wish I've ever had rolled all into one.

Maybe because, this time, he's actually mine.

He lets out a low groan against my mouth, and I swallow it down greedily. That same feral need has my hands gripping the hem of his shirt, tugging it upward as I guide him blindly toward his bedroom.

"Something you want?" Auden murmurs, amusement evident as he speaks against my lips.

"Strip, soldier" I mutter as we reach his bedroom. "Right fucking now."

"Someone's feeling bossy."

"I just know what I want. And it's you, naked with your dick in my mouth before you rail me into the mattress."

Auden's eyes flare with heat, and his dark, seductive chuckle goes straight to my dick, but not as much as the filthy promise falling from his lips. "Far be it from me to deny you a goddamn thing, baby."

Breaking apart, both of us tear at each other's clothes like starving animals going in for a kill. Shirts and pants fly in every direction until both of us are stripped bare and devouring each other's mouths all over again, and I love every second of it.

I drag him back toward the bed, dropping my ass on the edge, and bringing myself perfectly in line with his sinfully hard cock. Cupping the backs of his thighs, I urge him forward until his glistening crown nudges against my lips. My tongue swipes out along the head, lapping up the pre-cum before wrapping my lips around his length and immediately taking him to the back of my throat. Swallowing around his cock elicits a soft gasp from him, and his fingers dive into my hair as he holds me there until tears prick at my eyes and I'm forced to breathe through my nose.

"Jesus fuck. Do that again, baby" he groans, head rolling back.

I do as he says before moaning around his length, and the vibration has him twitching against my tongue. It's a heady, addictive feeling, to have this kind of power over a man like Auden. To be the thing that has his composure unraveling, to have him coming undone all because of *me*.

I continue lavishing attention on his dick, working him over until he's clawing at my scalp in a way that's more pain than pleasure, and I pull off him.

"Get inside me," I plead, wrapping my hand around my aching dick as I slide back on the bed.

Auden grins at me from above, wicked and sinful. "You feeling needy for my cock, baby?"

God, yes.

My gaze tracks him as he steps around the bed, heading for the nightstand where he keeps his lube. I swear, every second he takes to grab it drags on for an eternity. He knows it too, if the smirk on his lips is any indication.

Kneeling on the bed to my left, he urges me to turn over on my side, facing away from him, before he settles in behind me. His chest radiates heat against my back, and his shaft nestled between my cheeks has my own leaking more than it already was.

I press back against him at the same time he ruts forward, his spit-slicked length sliding up and down my crease.

"I'm serious, babe. Inside me. Now."

Auden's deep chuckle has my hair standing on end, but he wastes no time, flicking open the bottle of lube and coating himself before I feel his head pressing against me. One hand anchors on my hip as he pushes forward, crowning me slowly and drawing a sigh from my lips.

"Fuck yes," I groan as he slides all the way home, impaling me to the hilt.

His mouth moves over my shoulder in slow, open-mouthed kisses. Gentle and tender, something we haven't been able to be in such a long time. "God, I could make a home inside you."

It's clear from his tone—the love and adoration in his voice—he means more than just inside my body. And I feel exactly the same. Everything about this man is my home. His body, sure. But it's everything he is. Every thought in his mind and the beat of his heart and the essence of his soul are the places I feel most at home.

When we met in Cannon Beach, I was wayward and searching, and in the dim lighting of a dingy bar, I found the man I'm supposed to be; I found myself in him.

The first press he makes inside me has my dick twitching in my palm, the desire for him already building my need for release.

His hand on my hip tightens, and he presses into me, the thick head of his cock sliding all the way in until he bottoms out. Pelvis flush against my ass, Auden leans in and peppers kisses along my neck and shoulder.

"You're absolutely fucking perfect. And so fucking mine."

"For as long as you want me," I tell him, arching in his hold to press my lips to his.

Our pace is slow and leisurely, neither of us wanting to rush a moment like this. Because, despite this being far from the first time we've been together, it's the only time we've had something that was missing from all the others.

Hope.

For us. For more.

For a future that's as endless as my love for him.

And his for me.

Auden's teeth scrape over the side of my throat, skating along the skin until he reaches the place between my neck and shoulder. They sink into the taut muscle of my trapezius.

"You've never looked better in your life than you do right now, baby. My cock buried inside you, my marks on your skin."

A low moan slips from my lips as his teeth latch on to my trap again; the slight bite of pain causing my cock to jump and twitch some more.

If I thought the connection between us when we first met was intense, what we share now is explosive. There will never be a time when he doesn't reduce me to a pile of mush whenever he so much as glances in my direction.

"I love you, Pierce. So fucking much," he says against my skin. "It consumes me."

His words light me up from the inside out, my heart beating wildly against my rib cage. I will never tire of hearing those three words. Nothing compares to having the freedom to say them and the freedom to feel them.

"I wouldn't want it any other way."

I'd learned my lesson the hard way. Nobody will ever compare to him. Neither my love for him or his for me could be replicated or replaced. There was no substitute, and a different version of my life just won't do.

It's all or nothing.

We're all or nothing.

He smiles at my words before taking my lips again, sliding his tongue between the seam the second they collide. It rolls and twists against mine, dancing and dueling as our bodies move in a sensual rhythm.

This is it. How it's supposed to be.

This is worth the heartache.

I've never felt more sure of anything.

He swipes over that spot inside me that never fails to set me on fire, creating a swirling sensation of lust and need in my lower stomach. It builds and builds as Auden pushes us both up the cliff and toward the edge of impending ecstasy.

"Just like that, Will," I pant.

His name—*my* name for him rolls off my tongue with ease. Pleasure and ecstasy allowing me to claim him, in even the most simplest of ways.

We move together in perfect synchronicity, our bodies taking over and guiding us through the pleasure. Auden continues peppering open-mouthed kisses over my skin, and it starts becoming too much to bear.

"You're so fucking perfect, baby," he rasps. "So fucking mine."

His tongue spears between my lips, claiming my mouth the same way his cock claims my body. The same way his soul has claimed my heart.

My body rises and falls at his command, every part of me burning for him.

"I'm right there. Fuck, Auden," I gasp, edging closer to release.

"Then come." His teeth sink into my skin again, branding me as his. "Come for me, Pierce."

His thrusts are long and slow, the same way they were that final night we were in Cannon Beach. The night we said goodbye to each other, knowing it might be the last time we'd ever have this.

But this doesn't feel like the ending. It's actually the beginning.

Just like this isn't sex.

This is love.

This is *forever*.

"Let go," he murmurs, his teeth skating over my jaw until his lips reach my ear. "I wanna feel you, baby. Squeeze my cock while you come."

His grip on my waist tightens and he cants his hips up, the slight angle change allowing his crown to peg my prostate in just the right way that sends me spiraling into another dimension. My hand moves faster over my length, jacking myself until I explode.

Cum spills through my fingers as he continues thrusting into me, every pump of his hips effectively stealing the breath from my lungs. Auden's climax slams into him not long after, his movements becoming frantic and haphazard before filling me with his release. Bearing down on his length, I relish in that full feeling, enjoying the afterglow. If I could always live with him buried inside me, there would be no hesitation, wanting this closeness to him.

He stills, keeping his dick lodged inside me as he takes my jaw in his hand. Capturing my mouth in a kiss that's as possessive and owning as it is loving, I realize *this* is what would've been missing for the rest of my life if I'd stayed with his sister.

The feeling of being complete and coming home. The implicit certainty that there is nowhere else in the world you're supposed to be than with the person you love and who loves you just as fiercely in return.

Auden pulls from my body, and I clench at the sudden emptiness. His hand slides down my crease, and I feel his finger against my rim as he presses his cum back inside me. He does it a few times, and what little does manage to escape, he smears over the skin on my ass and lower back.

That last little reminder that I'm his.

"Enjoying yourself back there?" I ask.

"Oh, absolutely." His nose burrows into the crook of my neck before kissing the mark his teeth left on my skin. "Is it bad that I already want to do that again? Maybe let you try doing it to me next time?"

I arch a brow as I turn to face him, my eyes tracing over his face. "Yeah? You'd want that?"

"I want everything with you, Pierce. And I'm not just talking about sex." His fingers skate up and down my side, causing goosebumps to break out in their wake. "Every laugh and smile and secret and inside joke. All the little moments that make up a lifetime, I want with you."

Pure, unfiltered happiness fills my heart, and I grin. "I think that can be arranged, seeing as I'll be getting a divorce soon."

Auden's face falls slightly, and I instantly have the urge to kick myself for saying anything that involves Emily while it's still so fresh…or while we're still naked and dripping with cum.

"I'm sorry, I didn't mean—"

"No, it's not anything about that," he cuts in with quick reassurance. "Not entirely, at least."

I tuck an arm under my head and meet his worried gaze. "I'm all ears if you want to talk about it."

"I just worry it's gonna come off a bit...narcissistic."

My lips quirk, wondering where in the hell his line of thinking is going that'd ever bring him to that conclusion. "I sincerely doubt that, but go ahead."

"Do you think you fell in love with Emmy *because* she's my sister?"

"First of all, I don't think that's narcissistic at all," I murmur, my hand skating over his arm to his shoulder. "I've had a lot of time to think about this over the past few months, and it comes down to everything I love about her is everything I love about you too. I don't know if being twins has anything to *actually* do with it, but I can't deny just how many similarities there are between you two. Your loyalty, your dedication to those you love. The driven way you approach your careers. The way you're so optimistic and see the good in people, even if they might not deserve it. How you only want to help others, regardless if it means putting yourself last. All those are learned traits, whether they be from your parents, each other, or some outside source, and I don't think you sharing them is a coincidence." A shrug lifts my shoulder as I run my fingers over his scars, my eyes shifting to meet his. "I don't know. I guess...if I were to fall in love with anyone else on this planet besides you, it would make sense to be her. I'm not saying it's right or can excuse it, but it's the most sense I could make of it."

"No," he whispers, nuzzling his head against the pillow. "I think I understand. As much as I can."

Another tiny grin lifts my lips. "Then why do you still look unconvinced?"

My favorite laugh—the real, genuine kind—leaves him before he leans in to steal a quick kiss. "I just have a hard time accepting this is reality, I guess. After all the hurt, everything it cost us, it's almost impossible to imagine you're really fucking mine."

I brush my knuckles down the side of his face. "The romantic in me likes to think somehow we always would've ended up here." I press my lips to his, kissing him with the reverence a man like William Auden Thompson deserves.

"I've always been yours. I was yours even when I shouldn't have been, Auden. I'm yours now, the moment we fucking met, and every single day in between."

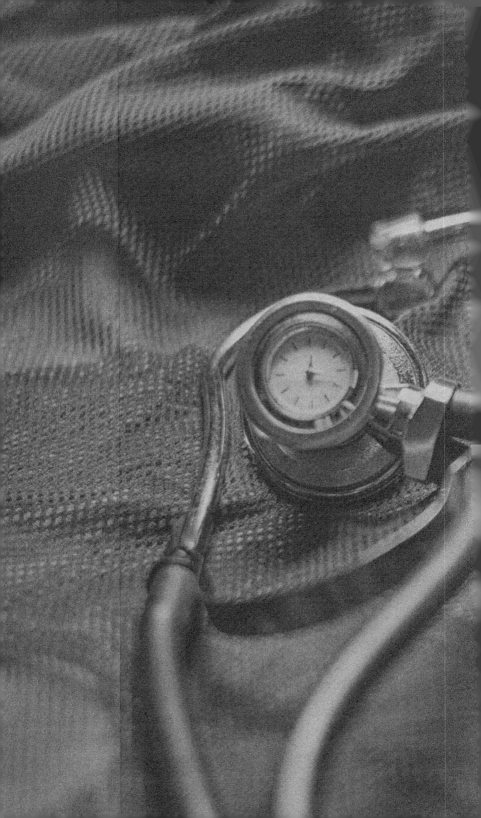

EPILOGUE

One Year Later

Auden

Pierce and I are finishing unloading the groceries when Emmy's SUV pulls into the driveway of the rental house just off the beach. *Our* rental house. Well, the same one that started the entire story between Pierce and me just over two years ago.

A guy, maybe an inch taller than me with sandy blond hair and deep brown eyes, steps from the driver's side of my sister's car before circling around to open the door for her.

I hand off the final grocery bag to my boyfriend, who's stare is locked on the vehicle like a deer in headlights.

"I really hope this goes as well as you think it will," he murmurs before his attention shifts to me. "Because the last time we were all in a room together, we all needed therapy after."

"I told her there was no obligation for her to come," I tell him, giving his forearm a gentle squeeze. "But if you're worried about it, go inside and let me break the ice."

As expected, things with Emily haven't been smooth sailing. They've been tense and awkward, filled with an immense amount of guilt, especially from me and Pierce.

We decided early on that the priority was Emily's and my relationship. And when I say *we*, I mean Pierce. While it made perfect sense, I hated that it also meant he was occasionally on the outs, and sometimes uncomfortable, like now.

I watch him retreat into the rental and then make my way to Emmy, meeting her halfway.

"Hey, Emmy." I grab the bottle of wine from her, unsure if I should pull her in for a hug. "I'm glad you two could make it down."

My sister arches her brow. "And miss out on Cannon Beach at Christmas? Not even an option." I feel my shoulders sag at the way she immediately jumps into conversation. "I'm kinda mad I didn't think of it first."

"It was Pierce's idea, actually," I tell her, only for a slightly pained expression to cross her face.

"Auden, this is my boyfriend, Alec," Emmy says, changing the subject and gesturing to the man she came with. "And Alec, this is my twin brother, Auden."

"Ah, the husband snatcher in the flesh," Alec says, a faint British accent rolling off his tongue.

I wince, though the nickname is the furthest thing from unfounded.

"Don't worry, mate." He extends his arm out for me to shake. "I'm happy you did it, otherwise I wouldn't have landed this gem."

I take his hand. "I'm glad to have…been of service, then?"

Oh, Jesus take the wheel. Maybe this was a bad idea after all.

"Don't mind Alec for wanting to break the ice in the most uncomfortable way possible," Emmy says with a laugh, and, God, how I've missed the sound of it. The way her eyes crinkle at the edges when she does. All the little things that make my sister all the more beautiful than she is naturally.

Changing the subject away from Pierce's and my indiscretions, I move to a much safer topic of conversation.

"Are Deacon and Julian coming down to join us?"

She shakes her head. "No, they went back to Montana. Victoria's baby is due any day now and they don't want to be away in case she goes into labor. It's just the four of us."

Pierce and I left the invitation open to our family and friends, knowing that Christmas is a time full of traditions, and we didn't want to impose on anybody else's by creating our own. With Alec and Emily here, the turn out is already better than I anticipated, but it will be even better when Pierce's parents arrive from Colorado tomorrow.

Pierce's parents have been the most supportive throughout this last year, loving their son unconditionally and welcoming me into their family without any hesitation. They lived by the belief that Pierce is man enough to make his own decisions—good and bad—and their job as parents is to support him through them, no matter what.

Despite not having that with my own family, I love it for him, and know their presence this Christmas will make Pierce feel like our world is finally moving forward.

The three of us head inside, where Emily introduces Alec and Pierce— only for Alec to break the ice even more awkwardly than he did with me by shaking his hand and saying, "Thanks for the fuckup, mate."

Pierce's face turns a shade of red I have never seen before, and if I hadn't already endured my own humiliation minutes earlier, I wouldn't find any humor in his embarrassment.

Luckily, Emily pipes in to save the day, opening her arms for Pierce in greeting, and any apprehension he and I were feeling dissipates immediately. They exchange a bit of small talk, and my respect for Alec increases tenfold when he places his hand on the small of my sister's back in support but still lets them have a conversation.

As they continue catching up, Pierce guides them to the kitchen, where I've been unloading drinks and snacks. I crack open the bottle of wine they brought, grabbing glasses from the cabinet and handing them each one.

"We're glad you decided to come," I say to Emily, then turn to Alec. "And you too."

"As am I." She pours herself a glass of wine before handing it off to her boyfriend. "I've missed you, Aud. A lot. And Christmas is the perfect time for fresh starts, right?"

I smile warmly, a spark of hope igniting in me at her words. "Absolutely."

The roller coaster of mending our relationship over the last twelve months has been completely understandable, seeing as my return to the States was the beginning of the end for her and Pierce; she just didn't know it at the time.

Space and time were two things I was more than happy to give. After all, she's not to blame for any of this. She was just an unfortunate casualty in something Pierce and I couldn't fight against.

But I'm taking her acceptance of this invitation as finally being ready for a fresh start. Turning the page to a new chapter in both of our lives.

Emily slides onto the stool beside me, watching as Pierce and her new boyfriend chat with each other out on the back deck.

Warmth floods my chest at the sight of it, knowing Pierce is feeling at ease and more like himself than he has since they announced they were driving down.

"He looks like he's gonna start an interrogation," she says with a laugh before her eyes shift to me. "And here I thought I'd have to worry about you instead."

"He still loves you," I say before quickly clarifying. "I mean, not like—"

She waves me off. "No, I get it, because I still love him too. It's just in a different way now. More of a fondness than anything else."

I nod, a small sense of relief spreading through me.

At no point in the past year did I think we'd get here, with Pierce, me, and Emmy in the same room, and her not either crying or screaming at us. It felt like an impossibility—a fool's dream.

Yet, here we are.

"Is this weird for you?" I find myself asking, my attention shifting back to her.

"Oh, absolutely, but not in an entirely bad way." Her green gaze lifts to meet mine. "I think I get it, why things ended up this way. I didn't understand at the time, of course. But now that I've met Alec, it makes a lot more sense. The way I loved Pierce...it doesn't compare to the way I feel about him."

I can see how much she means it—sincerity is written all over her face—and it brings another wave of relief washing over me. It's bittersweet at best, though, because I can still see the slightest amount of hurt and distrust lingering in her eyes when she looks at me.

And it breaks my fucking heart.

My hand cups the back of her arm, and I turn her toward me. "I just want you to be happy, Emmy. I never wanted to be the reason you weren't."

"I understand that, and I appreciate it. But, Auden…I'd never want my happiness to be at the cost of your own." Her head cants to the side, and she gives me a soft, sad smile. "There's no way I could live with myself if that were the case."

"Still…" I trail off, searching for the right words, only to come up short, because it wasn't too long ago I told myself those exact same words. "I just hope you know there's a part of me that'll never forgive myself for how things went down or how I hurt you."

Emmy shakes her head immediately, a complete rejection of that idea. The forgiveness she's so readily handing me feels undeserved, and part of me knows that might never change. But I know I'll stop at nothing to earn her trust back.

"This all worked out how it was meant to." She motions toward Pierce, who is now showing Alec around the rest of the house. "And watching you and Pierce together—how easy and seamlessly you work—is proof of that. He brings out a different side of you. A softer one that very few people know is underneath the war-hardened soldier you'd become, and I'm grateful for that." She lets out a soft laugh before adding, "Plus, if he keeps you on US soil, I'm not planning to object."

I can't help but laugh too. "Yeah, I never thought I'd see the day I'd be anything but a soldier."

"That makes two of us." Her gaze turns slightly analytical in nature but more layered with concern than judgment. "And are you happy now that you aren't?"

"More so than I've ever been," I tell her, unable to fight the smile taking over my face when I think about all the changes in my life over the past year. "It's kind of disgusting, actually. Like it almost feels wrong to be this happy when I've hurt you so badly."

"It's not, so don't think of it that way. You're allowed to be disgustingly in love, okay? Even if it is with my ex-husband," she says wryly before quickly moving the conversation along. "But I take it that means the new job is meeting your standards?"

"It's amazing, actually. Only a month in, and I love every second of it." Truthfully, I never thought I'd be fulfilled in a civilian job, even if it did mean having Pierce. It was even a point of contention for a few weeks before I made the final decision to not reenlist.

But as it turns out, there's not a whole lot of difference between working as a civilian flight paramedic and my old MOS in the military— besides the whole combat part of it. Though I'm starting to realize I probably help more people this way than I ever did on deployments.

It doesn't take away from the shit days or the people I can't save, but the ones I do are all the sweeter. Then again, maybe it's because I have someone to come home to after the shifts when I don't.

Someone to help shoulder the burden. Someone who allows me to take off the hard exterior I've been so accustomed to wearing and protects what's on the inside.

My gaze slides over to the front door, a small bout of curiosity coming over me about another person whose forgiveness will be much harder to receive.

"Is Mom still coming in for the holiday like usual?" I murmur, both hoping and dreading the answer is yes.

"She'll be flying into Seattle the day after tomorrow." Emmy must see the way my face struggles to pick an emotion, both disappointment and joy fighting for a place. Her hand reaches up, and she smooths out the worry lines creasing my forehead. "She'll come around to all this, Auden. Just give her time."

A sarcastic laugh slips out, and I shake my head—equal parts confusion and dismay hitting me. "I don't think I'll ever understand how you could get past it, but she can't."

"She'll get there."

If it's anything like my joining the military, I sincerely doubt it.

"I hope it's soon," I say instead, not wanting to bring down the festivities.

My knee starts bouncing, my pulse quickening, as I try to find the courage to tell Emmy of my plans.

Because nobody knows me better, she catches my gaze and places a hand on my thigh. "What is it?"

I clear my throat. "I'm gonna propose."

Emmy's eyes widen, and she quickly shifts her gaze over to Pierce. "Really?"

"Yeah," I murmur, smiling at my boyfriend from across the room. "And he has no fucking idea."

Emily and I watch him silently before she asks, "Are you planning to do it tonight?"

My attention shifts back to her, and I frown. "I wouldn't make you witness that."

"You're kidding me." When I don't respond, she backhands my shoulder and lets out a loud scoff. "It's not every day my brother decides to propose to the love of his life. Of course I wanna be here to see."

This woman never fails to amaze me with how big her heart is. And that's why I know she will always, *always* be the better Thompson twin.

"I say do it."

Her comment catches me off guard, but now that she's put it into the universe, along with her approval, it's the sign I was waiting for.

"Only if you promise you're okay with it."

"Auden, what happened was awful and painful and really shitty," she says, her voice resigned, like she's sick of repeating herself to me. "But I promise, it's okay." Emmy's hand cups my shoulder, and she gives it a firm squeeze. "Forgive yourselves and be happy. That's an order."

"Last time I checked, civilians don't take orders."

"Words I thought I'd never hear," she murmurs, lips twitching in a smirk. "Now, do us all a favor and go get yourself a husband."

"I'm just waiting for the right moment," I tell her.

"Every moment is the right moment to ask someone to spend their life with you." Emmy shifts her body, twisting on the stool. I mirror her actions and she takes my hands in hers. "You and I both know we only have so much time. Find an opening, and go make the most of it."

My throat tightens with emotion, and it takes everything in me not to cry. Sad tears for our past and tears of joy for my future.

Pierce chooses that moment to appear, a sheepish grin on his face. "You mind if I steal your brother?"

"Pretty sure he was the one who stole you," she says with a smile, followed by her gesturing to play the drums and cymbals. "Ba dum, tsss."

"And there's the embarrassingly awkward joke for the day," I mutter, glaring at my sister. "You really have a knack for sneaking those in."

"It's a God-given talent."

Pierce glances at me and smiles. "Wanna go watch the sunset on the beach?"

I don't have the chance to answer him before Emmy rises off her stool and kisses me on the cheek. "Looks like you've got an opening there, Romeo," she whispers.

I let out a soft chuckle and slip my hand into the pocket of my jeans. My finger fiddles with the black band resting inside. Always on a similar wavelength as my sister, I've been keeping it with me at all times, ensuring

I'm prepared and not missing the moment.

"Let me hit the bathroom real quick, and I'll meet you outside?" I tell Pierce, needing a moment to shake off the jitters.

He nods before brushing a kiss on my cheek, and I watch as my boyfriend walks away from me—no idea he's about to become my fiancé.

"Hey, Aud?" my sister calls before I can follow him out.

When I glance up, I find her beaming in Alec's arms, the picture of love and forgiveness. "At least he's ending up with the right Thompson twin this time."

The sun slips down past the horizon, casting a colorful glow of pinks and oranges across the thin veil of clouds overhead as Pierce and I walk along the beach together.

Glancing over my shoulder, I catch Emmy and Alec on the balcony of the rental. She waves when she notices us, and I've never felt as whole as I do in this very moment.

"God, I will never get sick of this view," he says, voice filled with wonder. "I understand why you love it here so much."

"Mmm," I mutter, nuzzling my nose against the side of his neck. "It really is one of the best places on the planet."

"What a way to spend the holidays."

A low hum leaves me. "Maybe we should make it a tradition."

"Any excuse to get back here, huh?"

I press kisses into the crook of his neck "Why wouldn't I wanna spend time with the love of my life in the place where he stole my heart?"

He chuckles, and I feel it against my lips. "You getting sappy on me now that you're living a civilian life?"

"Something like that." I raise my head and meet his beautiful, blue

WANT YOU STILL | 361

gaze. "Question."

Pierce's brows crash together at the center, and he cocks his head inquisitively, as if asking me to elaborate. I don't, instead waiting for the puzzle piece to lock into place. The second it does, his eyes light up with amusement and he laughs.

"Oh my God. Twenty questions." He shakes his head, a glimmer of amusement in his eyes as he pulls out of my hold. "You still have one left, don't you?"

"I know how to use them wisely, Evans. Unlike someone I know who is a bit more of the instant gratification type," I tease.

"It's called curiosity, but go on," he counters.

Here goes.

"This place has always been special to me, but it wasn't till I met you that I truly understood why. As if the universe knew something I didn't, bringing me back here time and time again, just waiting to meet you."

"That's not a question," Pierce breathes, his eyes filling with unshed tears.

"And when I met you, I told myself there's no way he's real. There's no way I'm having all these feelings for a man I met in a fucking bar."

This earns me a wet laugh.

"But I did, and the feelings were more than real."

Slipping my hand inside my pocket, I pull out the black band and hear the unmissable hitch of Pierce's breath.

Working my throat over, I try to swallow down my emotions as I take hold of his left hand and meet his watery gaze with my own.

"My feelings for you run deep. Your taste, your touch, your heart... every part of you is embedded in every part of me. Even when it cost me everything, it was you."

I place the ring at the tip of his ring finger, smiling at him. "As long as my heart is beating, there isn't a day on this earth where I won't want you still. Won't want to share this place with you—share every fucking moment with you for the rest of our lives."

My voice wavers as I finally ask him my final question. "Pierce Andrew Evans, will you marry me?"

The words barely leave my mouth and Pierce's hand is curled around my neck, bringing me to him as he slams our lips together.

His kiss is all-consuming, giving me all of him and taking all of me. A kiss full of old hurt, healing, and hope. Everything previously out of reach, now at the edge of our fingertips.

With his mouth molded to mine, I feel the depth of his answer and the weight of our love. In it, I hear the wordless response and know with truth and certainty that this is the first—and only time—I already knew his answer before even asking the question.

Yes. Yes. Yes.

the end

The end

acknowledgments

To our cover designers, Kate and Sybil. Thank you both for supporting each of our individual brands and identities with your designs, as well as putting up with our million tiny requests over the course of the project.

To our editing team, Shauna and Amanda. This wouldn't have been possible without your tireless work and dedication. Thank you for taking on our stress as your own and giving us a beautiful, clean manuscript for our readers to devour.

To our beta team, Janine and Jackie, for scouring this manuscript and making sure both our voices were well represented.

To Isaac and Chip, for helping us answer any military related questions we had, ensuring this story could hold as much accuracy as possible.

To all the men and women who serve in the armed forces, we thank you for your service. And to their families who are left at home, thank you for the love and support you show them on a daily basis.

And last but not least, to all of our readers who waited (im)patiently for this project to finally come to fruition. We hope the ride was worth it, and we promise, there's more where this came from.

— *CE and Marley*

about ce ricci

CE Ricci is an international best-selling author who enjoys plenty of things in her free time, but writing about herself in the third person isn't one of them. She believes home isn't a place, but a feeling, and it's one she gets when she's chilling lakeside or on hiking trails with her dogs, camera in hand. She's addicted to all things photography, plants, peaks, puppies, and paperbacks, though not necessarily in that order. Music is her love language, and traveling the country (and world) is the way she chooses to find most of her inspiration for whatever epic love story she will tell next!

CE Ricci is represented by Two Daisy Media.

For all subsidiary rights, please contact:

Savannah Greenwell — info@twodaisy.com

about marley valentine

Living in Sydney, Australia with her family, Marley Valentine is a USA Today bestselling author and a former social worker who uses her past experiences to write real life, emotional and heartfelt contemporary romance.

She enjoys mixing it up with all types of romance pairings, incorporating all forms of life, lust and love as her characters embark on their journey to their happily ever after.

When she's not busy writing her own stories, she spends most of her time immersed in the words of her favourite authors.

Marley enjoys interacting with her readers so please feel free to reach out to her via Facebook, Instagram, email and/or subscribe to her newsletter.

Marley Valentine is represented by Two Daisy Media.

For all subsidiary rights, please contact: info@twodaisy.com

Made in the USA
Las Vegas, NV
12 February 2024

85661665R00213